Armour

The Days are Numbered Book 1: Daystar
Published by Wombat Books,
PO Box 1519, Capalaba Qld 4157
www.wombatbooks.com.au

Decorative Initials by Rose SK
Cover Illustrations by Carmen Dougherty
Design by Wombat Books

© Anne Hamilton 2015
National Library of Australia Cataloguing-in-Publication entry
(pbk)

ANNE HAMILTON

Daystar
The Days are Numbered

To the special gatekeepers:
Dell, Janice, Janette

horn sounded, faint and far away.

It was answered by a ringing echo from high up the valley where the tallest pines pierced the sky.

Ansey smiled. The hunters had fallen for his ruse. He sighed with relief. 'Well done, Rigel.' He leaned forward to stroke the charger's mane. 'We've lost them.'

The air misted with Rigel's heaving breath as its restless hoofs stamped at the snow. As Ansey straightened, he felt its tense straining against the reins. 'They're too far away to catch us now.'

His words failed to calm the horse. Its ears were pricked and alert, its head twitched in agitation. Ansey glanced up.

Wind–tattered clouds, shaped like wolves' tails, raced across the sky and below them their shadows chased each other down the furrowed hillside. 'Just shadows, Rigel. Just shadows. Nothing to worry about. We're safe now.'

Another horn sounded, even more distant. *They're heading for Ysgarde. Trying to cut me off before I get to the pass.*

He reached out to pat the horse. Rigel's stamping became urgent.

He almost missed the signs: the wolf–tail shadows weren't following the path of the clouds; they were converging.

'They've found us!' He touched Rigel's flank with his rolled whip and, as it surged forward, he heard shouts behind him. The hunters were closing in. No concealment now. *How had they got so close without giving themselves away?*

Just one chance now: the swamps of the Mistmurk.

Rigel thundered down the hillside, leaping over pockets of late–fallen snow nestled in rocky hollows. Ansey felt he was flying over the pale heath. *Faster, Rigel, faster…*

Behind him, the roar of pursuit drew nearer. The hunters were so close. Unrolling his whip, he flicked the air near Rigel's left ear to signal a turn.

The horse wheeled mid–stride to head down one of the long wide furrows that spanned the hill.

'Faster, Rigel!' Ansey sensed the hunters reacting just a fraction too late. Their horses faltered, stumbling on the stony sides of the furrows as they turned after him. He'd gained half a second. *Will it be enough?*

He spotted the Mistmurk beyond a line of willows. It was stretched out, a flat gleaming expanse, swathed in wisps of grey gas. He gritted his teeth. *If I can reach the water first…*

He passed between the willows. Brown–capped reeds jutted like spears from the bank in front of him. A dark blur rushed past him and wheeled across his path.

He had no choice but to rein in as the black–clad riders of the King's Shield blocked his way forward. As they moved into a circle, Rigel reared and plunged.

Ansey bit his lip as he realised how close he was to the Mistmurk. Beyond the hunters, light glimmered on the sullen water. Brown rushes bobbed as a breeze parted the mist at the marsh's edge.

The captain of the King's Shield regarded him with an amused smirk. 'So, arrogant pup, anything to say for yourself?'

Ansey hung his head.

The captain tutted. 'Stealing the King's Royal Charger is a serious matter.' His grin broadened. 'What made you think you could get away with it?'

Ansey looked up, choked by disappointment. *The marsh is so close…* The captain's voice was an irritating buzz in his ears.

'Still nothing to say in your defence?'

The grin seemed to have detached itself from the captain's face.

Blurry and mocking, it swam in front of Ansey's eyes. All he wanted to do was to wipe it away.

He flicked his whip. As it struck the disembodied grin, he threw himself down, dived under the nearest horse and plunged into the water. Shouts and curses fouled the air behind him as he prepared to dive.

He was already leaping when a mailed hand grabbed his tunic and he lost his footing. He hit the water at an awkward angle. A moment later, he was hoisted into the air, spluttering.

'Fine fishing today, Captain?' A guard on the shore folded his arms and laughed.

'This one's a struggler.' The captain wrenched Ansey's whip away.

'Let me go!' The words came out as an undignified squeal.

The captain threw him over his shoulder and squelched back to the shore. Rigel kicked out. 'Keep that charger to the rear.' He thumped Ansey. 'I don't want this eel escaping again.'

As the nearest guard reached for the reins, Rigel reared backwards, hoofs out. Its nostrils were contorted, foam flecked its mouth.

Ansey knew there was no way they'd get it to the back of the troop. It would wound, perhaps kill, one of the guards, before it would submit to them. 'Rigel…' Ansey turned his face to the horse and breathed its name. 'No! Be at peace. Be courteous.'

Rigel settled at once, with just a shiver of its head. Ansey couldn't see the captain's face but the looks the guards shot him varied between stunned and awed. He saw one nudge another and heard an exchange of whispers.

'So that's how he managed that murdering beast.'

'He has the Flair.'

Rigel, meek and obedient, allowed one of them to handle its reins. As the captain flung Ansey over the pommel of his horse, it moved to the back.

The captain nodded in satisfaction, then holding him down, leapt behind him onto the horse. A moment later, Ansey heard a crack. It took him a few seconds to realise his whip had been snapped in two. He felt as if he had been snapped in two, along with it. His eyes blurred again and the disembodied mocking grin of the captain appeared in front of him, jiggling in silent laughter.

His hands gripped the muddy heel of the captain's boot as he flailed, trying to kick his way free. His feet just scissored the air.

The captain's horse cantered in a wide circle. 'Away!' At the captain's shout, the riders moved off, following the shore. The pace was an easy one, but before long, Ansey's ribs began to ache. Flicks of wind needled his ears and his head throbbed.

Soon the direction changed and the horses crossed sun–thawed fields, crushing the first pale flowers of spring underhoof. A wet corner of the captain's cloak slapped Ansey's cheek from time to time. His eyes watered, irritated by specks of mud flying off the captain's boot.

By the time the troop reached the narrow cliffway leading up the Harrowfell, he ached all over. *Why are they going back this way?* It might be the fastest, but the steep path was so tortuous, it was often the scene of fatal accidents.

'We've made good time.' The captain sounded surprised.

'Aye, too good,' came a reply. 'It's not as far to the Mistmurk as it used to be.'

'What's that mean?' The captain's tone was sharp.

'The land's cursed. It's folding in on itself.'

Ansey was startled. It was exactly what the finches had said, but they were so scatter–brained, he'd ignored them.

'Wild talk.' There was a warning edge to the captain's voice meant, it seemed, to deter more comment. It didn't work. More of the guards joined in.

'It's *her*.'

'Aye. It was never this way until *she* came, Captain Gratian.'

Ansey was even more surprised. *This isn't loyal talk. I'd never have suspected the King's Shield of this.*

Captain Gratian jerked his collar. 'Give me your word of honour, thief, that you won't escape and you can sit up.'

Ansey spat on his boot.

Gratian laughed and, as he did, Ansey felt a change in his

alertness. Or perhaps he was just becoming sensitive to the reactions of Gratian's horse. Could the Flair be used on a tamed beast? He'd never tried before; he'd only ever reached for wild things.

His mind was in ferment. As he considered his options, the ground shook. A small tremor, nothing like the quake at Summerheight, but it was enough to frighten the horses. Ansey seized the moment and slid backwards.

His feet almost touched the ground.

Gratian yanked him upright even while steadying the horse. All around, a restless wickering echoed off the rockface. 'Dark magic's on the move today,' a guard said, his voice sounding strange and hollow.

The captain pointed at the cliff path. 'Hurry!'

linking against the sunlight, Fern took off her glasses and rubbed her eyes. *I think I blacked out. Again.* She looked around. *Sports day. My least favourite day of the year.*

A starting gun went off, sending a blue puff of smoke into the air. The 100 metre sprint had just started. *Why didn't I just stay home? I should have remembered it was sportsday. I could've said I was sick.* She pulled at the tiny silver whistle around her neck. *But that would have meant drawing attention to myself. Fortunately it's easy to fade into the background with Elsa around.*

She twisted the whistle's silver chain as she watched Elsa marshalling her team down at the running track. *How did I get to live with someone so perfect at everything?* Elsa's long blonde hair swished as the wind caught it and threw handfuls to the hazy sky. Fern sighed and pulled at the whistle again. *It's one thing to have a step–sister who looks like a supermodel and just has to turn up the dimmer switch on her smile to get anything she wants. It's another to stay invisible and out of everyone's way…*

Her brain felt numb, her thoughts drowsy with heat. She jerked her head up. *Maybe I'm not drinking enough lately. Maybe that's what's causing the blackouts.* She decided to look for some water.

Before she could get up, a swirling darkness surrounded her. *No, not again. Stay. Don't faint. Not here of all places.*

There were voices nearby. *'Go quickly, Uller, before the Sleeper rises.'* A rough, rasping voice sent a chill to her bones. *'Take the sword and find the Daystar.'*

She felt dizzy as another voice broke like mocking waves around her. *'There is no Daystar.'*

'We have not looked far enough, Uller.'

The darkness parted. A whispering veil of mist shrouded the competitors at the starting blocks.

'Not looked far enough? In our father's time, the whole world was searched. In our own time, we have searched beyond the limits of the world.'

She could sense the suppressed rage in the voice. Its cold, scraped tone was just like her father's when the world didn't rush to fulfil his every wish. She twisted the chain holding the whistle. The voices became sharp and clear, as if she'd just found the exact frequency to tune a radio.

'I have been past the Isles of the Colossus and, with my brothers, walked the sunken lands to the Kingdoms beneath the Sea. Where else will we search, Freutim? Where else?'

This was worse than the blackouts. *Voices. I'm going mad.*

She put the whistle in her mouth as she raised her hands to her ears to block the sound. And almost jumped with fright. A giant with thistledown hair and silver eyes, like a sliver of moonlight, was in front of her. *I'm hallucinating.*

The giant spoke. *'We have not searched beyond time itself, Uller.'*

From behind her came the angry, violent voice. *'Beyond time itself?'* It was another giant. *'I have been to the City of Mages and copied their most secret scrolls. I tell you, Freutim, even the mages do not know how to reach outside of time.'*

'That is why you must take the sword, Uller—it will draw the Daystar to you.'

'I cannot take it. You will all be defenceless.'

She looked up. Uller's voice was coming from above her but all she could see was an immense shadow.

'It will not help us, Uller, if we do not find the Daystar. Not now we have lost the Helmet. We must hope the sword will draw the Daystar to it as moths are drawn to flame.'

'And if it does not?'

'Then if we are fortunate beyond all we deserve, we will die.'

Fern gasped. The whistle dropped from her mouth. The giant bowed and began to fade.

The fog deepened, turning to an unbroken white as smooth as pearl. Tinkling crystal sounds surrounded her and within the whiteness, tiny candles began to kindle by ones and twos. They cast flickering yellow shadows. Fern covered her face. *I'm going mad.*

A starting gun went off.

She peeked through her fingers. The fog was gone. Dazed, she took a deep breath and realised the 400 metre race was in progress. Her brain felt numb. Her hands and feet were needled with pain, as if blood were returning to them after being cut off.

'Didn't you get my text?' Elsa was in front of her, glaring, her pink mobile phone held up in obvious accusation.

How did you get there? You were down at the starting line. 'What text?' Fern reached for her pocket. She hadn't even felt her phone vibrate.

'We need you, shortstuff. Cato's twisted his ankle and we're a runner short.'

'You must be joking. Me? You know I'll come last.'

'It doesn't matter. We can't afford to forfeit ten points for not entering. You'll get one point, even if you walk it. You know that.' She produced a coaxing smile.

A distant cheer announced the end of a race.

Grabbing Fern's arm, Elsa pulled her up. *'Please.'* She smiled again, all dazzling teeth and sunlit eyes. 'I did give you a birthday present, didn't I?'

Fern's hand went to the whistle. *I still don't understand why.* 'This is supposed to be a gift, not a bribe.'

That was it. The moment I stopped being totally invisible. When Elsa remembered my birthday. When my step–dad and his new partner suddenly stopped being self–absorbed for long enough to realise I wasn't related to either of them. She'd been quieter and more compliant than ever, hoping they'd forget her again. Safety, security and a roof over her head lay in not being noticed.

'C'mon, shortstuff.' Elsa's tone was urgent. 'Just by entering, you could win this carnival for us. We're that close to catching the Blues.'

What's worse? Being noticed for entering a race or noticed because Elsa complains about me? She let Elsa drag her over to the registration tent. 'Fern McDey, thirteen years,' Elsa told the official.

I'm not thirteen for another two months. What's Elsa think she's doing?

Elsa tapped the desk as the official ignored her. 'This is urgent, Miz Ashe.' She rapped harder. 'I've got a replacement for Cato. So I want to register a late entry for the Green Team in the fifteen hundred metres.'

'Fifteen hundred?' Fern squeaked. 'You didn't say anything…' She broke off as Elsa pinched her arm.

Mrs Ashe looked up from the registration grid on her laptop. Her mirrored glasses reflected Elsa's long blonde waves of hair, lean tanned legs and blue eyes in a honey and gold face. 'Elsa, how many times do I have to warn you about bullying your fellow students?'

'I'm not bullying, Miz Ashe. I'm just attempting to bring out their innate competitive side.'

'Tomorrow at ten, Elsa, in my counselling rooms…'

Elsa slewed to Fern. 'Now see what you've done!'

'Stop, Elsa.' Mrs Ashe's tone was firm. 'Do you want to enter this race or not, Fern?'

Fern glanced at Elsa, then at Mrs Ashe. In her mirrored glasses she saw a stiff girl wearing plain spectacles which didn't suit her pale face. Her halo of tangled hair was speckled with grass stalks. *Me. Useless in every way. Except maybe to score the winning point for the Greens.* 'Yes, Miz Ashe.'

'I haven't seen you at youth group lately.' Mrs Ashe took off her glasses as Fern signed her name. 'If you need a lift, I'm sure one can be arranged.'

She knows mum's left. 'Youth group's not my thing anymore. It's kid stuff.'

'That's a pity.' Her tone was so kind and her eyes so caring, Fern found it almost unbearable. 'You used to be the real star of our Scripture memory quizzes.'

Is that supposed to make me feel better? Encourage me?

'There's an opening in the choir.'

And that's incentive to come back? 'I can't sing. I sound like a cricket.' *Leave it at that, Miz Ashe. Don't ask questions.*

'You know you can come and talk to me anytime, Fern. About anything that's troubling you.' Mrs Ashe smiled, but her eyes were narrowed.

Fern turned and fled. She was sure Mrs Ashe's ineffectual kindness was about to take a turn into asking probing questions about her life.

A call for competitors came over the loudspeakers. Guided by Elsa, she approached the chalk–lined start. 'They're all seniors! I have to withdraw.'

Elsa pulled her to the outside lane. 'Shortstuff, just do something useful in your life for once, hey?'

'Hi, Ellie.' The boy in the next lane finished tightening his laces and looked up at Elsa.

She ignored him.

Fern, feeling nervous, twitched a smile at him. 'Hi, Goliath.'

Goliath Jones was the shortest boy in school. And the fastest. She'd never really met him before but everyone knew him. She took a deep breath. His presence relieved her agitation. No one really expected to win against Goliath.

Known as Hobbit, Mouse and Squeak to his friends, he didn't mind being called a midget but would attack anyone who called him Golly. Fern found it secretly amusing he was named after a giant.

Goliath turned his attention from Elsa's chest long enough to flick a glance at Fern. 'Good luck.'

Well, you don't need any of your own. 'Thanks.'

His gaze had fixed on her and his expression turned to a scowl. 'Who gave you that?' He pointed to her whistle, then turned to Elsa. 'It–t–t was… for y–y–you.'

Oh no. She didn't. Fern felt a squeeze on her heart as she watched his face lose its colour. Another of Elsa's adoring worshippers betrayed.

'It–t–t's an h–h–heirloom.' Goliath looked crushed, as if he were unable to believe Elsa had no sense of his sacrifice or the value of the gift.

Fern fumbled with the catch to give it back to him. But before she could undo it, the starter's call rang out. 'On your marks…'

'Get ready.' Elsa pushed Fern to the line.

Goliath turned away and set his feet into running stocks, his face ash–white. His mouth was a thin grim line.

Fern didn't know what to say. *Should I offer to give the whistle back? Or would that make it worse?*

Her thoughts tumbling, she realised she was the only one without spiked shoes.

'Get ready…' the starter called.

At the crack of the pistol, they were off. By the end of a hundred metres, Fern was puffing. She began to slow down. Goliath matched his pace to hers. 'Are you alright?'

'Are you?'

Goliath's laugh was hollow. 'Just fine.'

'Then don't lose the race for me.'

With a nod, Goliath sped off to catch the pack.

As she watched him accelerate, she wondered about Elsa's agenda in bringing her down to the track. *Would she do it deliberately? Was this about giving Goliath a message, not about Cato's sprained ankle at all?*

Fern stopped, trying to make up her mind if Elsa really had played such a spiteful trick. *What happens if I just walk off? Will the Greens lose the point I just gained? Can I let the whole team down just because I'm sick at heart over what Elsa's done?*

She began jogging. The track turned but she didn't. She went straight on.

Across the field, through the side gate, down the hill… Hearing shouts behind her, she picked up her pace at the pedestrian crossing and ducked into a back street. *I'm going to keep going until…* She thought of the conversation between the imaginary giants. *…until I come to the limits of the world.*

'McDey! Come back!' The voices behind her were shouting her name and they were getting closer.

She put on a spurt of speed, finding reserves she didn't know she had and headed down a tree–shaded lane. *It's stupid running. I'm going to be in so much trouble.*

She slowed, noticing a bank of fine mist ahead. *Maybe I'll go back. Talk to Miz Ashe.* She pulled up the chain around her neck and examined the whistle. *I should've known.* It was delicate with fine etching across its silverwater surface. *Far too beautiful for Elsa to have ever really wanted to give me.* Yet, when she thought back to her birthday, she recalled unwrapping a whistle that had been lumpy and tarnished. It almost seemed to have changed as she wore it. *I guess I have to give it back to Goliath.*

The thought was painful. She put it to her lips and blew. *Just one go before I return it.* Nothing. It was disappointing. *Must be as high–pitched as a dog whistle.*

'Hey, McDey! Where are you?'

'Is that her? Hey, come back, McDey. The chaplain wants to see you in her counselling rooms.'

As Fern turned towards the two prefects who'd obviously been sent to retrieve her, the mist advanced. It billowed around her. Dense, white as a pearl, it swirled in bright eddies. A light as sharp as a needlepoint speared down towards her. She ducked, felt something snake its way around her waist and then yank her up into the sky. *'Uuah…! Hee…'*

Her scream was cut off as a frost–white bubble snapped into place around her. For several seconds there was silence. Fern felt as if her lips were moving, soundless and strange, like a gobbling fish.

She took a deep breath and tried to still the panic rising inside her. She could hear voices. They were all around her. Tinkling. Chiming. Whirring. *They're snowflakes.* She didn't know how she could be so sure. *Arguing over whether their designs are already copyrighted.*

She let out the breath she was holding. *This can't be happening. Snowflakes can't talk.*

The bubble bounced…

and bounced…

and bounced…

ursing, the King's Shield went single file up the Harrowfell. The path was wide enough for two horses but no one was taking chances. Ansey stared over the precipice, feeling sick. *This is madness. What if there's an aftershock when we're halfway up?*

The path was notorious for its dangerous switchbacks with black ice lying slick and invisible on slippery scree. A stinging wind swept across the face of the Harrowfell, battering the riders as they urged their horses on.

Ansey struggled to keep his eyes open against the biting gusts. In the distance, he could see the Mistmurk, glimmering grey even at this height. Beyond it, across the border into Fyrzentsou, a dust haze stretched to the horizon. *Still no rain.*

He felt a curious sense of relief at the sight. Fyrzentsou, once a kingdom of blue hills and silver rivers, was fast becoming an arid desert. *So Vircontium can't invade Fyrzentsou if their armies can't live off the land.*

He twisted his head to avoid the wind's relentless tattooing. Light dazzled him, glinting off the snow–topped peaks to the north. *They're too close.* Ansey was startled by the thought. By its impossibility. *How can mountains move? But what had the guard said? And the finches? 'The land's cursed. It's folding in on itself.'*

An image appeared in his mind: the furrows on the hillside as Rigel had raced down to the Mistmurk. *They're not furrows, they're folds. Folds in the landscape.*

'Folds? How can they be folds?' He hadn't meant to speak aloud. His voice broke into a splintery echo, bouncing off the cliff.

The horse in front shied at the sound and jerked back. Ansey tensed, sensing the panic in the captain's mount as it was crowded front and behind. 'Be calm, Mintaka.'

The horse's hooves scrabbled as it slipped, teetering on the edge of the precipice. He felt its effort not to panic. *Soothing, soothing.* 'At peace, Mintaka.'

Gratian pushed him clear, back onto the path. He hit an outcropping of rock headfirst.

Dazed, he pulled himself upright.

Gratian had leapt down and was soothing the trembling horse. 'How did you know her name is Mintaka?'

Ansey stared in shock as the captain turned to him. A blood–crusted gash extended from the corner of Gratian's mouth across his cheek, just missing his eye. It was recent, but not fresh. *What could have...?*

My whip. When I hit him back at the Mistmurk. 'I'm sorry, sir.' Ansey was appalled. 'I didn't mean to hurt you. I just wanted to distract you...' *And destroy the disembodied grin. Did I only imagine it?*

'It'll make a splendid scar.' Gratian's mouth twitched. 'You needn't call me 'sir', Your Highness. My name is Gratian.'

'I know. I heard your men.' He had already committed the captain's name to memory. 'I'll make it up to you, sir.'

'You're a strange contradiction of a whelp, Prince Ancelin. Someone ought to take you in hand before you're ruined completely.' His gaze seemed to reach into Ansey's soul. 'You didn't answer my question about Mintaka.'

Ansey hesitated. 'I guess I must have heard one of your men mention it.'

'You lie so very badly, Your Highness. I suppose that's something of a relief, given how exceptionally well your brother manages to do so.'

Tybold's not my brother. Ansey glared at Gratian.

He folded his arms and scowled at Gratian as Mintaka stepped up the path.

The guards had dismounted and were following at a distance. It was slow going. Tiny crumbling bridges crossed dark crevices. Precarious rockslabs loomed on either side of deep–cracked cuttings. Once they had to stop to clear their way through the remains of a small avalanche. Ansey jumped off Mintaka to help.

It's not just furrows and folds. The land's cracking. How come no one has mentioned this back at court? It's hardly invisible.

As they worked to remove enough of the avalanche to pass through, Rigel became agitated again. Ansey went to calm it. He could feel the eyes of all the guards on him as it settled at his touch. He knew what they were thinking: Rigel was notorious in the stables. He was regarded as impossible to handle.

Ansey felt Gratian's stare. It was intense. *I'm doomed. Everyone's going to know about the Flair.*

When at last they reached the top of the cliff and passed through the stone ruins of the Harrowgate, there was a collective sigh of relief.

Gratian shook his head. 'The Harrowfell is only supposed to be suicidal going down, not up.'

A trill of horns sounded in the distance. Powder–white spires towered above the trees.

'Spotted.' Gratian thumbed a command to Ansey. 'Up.'

As Ansey mounted Mintaka, Gratian turned to the King's Shield. His face with its bloodied gash was grim and forbidding. 'Guards of Auberon, I've been one of you for a long time. Today is my first day as your commander.'

Ansey wondered why he was making this point. It went without saying. In fact, it had been the inauguration ceremony which had served as the distraction for his own escape.

Gratian looked at each of the men in turn. 'You know I keep my word. Understand this: today your talk has been less than loyal.'

Ansey could see alarm spreading across the troop.

'But I could forget,' Gratian went on. 'My memory of your treasonable talk depends on yours about a certain flair possessed by His Highness, Prince Ancelin.'

There were looks of relief all round. The men nodded.

'Thank you, sir,' Ansey whispered as Gratian mounted behind him. *I owe you. I owe you big time. I may never be able to repay such a debt.*

The troop rode through the hedged gardens of the royal parkland. In contrast to the furrowed landscape behind him, the lawns were as smooth as glass.

I don't understand why it's so different. Is it magic? But how? Ansey sighed. He remembered the sturdy portcullis that had once loomed over the wide moat where the gatehouse now stood. He thought of the vigilant dogs that had roamed where peacocks now strolled past lily ponds.

The King's Shield clattered into the noisy courtyard. Geese and chickens scattered in raucous squawks. Servants scurried out of the way. Gratian swung down off Mintaka as an eerie silence descended.

Ansey could feel heat rising up his face as every gaze turned towards him. It was almost like an attack. *It's worse than I ever imagined.* He tried to look dignified as he dismounted but he realised he probably looked like the rat–boy who chased vermin out of the storerooms for the catchers.

He climbed the side steps into the castle, feeling rattled.

A cloud of tiny finches descended from the overhang of the roof. 'You can't help,' he whispered as they twittered in indignation. 'No, it's not the same rules.' He brushed them aside as they landed on his shoulders. 'Youngsters don't have to get pushed out of the nest if they're ready to fly.'

'Bird Flair too?' Gratian raised an eyebrow.

'Of course not. Just finches and herons.' Ansey realised even before he had finished speaking he should have kept it to himself. *I've just made it infinitely worse.* He hurried through the door.

The finches took off in a swirl of hazel wings. A babble of voices rose behind them as the servants resumed their chatter.

It isn't fair. Ansey allowed the fear he'd been swallowing to rise. It thundered to the surface as anger. Reaching the throneroom, he snarled as the chamberlain flung open the doors.

The throneroom was an airy vault with light streaming through silver–bordered windows. A sweeping staircase led to a balcony and a fountain court beyond. Tasselled banners and velvet tapestries lined the walls. Only three years previously, it had been a fortified stronghold.

War was a constant threat. But since the king had married again, making new alliances with old enemies, the battlements had become an art gallery, the throneroom a banqueting hall.

Ansey felt uneasy about the changes. Vircontium might just turn its predatory gaze to Auberon and forget about its claim on Fyrzentsou. Especially since the drought there meant there wasn't much worth claiming any more.

War could still erupt at any time.

He blamed his stepmother for addling his father's wits. She was there, under a silk canopy, her jewelled braids coiled about her ears and her pale face painted with blue accents. Her smile was gloating.

As soon as he saw it, his rage dissolved and he felt sick at heart. *I've played into her hands. But how…?*

'Ancelin!' The king stopped pacing the golden dais in front of her throne. 'I've been so worried.'

'Sire.' Ansey gave a formal bow. He didn't acknowledge the queen. He had finally realised, only a few days ago, she hated him simply because he existed. That's when he'd decided to run.

He knew she wanted to kill him. While he lived, none of her children would ever be Heir to the Kingdom of Auberon. Tybold would always take second place.

The king held him at arm's length. 'Why, Ancelin?'

'Why?' A stone seemed to lodge in his throat. 'I've told you a hundred times. I want to be a knight.'

'So you take the most dangerous horse in the Kingdom?'

Ansey was not about to be side–tracked. 'Every time I ask permission to begin training, you say "wait another year". I've waited six years now, and I'm not even a page.'

'That is beneath your station.' The king released him.

'It's part of the education of a knight. I can't skip it. That wouldn't be fair.'

'Many things aren't fair, Ancelin. I thought we'd agreed you finish your studies in statecraft and diplomacy. Those will be of greater benefit than all the arts of war.'

'I have finished them.'

'Seven years study in less than three?'

'I've worked especially hard. Even my tutors admit they cannot teach me more.' He took a deep breath and, to his horror, his voice trembled. 'You said I could start training if I showed some maturity. Last Winterdeep, at the feast, you gave your word.'

The king folded his arms. 'Today's effort is a demonstration of maturity?'

Ansey clenched his jaw. 'It's not fair. You've let Tybold be a squire and he's a year younger than me.'

'Tybold is obedient, chivalrous and dutiful.'

Ansey's mouth quivered. That was the most unfair thing he could ever remember his father saying. He felt tears welling. 'And I'm not?' He hoped his voice wasn't as broken and subdued as it sounded in his own ears. *I've worked so hard. I've done more than you've asked. More than you've dreamed.*

He tried to pull his thoughts together. They were heading on dangerous tracks. *How many princes know how to travel by night using only the stars for a guide? Or how to bake bread? Smoke fish? Speak the language of merchants? Or dwarves? Or finches? How many princes can calm a horse known for its violent rages?* 'I've tried to be patient, and never complain.'

'Behaving is much more than public politeness,' the queen said. 'Everyone in Auberon knows of your jealousy and the spiteful way you treat Tybold in private.'

'I *don't!* It's him!' The moment the words were out, he regretted them.

The queen came down from her throne and touched the king's arm. 'Maurtz, it's deliberate disobedience. Sterner lessons are required.'

'I believe you are right, Barbizca.' The king turned to her. 'I've been too tolerant. The boy has grown wild.' He turned back to Ansey. 'For your own good, I must place restrictions on you, Ancelin. I forbid you to entertain any further notion of knighthood. You are to stop—at once—this ridiculous behaviour of *practising* to be a page.'

'What?' Ansey felt himself shaking.

'Leaving food baskets outside the doors of the poorest villagers. Wasting the kitchen's time, ordering baskets of bread baked, using my flour, stealing my miller's work and sequestering my servants to work for lazy...'

'That's not true,' Ansey interrupted. 'I do the baking myself.' *Idiot, don't admit that.* 'And I didn't use your flour.' *Or that. Shut up, mouth, what do you think you're doing to me?* 'And the villagers aren't lazy, they're...'

The queen raised her hands and her voice. 'Not content with the humiliations of serving as a page, you sink lower than the kitchen help.'

'I'm going to be a knight of the people.' Ansey stopped as her hand slapped him hard across the face.

'You are born to be a king, to rule, not to serve.'

'A good king serves his people through his rule.'

'So...' The king shook his head, his face grey with sadness.

'...that's how you criticise me to your precious peasants.'

'I've never said a word against you, father.'

'That's not what I've heard.' The king pointed to the stone floor. 'Kneel, Ancelin, and give me your pledge you will immediately abandon this unseemly goal of knighthood.'

Ansey was shaking as if he were caught in the worst of land–tremors. He couldn't do it.

'Ancelin, We are waiting.'

He stared up at his father's grim face, his whole body numb.

'Your Majesty.' It was Gratian. Ansey had entirely forgotten he was there, a silent witness to his disgrace. 'Perhaps such a harsh sentence is unwarranted. Today's theft was only a boyish prank. His Highness has certainly caused anxiety but he hasn't disobeyed any explicit commands.'

Oh Gratian. Ansey was dizzy with relief. *One day I'll reward you for this. I owe you again. I owe you forever. And I'll never forget.*

He could see his father was swayed, even as the queen's eyes narrowed in anger.

Gratian placed his hand on Ansey's shoulder. It was a comforting weight. 'It's natural for a thwarted boy to run away. His Highness doesn't deserve so cruel a punishment.'

'Enough!' the queen ordered.

Gratian continued his defence, addressing the king. 'If Prince Ancelin were to give his word never to leave the grounds of Castle Auberon again, wouldn't that be enough?'

'You dare defy my orders to keep silent?' the queen demanded.

Ansey turned, terrified for Gratian. He knew the queen's venom like no one else.

Her voice rose to a shriek. 'You dare attempt to manipulate the king's mercy?'

Any hope the king would change his mind was gone. 'Your pledge, Ancelin. Kneel. Repeat after me: 'I will never seek knighthood nor…''

Ansey found his voice at last. 'No!' He had expected punishment, not injustice. 'Never.'

'So, the brat shows his true nature.' The queen's voice held a mocking lilt. 'Oh, his manners are fine enough if you pander to his every whim. But where are his knightly virtues now?' Her scornful gaze rested on him. 'If courtesy and obedience are thrown aside as soon as you encounter something you don't like, you vile little stain, then why swear to honour them at all?'

Thrown aside as soon as I encounter something I don't like? I've been courteous and obedient for years. 'You're twisting the meaning of honour…'

'Now he interrupts his betters.'

I haven't interrupted, Ansey thought. *You have.*

'Rude, undisciplined child. The boy has the heart of a serpent. He has won the favour of the poor with gifts of food; his plan is plainly to usurp the throne.'

'I was practising to be a page!' Ansey couldn't believe what was happening. 'Nothing more!' He gazed up into his father's eyes and saw suspicion. *How is this possible? We're arguing about knighthood one minute and treason the next.*

'There's no plot, then?' the king asked.

'No! Who'd say such a thing?'

'Tybold told me you'd asked him to join you.'

Ansey felt faint. He couldn't believe Tybold, for all his taunts about being elevated to squire, would devise this sort of trouble. 'This is Tybold's idea of a joke.'

'A joke?' The king was thoughtful. 'Tybold is a trickster. It would be just like...'

'Don't trust him, Maurtz.' The queen scowled. 'Tybold wouldn't joke about this. Remember, this is exactly how Rogin of Fyrzentsou was deceived by his own viperous son Emyr. He was fortunate to discover the real conspiracy just in time.'

Ansey shook his head in agitation. 'I'm not conspiring.'

'So you didn't flee because your wicked plan had been discovered? Do you think we're gullible, child? That we'll be tricked like Rogin of Fyrzentsou?'

Ansey saw his father was swayed by the queen's accusation. 'I'm not disloyal. I'd never betray you, father.'

'Then why won't you obey me?'

'Obey you?' Ansey's voice was as quiet as his father's was harsh. 'How could you believe I want to seize Auberon? You know all I've ever wanted is to be a knight. How can you ask me to give it up?'

'What I'm asking is you prove your loyalty. If you kneel and forswear knighthood, I will know you have not betrayed me. Is that so much to ask?'

Ansey was silent. If he did swear, he would give up the only dream that mattered to him. But if he didn't swear, he knew his father would never trust him again. He couldn't think about the first, but he couldn't live with the second.

He knelt.

'This is not honour.' His voice cracked. 'I yield to tyranny. But I will keep my word.' There were ashes in his mouth. 'I will never again seek to become a knight.' He looked up, hoping not to burst into tears. 'Please change your mind, father.'

'There's no possibility of that.'

'Can I go now?'

The king nodded.

Ansey rose and turned. He hadn't taken three steps when tears began to flow.

azed and dizzy, Fern woke. *Have I been out to it? Again?*

She emerged from the blackout into a cocoon of silk–white fog. *I've fainted. That's it. I've had a strange nightmare about being trapped in a bubble. I just need a drink and I'll be okay.*

There were voices in the distance.

She held her breath, listening. *Is it the giants or the snowflakes?* She hoped it was the prefects sent to retrieve her.

She pulled at the whistle around her neck. *Maybe I should try calling for help with this.* She blew, a long high fluting note, full of strange longing and heartache. *I wonder why I couldn't hear it before.*

'Stop that at once!' A heady waft of lavender, delicately undertoned with the scent of summer rosebuds, unlocked the bubble and floated over her, bringing other voices with it. 'Put it down! We heard you the first time!'

Something small and damp poked her face. A musky animal odour edged out the aroma of lavender. It was accompanied by a mellow voice. 'Oh, stop licking it, Hector. I'm telling you it's not a prince.'

Who's Hector? Another giant? Or another prince? Whiteness enveloped everything, whiteness with the smooth resplendence of a lily, whiteness drifting in lazy dream–like waves.

Something nuzzled her neck, tilted her chin up, dabbed at her glasses. 'Since when did you become our resident expert on princes?' It was a squeaky voice, different to the first.

'Hector, you're working up to a major disappointment.'

'Am not,' the squeaky voice retorted. 'It might be scruffy and worm–coloured, but look at these little plates over its eyes. Now what does that add up to?'

'What, Hector?'

'It adds up to Prince Emyr of Fyrzentsou, of course.'

'Oh, of course.' The mellow voice adopted a lofty sarcastic tone. 'I should have realised at once. Hector, be sensible.'

'I am,' the squeaky voice insisted. 'He's obviously in disguise. It's not a good disguise, I admit, since he's drawn attention to his eyes with the little plates, rather than away from them. But when you're on the run from Jotun assassins, you have to make do as best you can.' A sigh of contentment followed. 'Fortunately for my moment of destiny, he couldn't fool me.'

'Hector.' A gentle voice, different from the first two, spoke quietly. 'We're tired of hearing about your destiny.'

'You're just jealous because you don't have one, Ginevra.'

'Hector…'

'Oh, look,' the first voice interrupted. 'It twitched.'

'Where?' the squeaky voice asked. 'No! You imagined it, Boody.'

Fern was doing her best to do far more than twitch. She pushed and shoved, trying to brush aside the fog cocoon. It fell away in an abrupt shiver to reveal a fluttering silhouette. Fern blinked and squinted against the light.

A tiny white owl fluttered down to perch on her chest. It stared at her with shocked pink eyes. Fern stared back. *Do owls talk? Not normally. At least it's not a giant.*

A small snout thrust itself in front of the owl. 'Are you a prince?' a little fox asked.

Fern froze. *Foxes don't talk either.* Before she could say a word, the owl flapped its wing in the fox's face. 'Hector! Don't be so rude. Introduce yourself first.'

I'm dreaming. Hallucinating worse than ever.

'Name's Hector.' The fox's tone was brusque. 'What's yours, princeling?'

The owl's wing slapped more forcefully, sending Hector tumbling backwards. 'Trees will sprout feet before foxes find manners.' The owl spread its wings and leaned forward in an apologetic bow. 'May I introduce myself and my companions, wayfarer? My name is Boudicca's Chariot. My friends call me "Boody".' She gestured to her right. 'This is Ginevra–'ayelet–hashachar.'

And that's a mouthful.

'Peace, wayfarer.' A snow–white fawn bent towards Fern. Rose pink eyes, the shape of almonds, looked down on her. 'My friends called me "Ginevra".'

Right. Foxes, owls and fawns do not speak in the real world. So either I'm not in the real world and I've fallen into some place like Narnia or I'm delusional or this is a dream or... She looked past the talking animals at the tree above her. Its branches foamed with tiny white flowerlets and its leaves were pale green, edged with ivory. *...at least it's a beautiful place.*

'The individual with the atrocious manners...' Boody was continuing her introductions. '...is Hector.'

'Are you a prince?' Hector renewed his position.

Fern noticed he had studded leather cuffs around his white ankles. 'No, I'm not.' As she scrambled up, Boody hopped off her chest onto the grass. 'My name's Fern.'

'Fern...' Ginevra's tone was appreciative as her long eyelashes fluttered. 'Oh, what a lovely name! It conjures up thoughts of green shadows falling across leafy glades and midsummer light dancing along the forest floor.'

Fern stared at the little fawn. She'd always hated her name. She'd been called after one of her aunts who hadn't been fond of it either. It came from one of gran's favourite books. 'Why couldn't gran have chosen Charlotte after the spider?' Aunt Fern would mumble from time to time.

'There's no prince in any kingdom named Fern.' Hector's enthusiasm had soured. He thumped his tail and glared at Ginevra. '*Fern!?* What do you mean "leafy glades"? "Dancing in the forests"?'

He raised a leather–cuffed paw. 'What it really conjures up is hunters hiding in the bracken and don't you deny it.'

'Hector, stop it this instant,' Boody warned. 'It's not Fern's fault she isn't a prince.'

Fern knew she should be panic–stricken with worry but she couldn't help it. The fox's glowering snout and spitfire eyes looked so funny. She wanted to giggle. 'Are you always this cheerful?'

'Oh no.' Hector shook his head. 'Sometimes I get depressed. You're fortunate I'm in such an irrepressibly merry mood today. Nothing can dismay me.' His expression became even more glum as he cocked his snout at her. 'How long are you staying?'

Boody's wing flicked out once more, but he sidestepped it. 'I score—you missed.' Hector turned back to Fern. 'You're disturbing my date with destiny.'

Before she could answer, he was flung side–ways, his legs tumbling high in the air. A kick from Ginevra's hoof had connected with his rump. 'I score.' The little fawn inclined her head to Fern. 'Our apologies, wayfarer. Foxes are all obsessed with questions of identity and destiny. They search for the answers so busily and diligently they miss the best of life.'

'Whereas those of us who get on with life find destiny seeking us out.' Boody stared at Hector as he scrambled up. 'We don't have to wait around for it, it's there waiting for us.'

The fox was clearly unabashed. It was evident to Fern he had heard all this before. He sat up, his tail flat on the ground and his snout high in the air. 'Scoff if you will, but you'll be grovelling your apologies the day the prince arrives and invites me to help him save the world.'

Boody's pink eyes rolled skywards. Ginevra shook a dainty hoof and sighed.

Hector peered at Fern once more. 'So, when are you off? This is our tree, you see.' He tapped his leather–cuffed paw. 'Not that we own it, but everyone knows the White Tree belongs to the White Three. That's us, in case you can't count or have vision problems.' His paw tapped faster. 'You're disturbing the ambience of the locale, so the sooner you move on the better.'

Fern shrugged. 'I don't even know how I got here. And I haven't got a clue how to get back.'

Ginevra and Boody exchanged glances. 'How you got here is easy,' the little owl said. 'There was a high–pitched whistle which either preceded or possibly even precipitated a rip in the fabric between your dimension and ours.'

High–pitched whistle? Fern reached for the chain around her neck.

Ginevra nodded. 'She's definitely come from somewhere quite strange. I hope it's not the Plague Realm.'

'What's happened?' Hector was taking in the sidelong glances between them. 'Are we in danger? Never fear—Hector's here! Enemies, is it? I'll fight 'er for ya!'

'Hector, be quiet!' Ginevra raised her hoof at him, looking concerned. 'Boody, what is it?'

The owl scrutinised Fern with care. 'She seems harmless enough. But the dimensions don't just pluck people willy–nilly from one cosmos to another. Except in times of great peril.'

'Great peril?' Hector asked. 'Lead me to it! C'mon, c'mon.' His front paws were up in a belligerent pose. 'I'll send it packing. Yes, back to where it's come from, tail between its legs.'

Boody ignored him. 'There are accounts, preserved in the Wisdom Books of the Owls, about what happens when a dimension's very survival is threatened.'

'Very survival is threatened?' Hector began to look alarmed. 'That does not sound good. Of course, you are speaking in merely theoretical terms, aren't you?'

'The dimension itself may take desperate action. It will seek the perfect helper from another world and, when it finds that helper, it will put a needle of time through to the other world, thread the needle and stitch the two dimensions together to try to regain stability.'

The perfect helper? Fern threw up her hands. *Lucky this is a dream because this is a complete joke. Everyone knows I'm totally useless.*

'Fern is the thread?' Ginevra asked.

'She's not the needle anyway. She might be the stitch.' Boody's pink eyes narrowed into squints. 'At any rate, I believe she's in a multi–dimensional bubble.'

'There's definitely something odd about her.' Ginerva shook her head, looking dismayed.

'She's got no smell.' Hector sniffed Fern's shoes and socks while shaking his head. 'Why do you think I've been trying to get rid of her? I noticed it straight away.'

'She's in two places at once,' Ginevra said.

'Yes.' Boody nodded. 'In two dimensions simultaneously. What a desperate measure. Think how much energy it takes to stabilise an anomalous duality like this. We must be about to be plunged into a dreadful winter.'

Hector's gaze darted from one to the other. 'I don't like the sound of "anomalous duality", whatever it is. It's worse than "the dimension's very survival is threatened." So we're in trouble?'

'The biggest.' Boody nodded. 'The whole world's in trouble. I can't understand why we haven't noticed anything. Why there have been no signs.'

'There've been earthquakes,' Hector pointed out.

'There've always been earthquakes and the recent ones haven't been severe.' Ginevra looked up. 'Isn't the end of the world always accompanied by mysterious portents in the sky, rivers running with blood, mountains sheeted with torrents of flame?'

Boody heaved a sigh of relief and spread her wings. 'Too true. And we've had none of that.' She laughed, a brief self–deprecating chuckle. 'Imagine thinking someone has just popped on through from another dimension.'

Ginevra clicked her hooves together and joined in the laughter. 'Yes, imagine.'

'Hold on.' Hector squinted at Fern's glasses. 'What are those plates over your eyes?'

'These?' Fern touched her spectacles. 'They're glasses.'

'What do they do?'

'I can't see without them.'

'Are they magic?'

'No. They're just glasses. I'm short–sighted. They correct my vision.'

Several seconds of hushed quiet followed before Ginevra spoke. 'Does everyone have glasses plates for their eyes where you come from?'

'Not everyone. Only people with some sort of defect in their vision. Unless you've got sunglasses. You don't need to have faulty vision for them. They're for keeping the glare of the sun out of your eyes.'

'*Sun*glasses?' The word almost choked in Boody's throat. 'To keep glare out of your eyes?'

'Well, that's that, then.' Hector sat on his tail and folded his forepaws. 'She don't come from 'round here. I think the other dimension theory has my vote.' His smile was bright in an anxious, brittle way. 'I wish you the best of luck, young human. The very best. You'd better be off. No time to waste. If you're the perfect helper, you'd better go start helping.' He waggled his paws in a gesture of farewell. ''Bye!'

'You've got the wrong person if you're expecting help.' Fern's smile was thin. 'Besides I'm a stranger in this dimension. If it is another dimension, that is. So from my point of view, you're here to help me.'

There was silence. Hector leaned forward. 'We're not qualified to save the world…'

'Hector, she's got a point.' Ginevra nudged him with her hoof. 'Besides, you've always wanted to be a hero. Where's the brave little fox who's been waiting for the prince to come along so he could help defeat the powers of darkness?'

'Still waiting.' Hector threw up his snout. 'You've got the wrong idea entirely about my plan. I don't want to be a hero—I just want to tag along and make a minor contribution towards the prince's rite–of–passage adventure.' A woeful expression appeared on his face. 'You know, the moment I heard those words "anomalous duality", I had this sinking feeling there's a dark abyss out there which suddenly knows my name. I don't feel a sense of adventure calling—I feel something really evil's out to get me.'

'Hector, you're not afraid, are you?'

'Absoluuuutely!' the fox wailed.

'Oh, that makes me feel so much better.' Ginevra's smile was tremulous. 'I'm terrified. You might have had some ambition to save the world, but I've never had the slightest.'

'What shall we do?' Boody asked.

Ginevra raised a hoof. 'Let's take this straight to the king.'

'And hand over all responsibility?' Hector breathed a sigh of relief.

Boody seemed to have other things on her mind as she nodded. 'Sunglasses,' she said under her breath. 'Sunglasses.'

ver since he had returned from the throneroom, Ansey hadn't moved from his oriel window. He sat, hunched in the corner, unhearing, unseeing.

The window overlooked the smallest courtyard. A combat training session had been taking place in it for nearly an hour. Ansey hardly registered the noise or the dust. He knew it was a practice bout, using full–weight swords with blunted edges. He knew the swordmaster from Vircontium had just about shouted himself hoarse as he whipped out instructions to the squires.

But none of it mattered today.

His arms were wrapped about his knees. His heart felt dead. There were no tears left.

It wasn't just the unfairness of his father's demand, it was where the queen had apportioned the blame. His world had crashed around him.

'Tybold! Tybold!' The cheers drifted up from the courtyard. *Guess Toady is the champion. Again.*

A flicker of jealousy surged. Then crumbled. Ansey knew Tybold would have relied more on the strength and length of his arms than on any superior skill.

If I'd been able to get to Ysgarde, they'd have shown me how to use speed and agility, not brute force. He clamped down on the thought and flung it away. It's best to have no feelings at all. *No wants. No needs. No friends.*

Ansey stared at a patch of discoloured earth in the middle of the courtyard as if nothing in the entire universe were more important. *Is that what my father is trying to do? Teach me that I should be reliant on no one? That to be an impartial king who never shows favouritism, I must put my own desires aside?*

A shadow jumped onto the seat beside him in the oriel window. 'Have you finished tormenting yourself, Buttercup?' A dwarf with flame–coloured hair swept back into a single curled wave held up a dish of toffee–coated fruits. 'Your lunch is cold. So can I tempt you with one of these?'

Ansey waved them aside. 'I'm not tormenting myself.'

'Right.' The dwarf rolled his eyes and popped a toffee cherry into his mouth. 'So you're ready to hear the end of the story now?'

Ansey said nothing.

The dwarf stomped on the window seat and glared down at the combat. 'Five courtyards, but just coincidentally they pick the smallest to practice in. The only one your rooms overlook. Malice, that's what it is, Buttercup…'

Ansey turned away. His heart was coming alive again, despite his instructions for it to stay dead. He knew it was, because his chest was so painful.

'Trust me, Buttercup,' the dwarf said. 'You'll like the rest of this story.'

'It doesn't have a happy ending, does it, Candle?' Ansey wrapped his arms even tighter around himself.

'Can't answer for the book of real life, Your Highness.' Candle broke into a wide gold–toothed smile. 'Happily–ever–afters are only guaranteed in fairy tales—and not always then, these days. But this chapter panned out sweetly.'

'*Sweetly?*' Ansey spat as he turned to confront Candle. 'When the queen told Gratian to get rid of my tutors, she didn't mean to kick them out of the kingdom—you know what she meant.' He felt the fine nerves all across his face begin to jerk, just as they had when he first heard the news. 'She meant to execute them.' He buried his face in his hands. 'But they're not to blame.'

'But they *are* a bad influence.' Candle's grin became even wider. 'As for what she told Gratian, if she meant "execute" when she said "get rid of", she should've been more explicit.' He winked.

It took a moment for Ansey to understand. 'They got away?' He jumped up, clapping his hands. '*Away*! All of them?'

Candle nodded. 'Harper and Tobias and Doctor Much and the Professor, too.'

'Oh, Candle, why didn't you say so before?'

Candle planted one hand on a hip and reached out to pluck a cluster of toffee–coated grapes from the dish. 'You cut me off, Buttercup. Just when I was getting to the exciting part about the escape and the demon driver.'

'Demon driver?' Ansey frowned. 'What demon driver?'

'Oh, so you want to hear more now?' Candle crunched on a grape, his nose high with disdain.

'Please, Candle.' Ansey dropped to his knees. '*Please.*'

Candle looked down, his cold eyes softening. 'I always was a sucker for a prince with pretty manners.' He tilted his head. 'Oh, very well.'

Ansey jumped to his feet.

Candle tutted. 'Now, of course, when the carriage left the castle, the presence of the demon driver wasn't immediately obvious. The carriage ambled along as if there were nothing suspicious about its occupants or its route. You know how deaf Old Greywhiskers is? When he was told they had to flee for their lives, he thought a new species of bee in a hive had been found and he was being asked to identify it. He apparently thought the king and queen were finally beginning to appreciate the vastness of his knowledge.'

'Not this century.'

Candle laughed. 'No, not this century. So while Harper and Tobias and Doctor Much were hastily packing what little they could, he got out a beekeeper's suit and all sorts of equipment for catching insects. He was so happy his talents were being valued at last he began to sing.'

'Sing?' Ansey returned to the window–seat.

'Sing.' Candle's crest of flame–coloured hair bobbed up and down as he nodded. 'Perhaps I exaggerate. "Caterwaul" is more accurate. He was bundled into the coach with his nets and gloves and hooded gauze while singing a bee–catching song and instructing Doctor Much on the life cycle of the alpine moss bee. Much couldn't keep him quiet—which was a good thing, since the complete lack of secrecy about the departure dispelled all suspicion it was a desperate escape bid.'

'No one guessed?'

'Every time Much said, "Shh," Greywhiskers banged him on the head with his umbrella.' Candle's grin became wider. 'The umbrella came in handy as it turned out: Tobias used it to great effect knocking the lead riders of the King's Shield off their horses when the pursuit finally caught up with them.'

Ansey felt his heart lighten. It would be just like Candle to make up a story. However he was so obviously gleeful, it had to be true. Ansey smiled, imagining gangly short–sighted Tobias leaning out of a carriage and swiping at the black–clad riders armed only with an umbrella.

'But it was the driver who saved them,' Candle went on. 'Once his cloudshadow trick failed, he took the cliff road down the Harrowfell. The King's Shield had no chance to pass him there. He sliced round corners like a charioteer in the Vircontium stadium, cutting off their horses as they tried to overtake the carriage. It was a race to the Fyrzentsou border, touch and go all the way. Old Greywhiskers fainted when the coach leapt the broken bridge at Madder's Crossing.'

'You're making this up.' Suddenly Ansey wasn't so sure Candle was telling the truth. He thought of the switchbacks on the Harrowfell, the black ice, the narrow causeways, the cleared section where the avalanche had been. *Not even someone like Captain Gratian, who knows the dangers, could make it down safely.*

Candle laid a hand over his heart. 'True as I'm standing here. As for Tobias and Harper, they kept yelling for the driver to slow down before the coach overturned and he killed them all.' He grinned again. 'But their pleas fell on deaf ears. The driver kept going even when the back wheels fell off. He kept going even when one of the pursuing guards leapt onto the coach and tried to turn the horses.

Luckily Harper had enough sense by that stage to take the Professor's butterfly net and smack it over the guard's head. That gave the driver the chance to knock the guard unconscious.'

'You expect me to believe this?' Ansey withdrew, feeling an even deeper sense of crushing. *Fool. How could you have been so stupid as to give in to hope?*

Candle ate another grape. 'It's an eyewitness account. Bramble and Rubble saw the whole thing from the top of Fastness Height. Rubble said it was the cloudshadow drew his attention. It was going against the wind, not with it. Then he noticed the clouds had wolf–tail shapes. That was a giveaway.'

That's the same trick the King's Shield used on me. It's a neat deception: to hide in the cloudshadow. But who knows it? Could I bribe someone to teach me?

Candle folded his arms. 'It was Bramble who noticed the carriage careening down the Harrowfell. He didn't think it meant anything more than a reckless driver until he noticed the Pursuit.' He winked. 'Then he thought, "Aha! Prince Buttercup is making another run for it. Twice in one day! What determination! What boldness! What an idiot!"'

'He did *not*!'

Candle's grin faded and, for several seconds, he looked pensive. 'You're right, he didn't,' he admitted at last. 'What Bramble actually thought was, "Aha! Prince Ancelin Bedwyr Cai is making another run for it. Twice in one day! What determination! What boldness! What an idiot!"'

'He…'

Candle waved his hands to hush any protest. 'Bramble was just about to call out a dwarf troop to help you when he realised the driving was too good for any prince of Auberon, even one as talented in bread–baking and sparrow–speak as Your Highness. He wasn't sure if you knew the secret of making cloudshadow but he was sure the speed needed to soar across the broken bridge at Madder's Crossing needs a fine judgment and an even finer touch with horses. Three of the King's Shield wound up in the river rapids mistiming the leap, you know.'

Ansey began to feel curiously light–headed. *Could it be true? Could the queen's revenge have been foiled?*

'Bramble says he's never seen such a virtuoso display, even from the professional charioteers in the Vircontium arenas. And Bramble's a big fan of the arenas, so that, you know, is the highest praise.' Candle nodded his head and his thoughtful look was replaced by a sudden huge grin, followed by a deep frown. 'I never really liked Gratian, you know. We've had more than our fair share of differences. But I must say going down the Harrowfell took guts.'

'*Gratian*?!' Ansey felt his jaw drop. 'It was Captain Gratian? The driver?'

'Of course. Who else do you think would know every trick the King's Pursuit would throw at him?' Candle stared Ansey straight in the eyes, all trace of a smile gone. 'He knew exactly what he was being asked to do when he was told to get rid of your tutors. And it didn't involve escorting them safely out of the country. And he knew no one has ever outrun the King's Shield—but he had to reach the border before they did. The cliffs were the only way.'

How does an ordinary captain know how to make wolf–tail cloudshadow? 'Will he be all right?' Ansey's head and heart both started to thump at the same moment. 'In Fyrzentsou? Will they arrest him and send him back? What about my tutors?'

'They'll be all right.' Candle waved his hands in dismissal. 'Rogin will want to question them, but he won't send them back.'

'But what if he tortures them? He did that to his own son, didn't he? And sent manticore hunters after him.'

'That was a matter of treason.' Candle shook his head. 'This has nothing to do with Prince Emyr. Your tutors will be fine. Bramble's asked permission for a task force to protect them, if necessary.'

'The dwarves will help?'

Candle nodded. 'Haven't we always? Kindle, Humble and Toddle have been sent to Fyrzentsou to help Gratian and your tutors if required.' Candle's smile returned and he showed all his gold–capped teeth. 'Don't think we're doing it out of the goodness of our stony little hearts.'

'No?'

'It's all in hope of eventual reward.' Candle leaned back, gazed into his eyes and popped the last toffee grape into his mouth. 'A man of integrity and courage like Gratian is plainly destined to either die rashly in some noble cause or to become a great leader. It never hurts to have a future prominent leader indebted to you. Or to play the percentages about who's destined for greatness and who's not.'

Ansey's head stopped thumping and began to clamour for an explanation. 'If you and all the Cavern Kin are so coldly calculating in your relationships, then what are you doing here with me, Candle?'

'I'm assigned as Companion to the Heir of Auberon.' Candle eyed him without flinching.

'Well, you'd better get down to the courtyard and help Tybold then.' Ansey felt a chill come over him as he turned once more to look out the oriel window. The squires were gathering their weapons and filing out of the courtyard. He was filled with desperate longing to be with them. 'I want to be a knight,' he whispered under his breath.

'Haven't changed your mind?'

'I've ruined Gratian.' Ansey hung his head. 'And my tutors, too. After all their years of service, they could have expected a generous reward—if only I'd been more… more… patient.'

'Have you never heard about the frog in the cauldron?'

Ansey shook his head.

'It was a happy–hoppy frog, swimming about, making a splash in its own happy–hoppy way.'

'Is this story as true as the demon driver?'

'More so.' Candle folded his arms again. 'The water in the cauldron slowly lost its chill, became mild and balmy, then pleasantly warm, then unpleasantly hot—the temperature rose so slowly the water was almost boiling before the happy–hoppy frog realised the danger and had the sense to jump.' He reached out and clasped Ansey's elbow. 'Come on. Toad Gratian may have jumped, but you and I are still trapped in the cauldron.'

'Tybold's the toad, not Gratian.'

'How can you maintain such a profound innocence about reality, Buttercup? Ahh, no time for an education now. You'd better get properly attired for an audience. The king's about to send for you.'

He's heard the messenger's footsteps on the stairwell. We've got maybe a minute. 'Any idea what for?'

'I imagine his motive will be to show you how ridiculous your ambition is.'

'He's going to humiliate me in front of everyone.'

'The only person who can humiliate you, Prince Ancelin Bedwyr Cai, is Ancelin Bedwyr Cai.' Stepping off the window seat, Candle stumped across to a carved armoire closet on the far side of the room. He flung it open. 'But don't make the situation worse by keeping their Majesties waiting.'

Ansey jumped up. *Now Gratian's gone, will one of the King's Shield think it's safe to tell on me? How long is it going to be before everyone knows I have Beast Flair? They'll all think I'm a freak.*

He stripped off his linen shirt and replaced it with his best court tunic. 'Cloak or coat, you think?'

Candle pouted. 'Cloak may be best.'

Ansey stared at the choices, undecided. He hesitated between his velvet cloak with its tippets of gold and a plain hooded mantle whose only ornament was a sturdy silver clasp at the shoulder. *If it's a choice between looking like the king's heir and looking like a complete contrast to Tybold, I'll take the contrast.* He swung the plain hooded cape over his shoulder.

The heavy tread of a pair of boots sounded just outside in the hallway. Ansey watched as Candle flicked a short cloak from a rack near the door. He swirled it on while giving his crest of flame–coloured hair a quick smooth.

He opened the door and addressed the messenger. 'Their Majesties require Prince Ancelin's presence immediately?'

The messenger stood there, his hand raised, about to knock. 'Stop doing that! It gives me a right fright every time.' He glared. 'And you know it!'

'Now don't be bitter, boy.' Candle's voice was smooth as cream, topped with smugness. 'Bitter bulbs breed baleful blossoms, as one of the great dwarf poets said.' He nodded. 'But not quickly, of course.'

The messenger's glare became a peeved pout. 'Their Majesties require Prince Ancelin's presence at the Tourney Ground.'

'Tourney Ground?' Ansey felt his face crumple. 'Oh please no. They're not going to let Tybold gloat?'

'The Knights of Renown have come to Auberon.' The messenger ignored Candle and spoke straight over the top of his crest to Ansey. 'And the king supports their search.'

'Knights of Renown?' Ansey gripped Candle's shoulder. 'How? When? What search?'

'A tournament and fair.' Candle shrugged. 'Their usual enlistment lure. The Knights of Renown have been recruiting across the Kingdoms of Fyrzentsou, Malveraine and Vircontium. The king wants Ysgarde as an ally, so he's naturally he's letting the Knights put on their show here.' He snorted. 'I expected they'd turn up fairly swiftly once Gratian had gone, but not quite so soon.'

Ansey didn't know what to think. *What did the Knights have to do with Gratian going? But recruitment...!* 'I could have had my heart's desire, if only I'd waited. Just a few hours...'

Candle seemed unconcerned. 'Number one, destiny is not that easily thwarted. And number two, the king would've forbidden you to take part in the tournament anyway.'

The messenger moved aside to allow them to pass. 'But number three...' Candle led the way to a winding stairwell. '...you did make it easy for him.'

A new sense of dejection overwhelmed Ansey. When they reached the courtyard, the messenger left them. By that time, his thoughts were drowning in an anguished mire, even more trackless than the Mistmurk. A cloud of finches glided down from the battlements, and fluttered around him.

'You don't say?' Candle asked the twittering finches. 'The four-and-twenty blackbird pies are by far the best value for money at the fair—the venison sausages are mainly bread and eel meat.'

Ansey translated as the finches continued. 'The minstrels have got a scam going with the fortune teller, the baby dragon is really a lizard painted with phosphorescent dye, the monkey–king is a boy in a wolfskin suit, but the frost giant is probably the real thing.' Ansey didn't like Candle's scowl as he finished. 'Anything wrong? Did I get the translation wrong?'

'A *real* frost giant. And Gratian gone.' Candle's grim expression deepened as the finches become rowdier.

Nothing to do with the translation. 'What's a frost giant being here got to do with Gratian?'

Candle ignored him, turning his full attention to the finches. 'What's the weather forecast? Late afternoon snowstorm, yes? And early morning fog?' He nodded. 'You know, I believe it all, except the first bit about the blackbird pies. I don't know why you little guys don't give up this doomed marketing campaign. Your motives aren't half obvious.'

'What's the connection between Gratian and the frost giant?'

'None.' Candle shook his head as the finches continued to twitter. 'I'm sure the prince thanks you for volunteering, guys, but pecking the king's eyes out won't help. Truly. And strafing his kneecaps won't do any good, either.'

'No, no, no!' Ansey's hands jittered. 'Keep out of it, guys! It's my responsibility to deal with this.' He shook his head. Out of the corner of his eye he spotted a splinter of dazzling light. 'What's that?'

As they reached the castle gate, he pointed across the bustling fair towards the Tourney Ground. Another glinting sliver of light flashed out.

'What?' Candle craned his neck to see over the top of the silk pavilions. 'I haven't seen or heard anything except finch folly.'

Ansey saw the light again. *It's like a star window, opening and closing. A shimmer twirling in heaven.*

'I'm going to kill him.' Candle thumped his fist into his open palm. 'I'm going to smash the runt's face in. What's he thinking of? There's a frost giant around.'

Ansey stared. 'Who? What is it?' *A star? A firefly? An angel's wing?* 'Why are you keeping secrets, Candle? What is it about the frost giant?'

Candle harrumphed. 'What you see is nothing more than a reflection off a ground glass lens. What did you think I meant when I said Bramble saw Gratian's drive down the Harrowfell from the top of Fastness Height—that he was using magical sight?'

'I don't think I thought at all.' Ansey noticed a white deer, a white fox and a peasant girl with a white owl on one shoulder at the spot where the light winked. 'What's a ground glass lens?'

Candle stomped off towards the fair, the cloud of finches trailing after him.

Ground glass lens? Ansey took a deep breath. *Clearly a device for seeing long distances which emits bursts of brilliant light. How come no–one else has noticed it? The moment I get a chance, I'll ask the finches if they know why it shouldn't be used near a frost giant.* He set off after Candle, his thoughts pre–occupied. *And what Gratian's departure has to do with the coming of the Knights of Renown.*

ern was dazzled as she followed Ginevra and Hector. Boody was on Ginevra's back. Peering faces turned towards them as they made their way through the crowd. Their glances flicked from Boody to Ginevra to Hector's leather ankle–cuffs and then to her socks. Where they stayed. And stayed. *Like they've never seen anything like them before.*

There were dancers in flimsy silks, jugglers in fanciful jerkins and troubadours in velvet patchwork all mingling with the noisy crowds. Silence seemed to descend as Ginevra and Hector progressed down the lanes, before whispered talk started again once they were past.

There was so much to take in: silk pavilions with floating pennants, striped tents with bright tassels and elaborate booths of polished parquetry. Even the simplest of unroofed stalls had eye–catching gilded signs.

The comforting smell of cinnamon and all–spice competed with the aroma of new–baked bread and roasting meat.

'I could so go for a venison pie.' Hector licked his chops as they passed the pastry stall.

Ginevra flicked out a hoof but he dodged her kick with a deft jump.

'I score.' Hector winked at Fern. 'She thought I was serious.'

'People are looking at me.' Fern realised the crowds were parting to let them through and staring sidelong at her socks.

Boody hopped from Hector's back to Ginevra's neck and fluttered to Fern's shoulder. 'Sunglasses. The concept has merit…'

Fern glanced at her and then around at the leathers and fabrics, scrolls and chapbooks, perfumes, gold and silver ornaments in the nearby stalls. The eyes of all the stall-owners seemed to follow her, straying from their customers in an unnerving, curious way.

'Careful,' Ginevra warned. 'They're sizing you up as a prospect. Most everyone here has an outrageously priced under-the-counter miracle for sale.'

Fern was fairly sure the wary looks cast in her direction had nothing to do with wanting to sell her anything.

'Quite so,' Boody said. 'Don't get taken in by a simple herbal remedy or a posy of wishes.'

Fern smiled and wished she could become invisible. *I'm invisible at home. I've mastered the art of making sure no one thinks I'm competing with them or not pulling my weight or even breathing their oxygen. I melt into the background. If I can do it there, I can do it here.* She patted Ginevra's flank. 'Is there any way I could get some clothes that aren't conspicuous?' She looked down at her pleated uniform and the long socks below them. Then her gaze crossed the grass towards a pair of red jewelled slippers peeping out from beneath the embroidered hem of a velvet robe. 'People are staring at me.' She winced and kept her head down.

She could see long coarse mantles and muddy leather sandals, soft woollen cloaks and fine-tooled boots, but not a single pair of bare legs with socks. Except her own.

'No, no. It's not you.' Boody hopped from one foot to the other. 'They always stare at the White Three from the White Tree. They think we're magic and it's in our own best interests we do nothing to dispel that notion. It's our chief protection.'

Ginevra sighed. 'I suppose now we'll have to get you something white so we can be the White Four from the White...' She hesitated. 'Door? Floor?'

'Claw?' Hector offered. 'Jaw? Maw?'

'You have such a violent mind.'

'They're staring at *me*.' Fern felt herself getting redder.

'Sunglasses.' Boody brushed her wing against Fern's ear. 'I've given the concept a fleeting thought or two, and I think it's an idea whose time has obviously come.'

'We actually should get her something white before we go to the king,' Ginevra announced. 'How are we going to manage that?'

Fern looked around, puzzled. 'Couldn't you just ask? I'm sure if you explained the situation to someone, they'd do it for you.'

Boody looked at her in obvious consternation. 'A nice idea but there aren't that many people with Flair, you know. No one would understand what we were trying to explain.'

'What's Flair?'

'What you've got. In a very serious way.'

I've got flair? 'And what's that?'

Boody didn't answer. They'd reached the end of an avenue of stalls. Beyond it, a lawn stretched away towards the castle. Servants were pushing large marble rollers across it.

It's like a tennis court. They're flattening it. Fern thought of all the lumps in the fields on the way. They'd crossed furrows and folds and sometimes even wide cracks. Hector loved to get a run–up on them but Ginevra simply danced across them. Sometimes she pirouetted, sometimes she leapt. 'I wonder if the king and queen know what the countryside is really like,' she'd said at one point.

Staring at the diligent servants pushing their marble rollers, Fern thought it was very unlikely. She turned away towards a tent made of torn scraps of rag. Unlike the dazzling silk pavilions or the elaborate carved booths, it was faded and inferior. Long whitish strips of fabric fluttered in the breeze like bedraggled feathers. There was no sign on the tent.

'Sunglasses.' Boody leaned against Fern's ear. 'Actually I think it's an idea whose time is past due.'

'What's Flair?' Fern tried to bring Boody back to her last question. She was beginning to think the little pink–eyed owl was obsessed.

Without warning, her arm was grasped from behind. As she was whirled around by a crushing grip, Boody took to the air and Hector yelped.

'What bird–brained sparrowfart let you loose with a spyglass you haven't the sense to hide?' A dwarf was glaring at her.

Boody swooped down, claws raking. 'Bird–brain?'

The dwarf let go of Fern to try to fend off the screeching owl.

'Stop!' Fern threw up her hands as beads of blood appeared on the dwarf's forehead and hands. Boody whirled, talons still out. With a sideways swipe, she knocked off his hat to reveal hair combed up in a bright crest.

'You're not Bramble!' The dwarf stared at Fern with a grimace frozen half–way between dismay and apology. 'You're not Rubble, either!'

Boody landed on Fern's shoulder.

Rubble? Fern wasn't so sure. *Ow! My arm!*

'I'm so sorry.' A boy rushed up, apologising to her. He pushed the dwarf out of the way.

Fern stared at his pale face, partly hidden by the hood of a plain hooded cape with a sturdy silver clasp.

'Please forgive this terrible mistake.' He bowed to her as a crowd of on–lookers gathered behind him. 'Candle thought you were someone else. Please…' He looked up, his expression pleading. 'If there is any way I can make reparation…'

Maybe I can solve this problem of people staring. I'm sure it's my socks. If only I could hide them, then… 'Do you have a spare cloak I could borrow?'

A moment later, the boy had unclasped his silver cloak pin and swung off the hooded cape. Draping it over his arm, he bowed and presented both cloak and clasp to her.

The watching crowd murmured and strained their necks in obvious curiosity.

There seems to be a problem with fading into the background here. They're acting like this kid is some sort of royalty. Fern took the cloak and folded it. She didn't want to try to put it on in front of a gawping crowd. *This is not going to plan.*

A stir at the tent–flap in front of her drew her attention. A strange masked head poked out. 'Your Highness.' A little girl's voice came from the mask.

That explains it. Fern bit her lower lip. *He is royalty.*

'The wounds on your dwarf's face…' The girl in the mask pointed at Candle. '…they'll get infected, if not treated.'

'I'm not *his* dwarf,' Candle snapped at her.

Fern frowned. *You could've fooled me.*

The little girl stepped out from the shadows of the rag door and into the sunlight. Fern stared. The girl was dressed in faded trousers with a dark overdress. From her shoulders up all signs of the ordinary disappeared. Her black hair was braided with azure ribbons and gold–flecked cords. Woven into the intricate plaits were tiny silver bells, tinkling crystal droplets and blue lapis beads. The masked head–dress was so fantastic Fern blinked in disbelief. It was composed of brilliantly–coloured feathers, with an assortment of fern fronds, tangerine tulips, porcupine quills and even a dead azure–breasted kingfisher mounted on it.

She held up a tiny dark hand. 'I have balms and potions, poultices and lotions. Wounds should not be left until it's too late.'

'She's right, Candle.' The boy sighed and looked miserable. 'I don't want you scarred too.'

'Too?' Candle looked perplexed for a moment. 'Prince Ancelin, don't torture yourself with blame over what happened to Captain Gratian.'

'Prince Ancelin…' Fern whispered. *So that's his name.*

He must have heard her. He turned and smiled. 'My friends call me Ansey.'

Fern sensed it was an invitation. 'Ansey,' she said. 'Thank you.'

She realised the crowd was pressing closer, edging towards the rag tent in an attempt to see and hear better. A dark shadow fell across the sun and, in just a few seconds, the temperature plummeted. Pressing the warm cloak against herself, she thought seriously about putting it on.

'Brr…' Ansey shivered. 'What's this chill? When did winter…?' He broke off as he looked up.

Fern turned to follow his gaze. There, looming over the top of the rag tent, was an immense figure, blocking the sunlight.

'Pardon me, young sirs and young curs.' The giant inclined his head in polite greeting. 'Can you tell me if this is where I might find The King Who Guards The Gate?'

I'm going completely mad. It's him. That's his voice. The giant I imagined when I blacked out on the sportsfield. He was talking to Freutim about… was it a daystar? Fern felt Ginevra, Hector and Boody press against her as two jet–black ravens on the giant's shoulder peered at them with unabashed curiosity.

She glanced around and saw the crowd melt away. The masked girl disappeared in a tinkle of bells and crystals, pulling the flaps of the rag tent tight as she went.

'I don't think you'd be looking for the king of Auberon, sir.' Ansey craned his neck to look straight at the giant's ruddy face. 'At least not as the king who guards the gate. Our gateways are expected to guard themselves.'

A rumble of laughter started in the giant's belly. He pressed his huge lips together but his mouth twisted as if he was trying to keep his amusement from breaking out into the open. 'A task to which most gateways are unaccustomed.' With each word he spoke, the air became more brittle and glassy. Ice crystals started to form in the air. 'Just between you and me, young sir, the gateways here are inordinately lax.' He shook his head. Cold waves of mist rippled through the air as his tangled locks of hair swept back and forth. Snowflakes floated down onto Fern's shoulders.

'I think that's most unfair to the gateways, sir.'

Fern heard Candle's hiss. 'Don't talk to it.'

The giant had a twinkle in his eye as he observed Ansey. 'You may be right. All but the most magic gateways need sleep, after all. They can't be expected to be alert all day every day. Not like Captain Gratian, who was always alert and would never have allowed half the cutthroats and thieves here today anywhere within a hundred bowshots of the castle.'

Fern watched Ansey flick a glance at Candle. His eyes narrowed before he turned back to the giant. 'Are you here, sir, because Captain Gratian isn't?'

Candle's teeth were gritted. 'Don't talk to it.'

The giant stood up. Fern heard herself gasp. *He was kneeling behind the tent—kneeling!*

Icicles tinkled as he straightened to his full height; he towered over the highest pennon fluttering from the tallest pavilion. 'Thank you for your courtesy.' The giant's voice became a thunderous echo. 'It's a rare commodity. I haven't met it in many a long day. As for whether I'm here because Captain Gratian isn't, I'm afraid that while the King of the Dwarves is your counsellor, I'd rather not answer that.'

Ansey's head snapped around to face Candle. Shock was written on his face. 'King?'

Candle's return glare was fierce and indignant. Fern wasn't sure whether he was angrier at the giant or the prince.

She felt a heavy hand on her shoulder. Turning, she realised a company of knights had arrived. Their commander had one mailed hand on Ansey's shoulder and one on hers. 'Children, did the frost giant speak to you?'

Why don't you ask the giant himself? Fern looked back. The giant had gone. *How could it move that fast?*

'I'm not a child.' Candle folded his arms, fuming.

The knight bowed to him. 'My apologies, Cavern Lord. I was preoccupied and did not notice your esteemed presence.' His smile was grim. 'Did the frost giant speak?'

Candle snorted. 'It asked about The King Who Guards The Gate.'

The knight's smile disappeared in a deep frown. 'An old ruse, Cavern Lord. One we are both well aware of. It seemed too long a conversation for that.'

'It was trying to elicit information,' Candle said. 'Fortunately your company arrived just in time to scare it off.'

'Does it suspect, Cavern Lord?'

'Oh, yes, Lord Quystein. It suspects all right.'

'I offer you the protection of the Knights of Renown.'

Candle shook his head. 'That, Knight Commander, will only draw attention to all we've worked so hard to conceal.'

'Indeed.' Quystein bowed again. 'We cannot hope to match your subtlety, Cavern Lord.' He inclined his head to each member of the group. 'Our attempts to be discreet have already been thwarted.' Without a further word, he turned on his heel and left.

Fern stared after him. *At least I was invisible to him. I don't think he noticed my existence at all.* She took a deep breath and hugged her cloak closer. *This is starting to scare me. Really scare me. Right then, Boody, Hector and Ginevra, White Three of the White Tree. Let's high–tail it to the king and then get outta here as fast as we can.*

laring at the retreating company of knights in their rich embroidered surcoats, Ansey was deep in thought. *How can Candle be the King of the Dwarves? Why's he employed as my companion? Could he be the King Who Guards the Gate?*

He noticed several of the knights looking back over their shoulders. *They're here because Gratian's gone. But why?* Their shields were dazzling. Plain unadorned silver, brilliant even under the overcast sky, they were so bright he wanted to turn away. *That's it.* Ansey folded his arms. *The shields would be why no–one has noticed the light from the ground glass lens. They're like massed suns.*

He rounded on Candle. 'What was that about?'

Candle's teeth were gritted. 'Not now.'

'Are you the King of Dwarves?'

'It's not relevant.'

Not relevant?

'Does the King of Dwarves want ointment?' The fantastically masked girl peeked out of the rag tent. She held a leaf with a splodge of scented oil on it. As Candle reached for it, she disappeared back inside the tent. He threw the tent flap aside and went after her.

Not relevant!? Ansey felt more than irritated. *He's trying to evade me.* Something close to rage was building inside him. Intent on answers, he dived after Candle.

The interior of the tent was warm and smoke–filled. It seemed much larger inside than out. It took a few seconds for his eyes to become adjusted to the dim light. He wanted to sneeze.

A draught of frosty air chilled his ears as the tent flap opened beside him. Out of the corner of his eye, he noticed the bare–legged girl enter. She looked reluctant, as if she'd rather be somewhere else. Anywhere else. *I'm right with you on that one, girl.*

The fawn was by her side, the fox at her feet and the owl on her shoulder. *The magical white beasts of the White Tree. They look quite ordinary, actually. Except for those studded cuffs on the fox. I wonder if the Flair…*

The fox swivelled and leapt with bared teeth as a curious onlooker tried to tip–toe in. It nipped at the man's ankles while the owl batted the intruder's face with closed talons. The man fled.

That'll keep out nosey gossips. Good on you, little fox. Ansey reached up to grip his nose. *I'm going to sneeze.* He stifled it as a hiss came from the far side of the tent. It was Candle, gritting his teeth as his face was dabbed with ointment by the masked girl.

Ansey sniffed. *Where's this smoke coming…*

In the middle of the tent was a ragged boy, one hand gripping the central tentpole as he sat, watching a pot on a tiny fire. 'Heart or soul?' The boy took his hand off the tentpole just long enough to pull a forelock of hair in front of his eyes.

Ansey could hardly see his face. But he felt uneasy. The boy was inordinately dirty and lanky. Everything about him was drab, unkempt and poor. 'Heart or soul what?'

The boy's gaze didn't move from the pot. 'Do you want healing for your heart or your soul? A broken heart is one thing but a broken soul entirely another.'

A broken soul? Ansey caught his breath. 'Have you got a cure in the pot?'

'No, it's dinner.' The boy lowered his face even further.

'Are you with Ector, Ginevra–'ayelet–hashachar and Boudicca's Chariot?' The fantastically masked girl drew his attention away from the boy.

Who's she talking about? This girl with the bare legs? Nobody would call her 'Ector' surely. That means 'harasser'. But would anyone call her Ginevra—'ayelet—hashachar, 'ghostly white fawn of dawn'?

The bare–legged girl saved him from answering. 'I'm with them.' She smiled. 'My name is Fern.' Her smile broadened as she looked at the boy in front of the pot. 'And you are?'

If she's Fern, I guess Ginevra must be the white fawn.

The boy lowered his face even further. His hair was in danger of falling into the pot. He gripped the pole so tightly his dirty knuckles turned white.

'I'm Merry.' The fantastically masked girl laughed. Her braids swayed, tinkling and chiming as she moved. 'But everyone calls me Madmerry.' She jerked a thumb towards the boy. 'This is Dallan.'

'Hi Dallan,' Fern said.

He ignored her. Tilting his head towards Hector, his eyes still focussed on the pot, he mumbled, 'Bad fox. Bad, naughty, wicked. It is not right to break your vow.'

Is he just rude or plain stupid? How would a fox make a vow?

Hector sighed and rolled his eyes. 'I've only left the Tree under protest.'

'Did that fox speak?' Ansey felt his head spin. *The Flair has never operated on this level before. Or spontaneously.*

'Of course not.' The fawn shook her dainty head. 'Hector is merely my puppet and I am a master ventriloquist.'

'As if!' Hector wagged a cuffed paw at her. 'You! A master ventriloquist? Me: your puppet! Dream on, girlie!'

Ansey was stunned. *The fawn and the fox are speaking the same language. The Flair doesn't work like this. At least...* 'The finches said it's impossible for...'

'Finches!' the owl spat. 'Who'd believe anything those little jackboots say? They rarely deign to speak to anyone other than those able to assist their campaign.'

The owl too? Ansey frowned. 'Campaign?'

'A genocidal plan to rid the world of blackbirds, crows and...'

The owl paused, eyeing him with a wary look. '…innocent, harmless, affectionate owls.'

'Oh.' *Candle was on at them about the blackbird pies, come to think of it. I never thought of finches as pursuing an agenda. Have they got ulterior motives in being friends with me?*

Hector's snout was high in the air. 'Have you been informed of the anomalous duality?'

Ano…nomo…whatto? Ansey shook his head. *What does it have to do with the finches?*

'Sit down then,' the fox said.

Ansey felt bamboozled. He dropped to the floor, his eyes fixed on the fox. *What's happening? The Flair is usually more vague and formless. I have to guess a lot. But this is a crystal clear conversation.*

'Say 'hello' to Fern,' the fox ordered, pointing with his leather–cuffed paw to the bare–legged girl.

'I am honoured to meet you, Lady Fern.' Ansey bowed his head. 'I'm sorry for what happened. Please accept my humblest apologies for my companion's actions.'

Her smile was gentle and easy. 'Do you always apologise for things that aren't your fault?'

'No, my lady.' *I'm glad she realises it wasn't my fault. I like her.*

'Oh, he does,' Candle said. 'I'm surprised you picked up on it so quickly.'

'Anomalous dualities are really quick on the uptake,' Hector said.

'She's the anomalous duality?' Candle stomped across to Fern. 'Impossible! It can't be a living thing! The amount of energy required to stabilise an anomalous duality is unthinkable—vast beyond reckoning… '

'What are you talking about?' Ansey interrupted. *I've had enough of Candle's secrets. First Gratian, then a frost giant, then some secret between the Dwarves and the Knights of Renown… there are no answers, only more questions.*

'Merry.' Dallan pulled his hair over his forehead with a trembling hand. 'Can we pack up and leave now, Merry? They are scaring me.'

'Just keep watching the pot, Dallan.' Madmerry patted his shoulder.

'Merry, I don't think they want to buy anything. I asked about heart or soul. I asked just right but no one answered.'

'Keep watching the pot, Dallan.' Madmerry patted his shoulder again.

'I'm scared, Merry,' the boy whispered. But he nodded as she squeezed his upper arm. Taking a deep calming breath, he turned his attention back to the pot of broth and herbs as it bubbled over the fire.

Candle sighed as he looked at him. 'It's appropriate to be scared, boy. We're talking about the end of all things.'

Oh, come on. Ansey raised an eyebrow.

Candle frowned at him. 'I'm not exaggerating. When a dimension's very existence is threatened it may take desperate measures to try to survive and protect the life within it.'

Ansey rubbed his nose. *Puts my problems into a different perspective.*

'The dimension may create an insertion point into another dimension—to bring through a device called a perfect helper—an invincible sword, for instance, or a magic staff. Or a ring of power, an impenetrable shield—the perfect helper can be many things, but it's never alive.' Candle threw up his hands. 'At least, it can be alive in a sense—but not sentient, not a thinking, breathing being.'

All eyes went to Fern.

'There's a mistake. I'm not a perfect helper.'

'You're sure?' Madmerry twisted a braid of hair. 'Something's drawn that frost giant here.'

'Something unusual,' Candle agreed.

'We're going to take this problem to the king,' Hector said.

Candle folded his arms. 'King Maurtz will not want to know. He's closed his mind to the trouble long ago. Haven't you seen how the grounds are flattened to a perfect smoothness so as to give the illusion everything here is all right? Outside all may be warped and wrinkled but nothing can possibly be wrong in Auberon while the marble wheels just keep on rolling along.'

Father knows? Maybe that's the real reason why the Knights of

Renown are here… he's finally concerned enough to do something. Could this be why he won't let me train as a knight? He wants to protect me?

Candle shook his head, his teeth gritted. 'Why, he won't even allow a thorough search of Castle Auberon for the scrolls of prophecy which might help us all survive the coming darkness.'

Ansey was appalled. *That's going too far.* 'He won't?'

Candle raised his eyebrows and grinned. 'Don't worry—anyone who's anyone has managed to get round his interdiction.'

'How? What? Who?' *Anyone who's anyone? Does that include frost giants, Gratian, dwarves?*

Candle ignored the question.

Ansey sighed. *It must include them.*

Candle turned to bow to Fern. 'My Lady, the King of the Dwarves would be honoured if you would accept the protection of the Cavern Kin.'

'So you *are* the King of the Dwarves.' Ansey folded his arms. 'What's going on?'

'Enough, child! I don't know what's going on! Once I figure it out, I promise you—you'll be the second to know.' His eyes were black as he turned to pout at Dallan and Madmerry. 'I have to get a message to the Caverns and, until that time, I would like to be able to count on your protection for the Lady Fern. Will you guard her?'

You're asking Dopey and Dreamhead to take charge? Things must be desperate.

But Dallan looked up. His hair was still over his face but his voice was clear as he spoke. 'Yes. My life and service are at the lady's disposal.'

'Dallan's almost blind.' Madmerry's quiet announcement dropped like a stone in a pool. 'But don't let that fool you. He's protected me for years.'

Blind? And he's watching the pot? Ansey looked at Dallan in dismay. *Actually that's all he's doing. And all he has been doing since we got here.* He flicked a glance at Madmerry. *He's taken her instruction to watch that pot absolutely literally. He's not even stirring it. I'm not sure Dopey's all there in the head.*

Ansey put up his hand. 'I'll stay.' He turned to Candle. 'But you have to explain to me all that's going on as soon as you get back.'

'No!' Madmerry's mask jingled as she shook her head. 'You can't stay!'

I can't? What's wrong with me? 'I don't bite.'

'You'll bring the King's Shield here.' Madmerry's mouth was a grim line.

So you've got something to hide? He looked around the rag tent, trying to work out what it was. Nothing was obvious. *I'll just add you to my list, then, along with the frost giant, the dwarves, the Knights of Renown and Captain Gratian.*

Madmerry's mask tilted as she watched him. 'You'd better make an appearance outside soon, Your Highness, or a search party will barge in any minute.'

'Point taken.' Candle clicked his fingers. 'Let's move. No doubt there'll be complaints we're late. But fortunately, you do such pretty apologies.' He opened the tent flap just as a troop of the King's Shield arrived at the entrance.

Not a moment too soon. Ansey closed the flap behind him and smiled at the escort. Without a word, he fell in behind the leader and they set off through the avenues of stalls. *I need to make a list of questions to ask Candle. First, there's the question about Gratian. Or should it be about the scrolls of prophecy? Come to think of it, Candle must have allies working with him...*

Ansey's thoughts were interrupted by a mighty bellow coming from the Tourney Ground: *'Where is the king who guards the gate?'*

The bellow was followed by a scream. 'Heeeellllp!'

The King's Shield began to run. 'What's happening?' The leader unsheathed his sword as he dashed towards the combat field.

Ansey followed, Candle keeping pace with him. Dozens of people were rushing headlong from the Tourney Ground.

There was another scream and, high above the fairground, the figure of the frost giant appeared, blocking out the sun.

Tybold was bawling and struggling in the giant's left hand.

Candle stopped and clapped a hand to his head. The rearguard of the King's Shield passed him. 'The child's an idiot. He's got less brains than a sparrowfart. What kind of moron attacks a frost giant?'

Ansey halted beside him. 'Even Tybold wouldn't be that stupid.' He was appalled to see his step-brother shrieking and flailing ineffectually with his sword. One arm—his combat arm—was pinned against his body by the giant's grip. Ansey shook his head in disbelief. 'But he was, wasn't he?'

Candle nodded. 'Needless to say, dwarves and giants have been at war intermittently for centuries and, as far as I'm concerned, the only good giant is a dead one.' He shook his head. 'However I'll say one thing for them: a lone frost giant will never provoke anyone, and it takes considerable incitement to induce a murderous rage in one of them. Normally they throw off the first three dozen assaults as beneath their dignity.'

The fleeing crowds had thinned. Reaching the Tourney Ground, Ansey was surprised to see spectators all around, gazing on in fearless curiosity. At the far side of the field, there was a tiered box, set with two thrones. The king and queen were there, pointing in obvious shock. The frost giant took out a huge knife and held it at Tybold's throat.

'Help!' Tybold whimpered. 'Someone help me!'

Ringing the frost giant were the Knights of Renown, their silver shields a dazzling sunburst. Their swords were raised. At their feet were several squires who had been practising their skill at arms less than an hour ago in Ansey's courtyard.

One of them was clearly dead. 'Jens…' The name was strangled in Ansey's throat. The boy had been a shy freckled redhead. Once, after breaking his wrist in a practice mêlée, he had secretly loaned Ansey his sword for a month. *What have you done, Tybold?*

'Stay back.' Candle pushed Ansey behind him.

'Jotun!' Lord Quystein's voice rang across the field. 'Peace, Jotun! Let the boy go and we will allow you to depart in peace.' The Knights of Renown lowered their swords.

'I am not such a fool as to give up my hostage.' The frost giant held the knife closer to Tybold's throat.

'We are the Knights of Renown.' Lord Quystein took a step back. 'Look at our shields—you've heard, surely, of the shields of the Knights of Renown? How they reflect the state of our honour? How they show the inmost heart of the bearer and indicate if it is true or false?'

Ansey felt sure Quystein's patronising tone would enrage the Jotun further. But it cocked its head and seemed to be listening.

'See our shields are unblemished.' Quystein gestured left and right. 'That is your guarantee we speak the truth and will honour our word. Let the boy go. He's only a child, he can do you no harm.'

'Only a child?' the frost giant sneered. 'Will do me no harm? He's a vicious coward and I will keep him hostage.' He bared his huge yellow teeth at the Knights of Renown. 'Now, move back or you might find my knife slips and takes off the boy's ear or one of his lips.'

Tybold's wail was high and almost silent. The frost giant, moving backward, swung him round. In that moment, Tybold caught sight of Ansey. 'You! Ancelin! Help me!'

'Don't move!' Candle snapped his arm out. 'Don't say a word! Get back!'

'Jotun!' Tears of fear and desperation fell from Tybold's face as he addressed the frost giant. 'He'd make a much better hostage than me! That boy, there! He's the King's Heir.'

Candle's eyes never left the giant as he instructed Ansey. 'When I say "*run*", you are to take off as if the nine untiring avengers of a kin–slaying were after you and you are not to stop running until you're safe in my Kingdom or in Fyrzentsou. Got it?'

'Right.' *Safe in Fyrzentsou? You must be kidding. Rogin will take me hostage. He might even torture me. After all, he tortured his own son and sent manticores after him.* A terrible fear gripped Ansey as the frost giant caught his gaze and held it. He felt mesmerised, unable to move.

'Promise me.' Candle produced a stone knife, its blade gleaming like smoke–etched glass. 'Promise me you'll head for Fyrzentsou, not Ysgarde.'

'The King's Heir!' Tybold sobbed. 'A much better hostage than me.'

'Move back, unless you want the little coward damaged…' The giant snarled, shifting his weight.

'Run!' Candle pushed Ansey aside and, bellowing a dwarf war cry, rushed forward with his stone knife.

But Ansey, held under the spell of the Jotun's gaze, couldn't move a muscle.

The frost giant dropped Tybold from tree–height and swatted Candle aside.

Ansey could see the massive hand coming to scoop him up.

His feet left the ground. And then, before anyone could react, the frost giant set off with him across the field, crossing it in two earth–shaking bounds. The last thing Ansey heard as he was tucked under the Jotun's arm was his father's voice screaming in pain and loss. 'An———*sey*!'

nsey couldn't stop shivering. He was freezing and exhausted. *How can it be so cold? My bones are ice.* He shook violently as the world flashed by, upside down. He was reminded of the ride on Gratian's horse. *I'm going to die. I can't understand why it doesn't scare me.*

The Jotun slowed. 'Why are you so afraid, King's Heir?'

'I'm n…n…ot.' Ansey's teeth chattered. *But I should be. I should be absolutely petrified.*

'Then why are you trembling, King's Heir?'

'I'm c…c…old.'

'*Cold?*' The Jotun stopped and swung him up to stare into his eyes. 'I see you're speaking the truth.' He shook his head and swirls of white mist floated off into the air. 'Cold!'

Ansey nodded. As he looked past the giant's icicle–like hair, he noticed a finch weaving across the treetops. In the distance a tiny brown speck darted up and down. *Little friends. They're trying to follow.*

He sighed. *Don't,* he wanted to tell them. *It's no use.* He realised there was a line of little brown specks bobbing up and down. *They're marking a trail across the sky. They're showing the direction the Jotun's travelling.*

As long as they kept high enough, the pursuit wouldn't falter. Ansey glanced at the giant. *I wonder when he'll kill me. Rescue will surely come too late.*

With a grunt, the Jotun drew him closer and settled him into the crook of his elbow. Then he wrapped him in a tuck of his jerkin. 'Still cold?'

'It's better.' Ansey was surprised.

The Jotun began to run again.

It's much *better.* Ansey was puzzled to find it was quite warm in the Jotun's coat. He leaned back. *Warm,* he thought. *Dark,* he thought. And then two other, much more surprising thoughts occurred to him. *Comfortable. And protected.*

He began to sense the rhythm of the Jotun's running. Up, down, one, two. High, low, three, four.

He felt himself bobbing with each long stride. He could hear the Jotun's heart beat. Up, down, one, two. High, low, three, four. The gentle swaying, together with the hazy pleasant warmth, was so soothing he began to feel sleepy. He tried to stay awake, but the Jotun began to sing a soft murmuring tune and his eyes shut. *Maybe he's singing this lullaby so he can kill me when I'm unconscious.* He blinked, jerking awake in the darkness, but after a few seconds it made no difference. He thought he heard fluttering and tiny shrill cries, but it seemed so far distant and his head so heavy he couldn't be sure it wasn't a dream.

Up, down, one, two. High, low, three, four. Up, down, one, two. High, low…

He woke with a start. And realised at once he had slept for hours.

The sky was overcast. Fireshadows flickered across gnarled tree trunks; mist hung from crooked branches. Stiff and sore, he sat up, a covering falling from him as he straightened. He had been wrapped in a mossy blanket.

A whiff of some foul smell reached him. *The Mistmurk.* He recognised the stench. *We're in the depths of the Mistmurk, where no one can track us.*

He looked around. The Jotun was sitting by a fire, turning a rabbit on a spit. Perched on his shoulder was a raven with eyes as red as burning coals. And hopping along the ground next to him was a second raven, its glossy feathers tinged with the scarlet glow of the fire. 'Hostage is up,' the first raven said.

Now ravens as well. *Is this how the Flair was always meant to be? Maybe I wasn't tuned into it properly before.*

The Jotun turned towards Ansey and smiled. 'Good evening.' His voice was polite and smooth as creamed honey. 'Would you like to share our fire?'

Ansey was wary but he came forward. 'Thank you.' He sat down. *Why is he being so civil? Are giants especially courteous just before killing you?*

'May I introduce my messengers?' The Jotun indicated the ravens. 'This is Munin…'

'Delighted, I'm sure,' squawked the bird on his shoulder.

'…and Huginn.'

'Likewise, natch,' clicked the bird on the ground.

Ansey decided he should appear surprised. 'You talk!'

'Natch,' said Huginn.

'Quite so,' Munin agreed. 'So do you! But people rarely engage us in conversation.'

''e's got the Flair, ain't he?'

'Indeed he has, Huggy boy.' The raven's beady eyes were fixed on Ansey. 'And now we have introduced ourselves, won't you tell us *your* name?'

Ansey paused. *Is it a trick question?* 'Ansey.'

Huginn clicked in obvious disapproval. 'Nain't never heard of no king's brat name of Ansey.'

'Are you indeed Heir to a kingdom?' Munin sounded suspicious.

'I was.' Ansey shrugged. 'Things have probably changed by now.' He paused. 'My full name is Ancelin Bedwyr Cai.'

'Crown Prince of Auberon?' the Jotun enquired.

When Ansey nodded, he reached inside his jacket and removed two pieces of parchment. He unfolded them, put them on the ground and smoothed them out. 'I've a contract here with your name on it.'

'Contract?' Ansey frowned. 'What sort of contract?'

'A contract to kill Prince Ancelin of Auberon. How convenient you were available to be so readily abducted.'

Ansey stared into his ice–white eyes. 'You knew who I was all along. You're just trying to scare me.'

'I did know. At first I thought you might be a fake. That little coward at the fair would have tried to finger anyone as the King's Heir if it meant he was off the hook. He was wetting himself with fear.' Stare for stare, he scowled at Ansey.

He's trying to make me flinch, to blink first.

After several seconds, the Jotun broke into a broad smile. 'Then I realised you weren't a fake and it occurred to me the relative smoothness of your abduction smelt of a set–up.' He pointed at the two pieces of parchment. 'A fortune. Either of my two current assignments would double the contents of the Jotun treasury. And, when I come to think of it, the promises of incomparably vast riches are *so* incomparably vast there is probably no intention of fulfilling them.'

The sigh he gave was so exaggerated Ansey knew he was supposed to sympathise. *Not a chance.* 'You said two assignments. Is your second one for the King of Dwarves?'

'That little runt? I don't need a contract to kill him. I'd quite happily do it for free.' His smile returned. 'You're curious about why I told you about Candle?'

Ansey nodded.

'I wanted to know if you knew. Your reaction told me everything. I obviously have to return to Auberon to find out what those pesky dwarves are plotting.' He held up the parchment. 'As for the second contract… This is the most difficult and frustrating assignment I've ever had. Already I've been working on it nearly two years and I'm no closer to success than I was on the day I started.'

'I can't say I wish you luck. Who's it for?'

'Prince Emyr of Fyrzentsou. The most cunning and elusive target I've ever tracked. I'm certain his trail leads to Auberon. You wouldn't think a cosseted and sheltered prince could live off the land, would you? Or hide himself so effectively not even Huginn and Munin have been able to find the slightest trace of him?'

''e's carked it,' squawked Huginn. 'Manticores got 'im.'

'No evidence,' Munin said.

'Evidence schmevidence,' Huginn squawked.

The Jotun tilted his head to give Ansey a speculative look. 'It seems to me a tender young prince would seek sanctuary with his own kind. And it might be to some King's political advantage to take in the son of a rival. He wouldn't be hiding at Castle Auberon, would he? Taken refuge with his good friend Ansey?'

Ansey shook his head. *So this is why the Jotun's keeping me alive. He's trying to pump me for information.* 'Emyr isn't a friend of mine.'

'No?'

'No. Even if he was at Castle Auberon, I wouldn't recognise him. I've never met him.'

'Are you sure of that?' the Jotun asked.

'Nain't no need to meet 'im ta recognise 'im,' Huginn clicked.

'He's got one green eye and one blue eye,' Munin said. 'That's how he can be recognised.'

'And 'e's a chubby lump,' Huginn added.

'That could have changed,' Munin said.

'Have you ever met a fat boy with one blue and one green eye?' the Jotun asked.

Ansey shook his head.

'What colour were that boy, Tybold's, eyes?' the Jotun asked. 'He was plump enough.'

Ansey just stared at the Jotun. 'I don't know.'

'Don't know?' A tone of disbelief edged the Jotun's voice.

'I've never really noticed. I try not to have much to do with Tybold.'

'Who is The King Who Guards The Gate?'

Ansey shook his head. 'I don't know.'

'Not very knowledgeable, are you?' Munin asked.

'Especially,' the Jotun commented, 'about affairs that affect a realm you'll rule one day.'

'I won't be ruling Auberon.' Ansey felt as if a pebble had lodged in his throat.

'Won't ya?' Huginn asked.

'Why not?' Munin added.

Ansey looked calmly at the giant. 'Because you're going to kill me.'

The Jotun burst out laughing. 'Whatever gave you that idea?'

'You're an assassin, aren't you?'

'Indeed I am,' the Jotun admitted, still chortling. 'The best there is.' There was a twinkle in his eye. 'Uller Princekiller is my name, and royalty's passing is my game.' His expression became solemn. 'However, for you, Ansey—I may call you, Ansey, mayn't I?—for I'm not fond of the name Ancelin. It brings back bad memories of a knight who slaughtered my two brothers many years ago. But, as I was saying, for you, Ansey, I'll make an exception.'

'Why?'

'Ahh, well now, that's hard to answer. Perhaps I could say I owe you a debt. And Uller is not so far gone into the clutches of evil he fails to pay his dues.'

'Debt?' Ansey was puzzled.

'You were polite to me. And that is rare enough that I wish to reward it. When I asked a question at the fairground, you answered me with dignity and humour.'

Ansey frowned. 'And for that you're not going to kill me?'

'You were also brave and humble. You didn't wet me, like the snivelling coward did, you didn't have anything trickling down your leg and you didn't smell as if you needed to change your underwear.'

Ansey laughed. 'He didn't, did he?'

The Jotun shuddered. 'It was disgusting. I don't like to seem too refined or delicate, but good clean killing is Uller's specialty. I hate it when things become messy.' His sudden smile was as broad as a sunbeam.

I don't believe a word of this.

'Boss,' Huginn said. 'He don't believe a word of it.'

Ansey stared, disconcerted. *Can the bird read my mind?*

Uller laughed. 'No, he can't. But he's sensitive to reactions.'

Ansey felt his eyes bulging. He wasn't sure what to think.

Uller blew out his cheeks. 'To be honest, I'm not entirely sure why I'm letting you go. I'm not even sure why I'm being honest with you. The fact is I've always been proud to rid the world of its surfeit of arrogant, selfish princes. However, Prince Ancelin Bedwyr Cai may be that rare prize, as unusual and, dare I suggest, unique as a dragon's sweet tooth or violet snow? You might be a genuine prince charming.' His brow creased. 'You have the Flair. So I wouldn't want to make a mistake and knock off a prince who might grow up to be a decent king.'

This sounds odd. 'There are lots of decent kings.'

'Not from my point of view. There's not one who will give a Jotun ambassador an audience, let alone a serious hearing about gaining access to a public library or a scrollroom specialising in prophecy.'

Is he on about the same thing as Candle? 'We don't have public libraries in Auberon. Or scrollrooms specialising in anything.'

'But there used to be several. Up until about ten years ago.'

Did there? I wonder what happened to them.

Uller scratched his icicle–hair. 'When it comes down to it, the reason I'm letting you go is that it never hurts to have a future king indebted to you. Or to play the percentages about who's destined for greatness and who's not.'

That's almost exactly what Candle said about why the dwarves were going to help Gratian. Hmm…

'Of course,' Uller continued, 'you understand I still have my contract to fulfil and my reputation to uphold, so if we should ever cross paths again, be warned—you are a dead prince!'

Ansey considered Uller's words. There was a lot of contradiction in what he said but maybe frost giants were like that. 'I think I should thank you.'

'Oh, don't go complicating the matter with gratitude,' Munin said.

'Time to be off,' Huginn added.

The giant looked up. Ansey followed his gaze. Through a drift of mist, a pale crescent of moon could be seen in the darkening sky, high above the twisted trees.

'So it is.' Uller nodded. 'It'll be nightfall soon.'

'Farewell, Ansey Jotunsfriend,' Munin said.

'Ta ta, kiddo,' Huginn clicked.

'You're leaving me here?' Ansey was astonished.

Uller nodded. 'I have other business to attend to, Your Highness, believe it or not. I doubt if it will surprise you to know that the killing business is merely a front which enables me to go unmolested through a great many kingdoms that use my services. My real work is searching for The King Who Guards The Gate.'

'There can't be that many kings you'd have to investigate.'

'In every generation the search has to start again. And become wider. In my grandfather's time, the whole world was searched. And in my father's time, we searched beyond the limits of the world into the near dimensions. In our own time, seekers have gone to the far dimensions and given their lives in the quest. In the next generation, if he is not found, we will have to search beyond time itself.'

Ansey stared as Uller's voice dropped to a whisper and he seemed to be caught up in some private debate. 'Have we done all we could or will it all be in vain? I myself have been past the Isles of the Colossus and, with my brothers, walked the sunken lands to the Kingdoms Beneath the Sea to search for the King. Where else can we seek? Where else?'

Uller's voice became almost anguished as he pounded the ground. 'I have been to the City of Mages and copied their most secret scrolls. I tell you, even the high mage himself does not know who the King is or how to reach outside of time.'

'So this is the real reason you're letting me go? Because you won't have an excuse to stay in Auberon if you fulfil the contract on me?'

Uller's face changed. The pain and desperation disappeared and he winked. 'I'm letting you go because I like you. How could you think anything else?' He leaned back, observing Ansey. 'Keep the fire up through the night. Don't try to find your way through the swamp in the dark. When dawn breaks, feed it lots of damp wood. That will give plenty of smoke for a signal and enable rescuers to find you.'

Ansey blinked. 'But…' He pointed to the fire and the roast rabbit on the spit. 'What about your meat?'

'It's for you.' Uller stretched as he stood up. 'I'm a vegetarian.' He laughed. 'I thought you knew the fire was for you. I'm a frost giant, after all.' Without warning he leaned towards Ansey, dropping a collar of fine silver–grey chainmail over his neck. 'Wear this always. It has power to protect you.'

'Is it magic?' Ansey tried to hide the doubt in his voice as he looked down at the watersilver links. They seemed to flow into place and mould themselves to his throat and upper shoulders. *I don't like it.*

Uller shook his head. 'Hardly. It belonged to a servant of Ruēl.'

'You stole it?'

'More than a century ago. It has been two hundred years before that since it was last given as a gift. So it will be well–remarked. And those who recognise it will know to pass on the favour you have done to me. Therein lies its magic, if it has any at all.'

A whirr of wings sounded in Ansey's ears. 'I haven't done you any favour.' He stared at the gleaming watersilver links, realising that they were so light he couldn't feel their weight. 'I don't think thanking you counts.'

There was no reply. He looked up.

There was no one else in the clearing. Uller had gone, disappearing in complete silence. The ravens had vanished.

He stared at the collar once more. He began to lift it off, when a glint caught his eye. Dropping the collar back, he swivelled around to face a new threat.

But there was only a sword in a sheath, resting against a boulder. Its hilt had caught the last rays of sun as it angled through the bent and twisted trees. *Uller's forgotten it. He'll be back shortly.*

Ansey picked up the sword. There was a buckler with it. He drew the sword from the sheath and dropped into a practice stance. *I could go to Ysgarde. In disguise. No one would know who I was. If I had a sword like this, would they turn me away?*

He swished the blade left and right. *Take that, you villain.* A frond of hanging moss dropped to the ground with a plop. *And that.* Slicing to and fro, he had soon beheaded a a row of myst–beard flowers.

He stopped, breathing hard, and dropped the sword. *Uller,* he thought in sudden alarm, *said that the next time he saw me he'd kill me.*

It was hard to know whether that was true or not. *But it's not worth chancing it. 'Next time' could be when Uller returns for the sword.* He picked the buckler and tried it on. It was far too big. He threw it aside, attaching the sheath to his own belt.

Then he picked up the sword.

Looking around, he wasn't sure which way to go. It was dangerous to try to cross the Mistmurk at night. But he knew he had no choice. Grabbing hold of the bole of a tree, he pulled himself up so that he could stand on a gnarled mossy knob. All around was mist, coiling and writhing over the swamp.

Then, as he looked higher, he noticed a ridge jutting above the marshland. *Mistmurk Height.* He took a deep breath. *If I don't delay, I can make it to the ridge before twilight is over. I need to get my bearings.*

Stopping just long enough to stamp out the fire and retrieve the roast rabbit, he set off through the swamp. It wasn't long before a conviction grew on him that he was under observation every splash of the way.

y sundown, Fern's nerves were frazzled. *I've got it*, she finally decided. *He's not stupid. Just autistic. You can't talk to Dallan like you can talk to a normal person. You've got to think about every word you use.*

She thought back to the nightmare that getting out of Auberon had been.

Don't say, 'Can you hand me that tent pole?' because he'll say 'Yes,' and do nothing because he doesn't get that you actually want him to help pack up and leave. Say, 'Please hand me that tent pole,' and he'll rush at you, eager to help.

Fern had felt as if she wanted to explode with frustration. Somehow she'd kept her cool. In the turmoil that followed the Jotun's escape, Madmerry had grabbed her potions and begun to help the wounded out on the open field. Dallan worked as her assistant, following her every instruction to the letter. *Which should have been a warning sign. I should have known.*

Her science teacher had partnered her with a new boy early in the year. No one had said he was autistic, but everyone knew.

'Be intentionally present to him,' the teacher had said, 'and you'll be fine.' *And I have no more idea of what 'intentionally present' means now than I did then.* Fortunately Quade had gone off to a special school after two weeks.

I don't think Dallan is as anti-social as Quade. But I really should have got it the moment he said, 'Bad fox. Bad, naughty, wicked.' For him, the rules are the rules, even if they're self–imposed ones. You don't break them in any circumstances. If there's an exception, you should have already made that perfectly clear.

The tournament had been called off as the Knights of Renown set off to rescue Ansey. Confusion began to give way to order. Then a rumour started that the king had had a heart seizure.

Madmerry had turned to Dallan at that moment. 'Barbizca will rule in his stead.'

Dallan's face had turned a pasty colour.

'We must go without delay.' Madmerry's mask had jingled as she'd turned to gaze at the field of wounded. 'We must leave before she closes the borders.'

'There's nowhere to go.' Dallan's voice was edged with panic.

Madmerry had pointed to Candle, lying unconscious not far distant. 'Yes, there is.'

Dallan had looked perplexed for a moment and then, slowly, tremulously, he'd smiled.

And after that the nightmare had simply got worse, as far as Fern was concerned. She hadn't been able to regain her invisibility no matter how hard she tried. She'd exchanged the silver clasp on Ansey's cloak for a pony and cart. She'd thought about trading her mobile phone instead but left it in her pocket. After arranging the deal, there was no turning back. Madmerry and Dallan just seemed to expect her to help.

So here I am, driving a tumbrel. She knew she was gripping the pony's reins too tightly. And she was probably sitting too stiff and upright. It didn't really matter that they were going slow. The road got bumpier the further they got from Castle Auberon.

She tried to soak in the golden haze hanging over the heath and mountains ahead, tried to draw its calming aura to herself. But her gaze darted away from the forested peaks and settled with rigid attention on the pony pulling the tumbrel.

'I take it you know where we're going?' Hector leapt onto the seat beside her.

And you're not helping my mood, Hector. He sounded as disgruntled as she felt.

'Hey, c'mon girlie. Gimme an answer. Where are we going?'

She didn't respond.

'Hey?'

'Why don't you ask them?' She jerked her thumb towards the back of the tumbrel where Madmerry and Dallan were still giving all their attention to Candle's injuries.

The pony stopped.

I jerked my thumb and forgot to let go of the reins, didn't I? This is so hard and so humiliating.

'Maybe you should loosen the reins a little,' Hector suggested. 'I don't think Zippy is going to run away. She doesn't even seem to object to a fox smell.'

'Zippy?' Fern eyed Hector. 'Did you name her that?'

Hector raised one leather–cuffed paw. 'You're holding on too tightly. She thinks you're trying to pull her up.'

Thankful for his kind tone, she turned to smile down at him. But as she did, her arm followed the movement of her head. Zippy tried to back up. She could have screamed.

Utterly humiliated. Fern felt her teeth grinding together. *Not even Elsa managed this.*

'Dallan.' Madmerry was inspecting a weeping bandage on Candle's leg. 'Go to the front and show Fern how to drive.'

Dallan got up at once. He jumped from the back of the tumbrel to the front seat.

'Can you drive for me?' Fern beamed with relief as he hustled Hector off the front seat. 'I mean, please drive for me.'

'I need you to serve as my eyes.'

Fern took a deep breath. *Intentionally present.* 'I can do that. Sorry, I *will* do that.'

He held out his hands. Without a word she put the reins into his hands.

Hector jumped onto her lap. 'Do you know where we're going?'

he asked Dallan. 'It's not an unreasonable question.'

Dallan whisked the reins twice and the pony set off, settling into an easy walking pace.

Fern sighed at how easy it seemed.

Boody hopped onto her shoulder. 'Now, Lady Fern…' Dallan began. 'Watch what…'

'I'm not a Lady!' She pulled Ansey's cloak tight around herself. 'I'm just an ordinary girl.'

'Is that right?' Dallan tilted his head towards her. His ragged fringe of hair still covered his eyes. 'You know, at the time when words were just acquiring meanings, "lady" didn't mean *nobility*, it simply meant *gift–giver*. Now since we wouldn't have either Zippy or this cart without you, Ordinary Girl, you will always be Lady Fern to me, like it or not.'

Fern felt her dejection lift. 'I'm watching what you do…'

'Hold on!' Hector raised his paw. 'Nice speech, Boy Wonder. But it's not impressing this little vulpine.' He glared, his eyes intense and his snout furrowed. 'Stop being evasive. Ever since we left Auberon, all I've wanted is a simple answer to a simple question: *where are we going?*'

Dallan shrugged. 'Oh, Ector. It's obvious. Out of Auberon.'

'See what I mean?' Hector thumped her knee. 'Even you knew that, and you're from another dimension.' He rolled his eyes and then scowled at the plodding pony.

He licked his chops.

Boody's wings fluttered. 'Before Hector announces he's starving and could eat a horse *and* decides to act on it, just tell us where we're going, Dallan.'

'Out of danger.'

It took Fern a moment to realise Dallan really was avoiding a direct answer. *Is he being deliberately obstructive or are we failing to ask the right question?*

Hector rose on his haunches and whacked Dallan on the shoulder. 'Let me explain it in simple terms, Boy Wonder. It's like this: I have a rendezvous with destiny which this little interlude may be seriously disrupting. I have to get back to the White Tree a.s.a.p. Are we going in that direction?'

'No.'

Hector sighed with exaggerated patience. 'Can we cut across country?'

'No.'

Be intentionally present. Find the right question. Fern put on one of her best smiles. 'Are we going in the opposite direction to the White Tree, Dallan?'

'Yes.'

Hector fell back against Fern. 'I'm ruined. My life is over!' He began to howl.

Fern stared. She tried stroking him but his wailing grew worse. 'Hector, it's okay. It'll be fine.' *I'm as ineffectual as Miz Ashe.* Hector raised his snout and howled at the first evening stars.

How strange, Fern thought. *Stars are different here. They're unfolding like tiny flowers.*

Hector set up a prolonged yowl, bringing her attention back from the sky. *What can I do to comfort him?*

Boody hopped off her shoulder to swat him with her wing. 'Stop that, you baby! You've no idea whether your date with destiny is jeopardised or not.'

Hector stopped and folded his paws.

Fern was hard put not to laugh. The black leather cuffs looked so silly against his white fur.

The look Boody turned on Fern was soulful and apologetic. 'Hector's never been the same since he was kicked out of his den, you understand. No doubt you've noticed that he's white. Well, so did everyone else.'

'I didn't,' Dallan said.

And that's another thing about some autistic kids. Fern shook her head. *They have to correct you.*

'He looks like a fuzzy grey ghost to me,' Dallan went on.

'Everyone looks like a fuzzy grey ghost shape to you.' Madmerry's voice echoed from the back of the cart.

'No, they don't.' Dallan pouted and sounded upset.

Fern eyed his long hair. *If you ever got your fringe out of your eyes, you'd have some chance of seeing properly.*

Boody shook her head at Dallan. 'Well, dear driver, you're the only one *not* to notice his pristine snowiness.'

'We're on a straight stretch, Dallan. And the bumps have gone.' Ginevra, her nose stuck between the top of the tumbrel and the seat, was clearly ignoring the argument. 'There are gentle rises and falls now.' She sniffed. 'So set the pony to a trot.'

'Yes, Ginevra.' Dallan flicked the reins.

That's what he means by being his eyes, Fern thought. *I'm just useless.*

'And of course being white…' Boody went on as if her story had never been interrupted. '…means he's highly visible to hunters. "Hector the Spectre" they called him and said he brought bad luck. So the den asked him to leave.'

'Asked?' Hector's paws became fists. 'Threatened. Said they'd rip my throat out if I didn't go.'

'The den *asked* him to leave,' Boody repeated. 'They sent him off with half a rabbit leg, a prophetic blessing and a warning never to come back.'

'Prophetic blessing…' Dallan mumbled under his breath. 'Is that why Ector thinks he's got a destiny?'

'I don't *think*,' Hector snapped. 'I know. One day I'll meet a prince under a white canopy. He will become my protector and I will become his.'

No one spoke for several seconds. Fern didn't know what to say. To her surprise, Dallan broke the silence: 'Do you help him save the cosmos?'

'Don't be flippant.' Hector swiped Dallan's shoulder again. 'We're just a mutual help to each other, that's all. I suspect we become friends.'

Boody looked skywards. 'Of course he helps the prince save the world. The prophecy is quite detailed—it even goes on to predict Hector will become famous and be named Protector of the Realm.'

'One of Seven Protectors!' Hector batted his paw towards the owl. 'It's not as if I'm lording it over everyone. Get it right, girlie!'

Fern could only just hear Boody's whispered retort: 'Girlie! Mind your manners, buster.' A moment later Boody raised her voice: 'Hector's problem is that, despite his early childhood experiences, he still believes in the happily–ever–after. I'm sure it's part of the obsession.'

'Good try, folks.' Hector balanced himself right on the edge of Fern's knees. 'But I'm awake to your little scheme. You're all trying to distract me. It's not going to work. As I have made it abundantly clear, I would like to get back to the White Tree—the white canopy of prophecy, as I'm sure you've all guessed. Here I am risking the ruination of my hopes, my future and my fortune to accompany my friends somewhere I don't want to go and all I want for my sacrifice is an answer. Is that too much to ask?' He turned with a growl to Dallan. 'Where are we going?'

Dallan ignored him. 'Merry!' he exclaimed. 'Is this what you tried to tell me? When you said friends are more important than rules? I'm getting it now.'

Hector rose up with a snarl. '*Where* are we going?'

'We're going home.' Madmerry's voice came from the back of the tumbrel. 'My home.'

Hector was silent for a moment. 'Where's that?'

'The main problem with answering your question, Hector,' Madmerry said, 'is that we can't be sure of the way because it's changed.'

'The way has changed?' Hector cleared his throat. 'You really expect me to believe that?'

Madmerry nodded. 'The land is folding. Auberon might be using marble rollers to create the illusion everything's all right but I'm sure you know it's not. Haven't you noticed that every earth tremor is changing the landscape? Towns are closer together. It's not nearly as far to the Mistmurk as it once was. And it used to be a day's hard ride to the Wreathwatch Mountains but now you can make it in half that.'

Hector's gaze slid to Boody, then to Ginevra. 'Oh.' His belligerent attitude vanished in an instant.

'That's probably a fair answer,' Ginevra pointed out. 'You know, we might not be as far from our Tree as you think.'

Hector nodded to her, then to Boody. 'Let's go, girls. Pluuuease. *Now.* Before we get caught up in something really bad.'

'Isn't it a bit late?' Ginevra asked.

I'm going to do it. It's a risk but it might be worth the tantrum. Fern took off her glasses.

'Stop…!' Dallan yelled. 'What are you doing?' The cart came to a stop as he jerked the reins. 'Don't touch me…' He pushed her away.

'Calm down. I just want you to try my glasses.' She pushed her spectacles onto his nose, brushed aside his fringe and positioned the frames around his ears. 'Your eyes are different colours, you know?'

There was silence as he looked around.

In a world where there are no glasses, then they should make at least a little difference. Fern watched him peer along the winding road, across the heather–clad hills towards the distant mountains, then down at Hector and Boody perched on her cloaked knees. His eyes became wider. 'I can see.' His voice was so low as he stared straight at her that his breath it would barely have stirred a feather. 'Not the distance but close by. I can see blades of grass and leaves on the trees and not just flowers, but petals too…'

There was a sudden cheer from Madmerry. She jumped up in the cart and ran along the back of the seat. She seemed surprised at the astonished faces looking up at her as she danced out a damburst of joy. 'Well, doesn't this change everything?' Her mask jangled as she twirled and star–wheeled.

'Oh, Lady Fern.' A single teardrop ran down Dallan's check.

Madmerry stopped her dance to peer at the spectacles. 'Curved glass. We could probably make it ourselves.'

Boody raised a wing in the air, shouting in victory: 'And then there were sunglasses!'

Hector glared at her. 'And *you* have the absolute effrontery to call *me* obsessed!'

'This remakes my world.' Dallan glanced from Madmerry to Fern. 'Restores all choices. Beyond all hope.' His face seemed to withdraw into shadow. He pulled his fringe down over the glasses. 'I might be able to go home.'

Madmerry laid a hand on Dallan's sleeve. 'If you go home, who will you choose to be? Consider carefully before you become the cleansing, slaying whirlwind.'

Fern listened with increasing misgiving. *Who will you choose to be? What's that mean?*

Dallan whisked the reins without replying. The cart jerked and the pony started up the road once more.

'Hey, Boy Wonder, where *is* your home?' Hector demanded.

Dallan said nothing.

'Where am I?' a groggy voice asked from floor of the tumbrel. 'Who do I have to thank for saving me from the leech–surgeons of Auberon?' Candle stood up, unsteady on his feet.

Dallan disentangled Fern's glasses from his ears. He held them out to her.

She hadn't realised how delighted he'd been until his quiet happiness disappeared, like mist in bright sunlight. A closed impenetrable expression came down like a shutter. *However, I think the key is intentional presence. Give him your undivided attention and think about what you're saying and it'll be okay.*

Madmerry had turned to Candle. 'You've made a remarkable recovery, considering your wounds. As for your rescue from the leech–surgeons, you may thank Lady Fern.'

Fern swivelled on her seat. 'I didn't do much.' She was disconcerted by Candle's scowl. *I suppose he's not sure what he's doing here or why he's with us. Come to think of it, I'm not sure why Madmerry wanted to bring him along.* 'All I did was sell the silver cloak pin to buy this pony and cart. It was Dallan got you off the field with the help of Hector, Boody and Ginevra. He and Madmerry treated your wounds.'

Candle shook his head. His flame crest was a tangle of red curls. 'You fail to mention Prince Ancelin in this tale.'

'The Jotun got him,' Madmerry said. 'But the Knights of Renown were on the trail at once.'

'Which way did they go?' Candle asked.

Dallan pointed backwards. 'The other way.'

'We must turn around then.' Candle sounded agitated. 'We must pursue the Jotun.'

'The Knights of Renown are already doing that,' Madmerry said.

'Quystein's a good man, but he doesn't understand the wiles of the frost giants. They'll take off one way, then sneak around to head in exactly the opposite direction.'

'Like we're going now?' Dallan asked.

'Yes!' Candle stabbed with his finger towards Madmerry's mask. 'No!' He turned in a circle. 'Who knows? You can't just guess like this. We have to gather information. You need to look for a line of finches across the sky. Stop this cart! I want to get off.'

Dallan shook his head. 'No!' He increased the pace.

No, don't dig your heels in. Don't throw a tantrum. Fern could see Madmerry was trying to calm Candle. 'You've had concussion for hours and, as your physician, I advise you not to go anywhere without supervision.'

Candle lost his temper. '*Physician?*' He spotted a tent pole on the floor of the cart. 'Stop this cart, I say!' Grabbing the pole, he advanced in a threatening manner.

Madmerry tapped Dallan on the shoulder. 'Doesn't matter what happens back here, don't you stop this cart, whatever you do.'

Oh, dear. He won't. Candle, you're not going to persuade anyone like this. You got to understand about dealing with autism.

Ginevra leapt towards Candle as he swished the pole towards Madmerry.

'Out of my way, you snivelling fawn!' He kicked her aside but she was at him again almost at once.

Fern realised he was distracted. Lunging backwards, she grabbed the pole and yanked it out of his hands. *I don't believe I actually did that.* She nearly fell off the seat.

Dallan reached across and pulled her back.

Candle grabbed another tent pole from the floor of the tumbrel. Balling his fist, he slammed Ginevra against the far side of the cart and turned to jump.

Hector snarled as he saw Ginevra fall and launched himself at Candle's head. 'There was no need for that. She was just trying to stop you hurting yourself.'

'Get off me, whelp of a devil vixen.' He tried to thump Hector but only hit himself.

Hector wrapped himself around Candle's head. 'Don't you talk about my mother like that!' He swatted Candle's eyes with his tail. 'Is this knocking some sense into you?'

Candle snatched him down, grabbed him by the tail and pounded his snout against the tumbrel. 'And is this knocking sense into you?'

'Enough!' Dallan brought the cart to a halt.

Fern was stunned. She'd have thought Madmerry's command would have kept him going indefinitely.

Dallan's voice was full of cold anger. 'Is this how the King of Dwarves repays his debts? By beating defenceless children who are only trying to help him?'

Candle froze. He dropped his tent pole.

Madmerry went straight to Hector.

'Look!' Hector's head was lolling to one side. 'Exsploding shtars! It'sh a supernova! And I dishcovered it! Maybe they'll name it after me.' Madmerry picked him up and held him against her shoulder. She stroked him as she went to examine Ginevra's injuries.

Candle took several deep breaths. 'You are indeed only children. I'm sorry.'

'Sorry?' Madmerry touched a bleeding gash on Ginevra's flank. 'You've a wicked temper, so I hope that means something.'

'Oh, it means something, Mistress Wildling.' Candle made a tight formal bow. 'The King of Dwarves has never apologised to anyone in his life before.'

'He hashn't?' Hector groaned as he straightened his neck. 'Ooh, I think I've crinked it.'

'I was—*I am*—worried about Prince Ancelin and, as a result, I became very angry when my will was thwarted. My anger was unjustified and I ask your forgiveness for my unreasonable behaviour.'

Hector sniffled. 'You think the prince of prophecy will mind me having a crinked neck?' He looked so piteous, Fern put her arms out for him. Madmerry handed him over and went back to Ginevra.

Candle was staring up the road ahead. 'Why are we taking this forbidding route? Where are we going?'

'That *is* the question.' Hector snuggled against Fern. 'I wish you luck with it.'

'We're going to the Wreathwatch.' Madmerry took a tiny flask out of her pouch and poured the contents over Ginevra's flank.

'Ahhh!' the little fawn gasped. 'It didn't really hurt until that. Ahhh!'

'Wreathwatch Mountains?' Candle folded his arms. 'Why didn't you say so before? It would have saved a great deal of misunderstanding. I will be able to contact the Cavern Kin easily there and get help.'

'Wreathwatch Mountains?' Boody hopped onto Dallan's shoulder. 'Why was that a secret?'

'Madmerry said not to alarm anyone.'

'We're not going over the Pass?' Hector raised his head. 'You've scared me so much I'm uncrinked. The winds, the snow, the cold, the demons—and that's on the good days. Oh, I forgot the avalanches. Tell me we're not going over the Pass.'

'Of course not,' Madmerry said. 'We're not that stupid.'

'Or that desperate,' Dallan added.

Candle glanced from one to the other, finger-combing his tangled fire-coloured hair. 'Then how are you going to cross the glacier?'

'We're not,' Dallan said.

'We're going to go under it,' Madmerry added.

There was a moment's silence. The finger-combing stopped. 'And how do you propose to do that?'

'You're going to show us the secret way.' Dallan paused, and waited a moment, before adding: 'Your Majesty.'

 limbing a tree overgrown with shaggy sedge, Ansey felt the sword bump against his leg. *This might be the worst mistake I've ever made.* Mistmurk Height was closer, much closer. *But was it near enough to reach before the light failed completely?*

The golden haze of early twilight had passed and now a silver–grey gloaming mantled the sky. *I can't go on. It's getting too dark.* Ansey drew a deep breath. The foul smell of the Mistmurk seemed even stronger as the night grew colder. *But I can't stay here.* The sense of something watching him, tracking his every move, had not faded. It had grown worse.

Ansey almost fell off the tree in fright as a dark shadow plummeted towards him.

It took him several flustered and fearful seconds to realise it was only a finch. Exhausted, the tiny bird dropped onto the branch in front of him.

'You nearly scared the life out of me.'

The finch hopped up and began to twitter.

'There are ravens following me? I'm not surprised…'

The finch chirruped.

'No!' Ansey was startled. 'Don't even think about it. It's suicide to try to distract them.'

The finch gave a furious flap of its wings.

'Of course, I appreciate the sacrifice. Don't get me wrong.'

The finch twittered again.

'But if the ravens are following at a careful distance,' Ansey said to it, 'then obviously they're not trying to catch me. If you little guys really insist on helping, could you make me a trail pointing to Mistmurk Height?'

The finch pumped out its chest, flicked up one wing in a move that almost reminded Ansey of a salute and sailed off into the sky. He watched it go.

'I'll take that as a "yes",' he sniffed. He began to climb back down the tree.

allan's stare was so unnerving that, after almost a minute's silence, broken only by the clip-clop of the pony's hooves, Fern wanted to cry. *And it's not even me on the receiving end.* She didn't know how Candle could stand it.

It was nerve–wracking just to watch the wordless contest of wills between the two of them. Candle was the first to crack. 'What makes you think there's a way under the Wreathwatch?'

Dallan flicked a strand of hair across his eyes. 'Certain very old maps call this area Auberon–Zamberg. They date back almost to the Englobing, way before the division into the present kingdoms of Auberon, Malveraine, Fyrzentsou, Lyndark, Vircontium and the Sovereign Isles. Clearly marked in those maps of Auberon–Zamberg was an englacial stream through the middle of the Wreathwatch.'

'Such ancient maps are only to be found in the City of the Mages. Are you a mage?'

'Of course not!' Madmerry snapped. 'Would we be using a pony and cart to get to the Wreathwatch if he was?'

A tiny smile formed in the corners of Dallan's mouth. 'So there really is a stream that has hollowed out the heart of the glacier.' He nodded to himself.

Fern re–assessed him. *He's autistic, but he's also intelligent. He trapped Candle into an admission there.*

Candle leaned back. 'Any such map you might have seen,

boy—though I can't imagine how or where, if you're not a mage—is centuries old. The englacial stream is long gone.'

Dallan's tiny smile broadened. 'It's bad to tell lies. A dwarf highway passes through the Mountains. The ice caves once sculpted by that englacial stream now form an important part of that underground route.'

'Unfounded rumour,' Candle said. 'You can't believe everything you hear whispered on the wind.'

Flicking Zippy's reins once more, Dallan turned to look directly at Candle. 'It seems to me that, of all dwarves, the King would be most likely to know the entrance to the old englacial stream.'

Boody blinked. 'I thought we brought Candle along out of the goodness of our hearts! Are you telling me we have a secret agenda?'

Hector put one leather–cuffed paw to his temple. 'I salute you, Boy Wonder! To think this was in your mind when you dashed onto the field and pulled Candle out from amongst the wounded!'

But Madmerry told him to. Fern tried to remember exactly what happened. *If it was in anyone's mind, it was in hers.*

Ginevra seemed to be recovering. 'I thought the plan to buy the pony and cart was so we could run for our lives. You mean it isn't?' She drew back, her eyes fixed on Dallan. 'I think I'm more scared than ever.'

'I doubt if a Master of Intrigue could do better at arranging events.' Hector looked thoughtful. 'You're not a mage, Dallan?'

'I *am* a Master of Intrigue,' Candle said, 'so let me tell you he's revealed his hand too early.' His tone was scornful. 'I see it's futile to deny the existence of the dwarf highway. You won't believe me, whatever I say. However, there is no threat or reward—not all the gold in the treasury of Auberon nor all the tortures of the dungeons of Fyrzentsou—can induce me to reveal the secret of the Wreathwatch Way.'

'We're not going to threaten you.' Madmerry sounded affronted. '…or try to bribe you. Tell him what we're going to do, Dallan.'

'We're going to persuade you.' Dallan's smile became broader still.

Candle roared with laughter. 'You will never succeed. *Never.*'

'We'll see.' Dallan's tone was calm and equable.

'Not a chance.'

Madmerry tapped Dallan's shoulder. 'He won't be easy to convince.'

Dallan's smile became so beatific that Fern knew, if she'd been the one on the receiving end, it would be almost maddeningly provocative. 'We'll see,' he said again.

Candle was seething. His fists were balling.

Don't provoke him. Don't make him incensed. Don't doubt his word. Don't challenge his ability to withstand your persuasion. You're doing just what mum did with dad before… Fern cut the thought off, unwilling to go into the pain.

She turned to Dallan, trying to frame the right words. His smile vanished in front of her eyes and, without warning, his body shook with such a violent spasm that he lost the reins. His eyes rolled and he began to fall sideways.

He's blacked out. She grabbed his arm.

Madmerry pulled him up by his collar. 'Dallan!' Her voice was edged with panic. 'Dallan!'

With a shudder, he righted himself. 'I'm f–f–fine. Fine…'

'No, you're not,' Fern said.

'Y–y–you're right.' He turned to Madmerry. 'We mustn't delay. She knows we're coming. I begin to feel her.' He shuddered again.

'*She*?' Hector asked. '*She* who?'

Dallan gripped Fern's arm. 'I need the reins. We must hurry.' She could feel his trembling. Gathering up the reins, she put them in his hands.

'*She* who?' Hector persisted.

'Perhaps it's not wise to press on,' Madmerry said. 'Should we go back?'

'We can't turn around now,' Dallan said.

'*She*?' Hector's teeth were gritted.

'It might be best.' Madmerry laid a gentle hand on Dallan's shoulder.

'I don't know why I never quite get used to everyone ignoring me.' Hector stretched his paw and hit Dallan on the upper arm. 'She who?'

'It's not best.' Dallan glanced at Madmerry as he whisked the reins to set Zippy at a trot. 'The Jotun's not likely to hurt Ansey. Not unless it's particularly stupid and that one seemed pretty bright to me. But if Barbizca's in charge, she might take the opportunity to ensure Ansey doesn't get back safely.'

'How could she possibly do that?' Fern re–assessed Dallan's intelligence up another notch. *He's thought this through carefully.*

'Yes, how could she possibly do that?' Madmerry repeated. 'The Knights of Renown are way ahead of any assassin she might send.'

Dallan's voice dropped. 'What if she sends manticores?'

Madmerry gasped.

'Manticores?' Ginevra looked stunned. 'She's a nasty woman with a twisted mind but I find it difficult to believe she'd go that far.'

Candle nodded. 'Indeed. Well said, young fawn.'

'What are manticores?' Fern leaned over to whisper to Boody.

'They are blood–coloured lions with human faces, scorpion's tails and the malice of a sphinx.' The little owl hopped onto her shoulder. 'They ask no questions, they take no prisoners, they just kill their target and whatever stands in the way of it. Once they have the scent of their prey, they are relentless.'

'How would they get Ansey's scent?' Even as she asked the question, Fern realised how foolish it was.

'Any item of clothing will do,' Madmerry said.

Hector raised himself on his haunches and, without a word, pointed to the cloak around Fern's shoulders.

'Double jeopardy,' Madmerry said. 'If you're right about the queen, that is, Dallan.'

'What *double* jeopardy?' Candle gestured to Fern to keep the cloak. 'Don't remove it, girl. I have grave doubts about this theory. Barbizca is not all sweetness and light, I grant you, but I find it difficult to believe this tangled tale of conspiracy.'

'You don't think she's that ambitious or manipulative?'

'She's not a Master of Intrigue. She's not even as devious as a frost giant.'

'I think you underestimate her,' Boody said. 'Frost giants are all brute strength without brain.'

'A common mistake of perception.' Candle clambered over the back of the seat and squeezed himself in between Fern and Dallan. 'They're cunning. Even Quystein is willing to admit that. But the depth of their plotting is something he really hasn't come to terms with. You've heard of the Helmet of Providence?'

Dallan didn't say a word. Candle glared at him when he didn't answer.

But you didn't really ask a question. It was more like a statement. Fern could feel Dallan's retreat back into himself. He clearly disliked Candle sitting pressed up against him and was trying to pretend he wasn't there.

Fern felt closed in herself as Madmerry climbed onto one of the slats of the tumbrel behind the front seat.

She stood there, her mask towering over them. 'The Helmet of Providence is the symbol of sovereignty of the Kingdom of Fyrzentsou.'

Candle glanced over his shoulder. 'Indeed, Mistress Wildling. But not merely a symbol. It is also one of the Seven Powers. It draws on the very flux that flows between the paths of time: its power is unimaginable.'

Dallan nodded but kept his gaze fixed on Zippy. Fern wondered if he could see anything more than a vague outline. Perhaps it didn't matter. Zippy seemed quite capable of following the road.

'The Helmet of Providence fell into the hands of the Jotuns four hundred years ago at the Battle of Tariquhaven. Do you know how Rogin of Fyrzentsou got it back?'

Dallan shook his head.

'A morality tale demonstrating just how devious the frost giants are.' Candle gestured to Fern to hop into the back of the tumbrel.

Absolutely not. She folded her arms and shot him a mutinous glare.

That slimy arrogant little manipulator… he's at the front and he's trying to take over. She was angry at how simply Candle had managed to get his own way. *Can Dallan see it?*

'The Citadel of Mages has never been breached, protected as it is by sorcery.' Candle's voice had changed. It was obvious he enjoyed telling stories. Leaning back, relaxed, he took a pipe and a tinderbox out of his pocket.

Don't be fooled, Dallan. He'll take any chance he can.

'The spells and enchantments, mazes and mind–traps guarding their Onyx Towers have never been overcome.' Candle placed a powder wad in the pipe. 'Except by trickery.'

Dallan's silence was almost oppressive. Madmerry filled the gap. 'Oh?' she asked, her braids tinkling.

'Aye, trickery, Mistress Wildling. A Jotun, a master of illusion, took the form of a merchant, a jolly trader who plied his goods weekly at the citadel gate. For ten years, he let his face become familiar; he laughed and joked while trading news and gossip with the porter. He never asked to be allowed into the city, just produced the occasional rare item for sale and sold it for a reasonable price. Ten years he waited.'

'Do dwarves have such incredible patience?'

Candle ignored her question. 'Slowly he undermined the porter's caution and vigilance. Once he was ready, he spiked his wares with something really tempting: the Helmet of Providence, one of the Seven Powers. Said he'd bought it from a sailor who'd fallen on hard times. The porter recognised it instantly, but the merchant said he'd already got a buyer. Still he hinted that the mages could negotiate a deal over dinner.'

Madmerry gasped. 'Dinner!'

Candle laughed and nodded at her over his shoulder. 'You see how clever it was? All the ward–spells in the world won't help, if you invite the enemy in.'

Dallan spoke at last. 'Did the mages do that?'

'Yes, they succumbed to the bait and invited the Jotun into their citadel.' Candle smiled as if Dallan had succumbed to his bait. 'And the Jotun got what he'd worked ten years to achieve: access to their Scroll Room.'

'He got into their library and stole all their magic spells?' Madmerry's hand went to her mouth.

'No. He stole a single parchment. It wasn't a scroll of magic, it was a prophecy called *The King Who Guards The Gate*.'

'What's in the prophecy?' Hector tapped Fern's knee as he looked Candle straight in the eye. 'Professional interest, you understand.'

'No one knows.' Candle shrugged.

'What?' Hector glared. 'Piffle! Someone knows.'

'The mages don't. They're interested in power and magic, not in prophecy.' Candle tried to elbow Fern.

'But knowledge is power.' She elbowed him back. *I'm not moving*. 'At least, that's a saying in my world. So knowledge of a prophecy would be power.'

Candle shrugged again. 'Nonetheless, the mages have no idea why the Jotuns sacrificed the Helmet of Providence.' Candle held up his hands. 'When Rogin of Fyrzentsou demanded the Helmet's return, the mages agreed, but not before studying its rune–lore. If there's one good thing come of it, it's that the Helmet has returned to Fyrzentsou. I feel much safer knowing that one of the Seven Powers is guarding my borders.'

Dallan's brow beetled in a deep frown as he turned to face Candle. 'Don't you have one of the Seven Powers yourself? Isn't the King of Dwarves the Keeper of the Belt of Veracity?'

'What an impertinent question. The moral of the story is of course that all the protection in the world, magic or otherwise, won't avail you, if you ask the enemy in.'

'You've got the Belt on you!' Dallan pulled on the reins and brought Zippy to an abrupt halt. 'Haven't you?'

'This is trouble.' Madmerry sounded appalled.

Fern couldn't understand what they were concerned about.

Neither, it seemed, could Candle. 'Trouble?' He looked at them in obvious perplexity. 'No, safety! I've worn it for years. It's protection!'

Dallan's head drooped. He was so still Fern thought he was turning into a statue.

'Look!' Madmerry pointed ahead. Just visible in the silver gloaming were two flying shapes like shadowy arrowheads.

Dallan raised his head. 'What is it?'

Two birds cawed as he spoke.

'Ravens.' As Madmerry identified them, the birds wheeled, circled twice and then headed off towards the mountains.

Candle expelled a deep breath. 'Those weren't any ordinary ravens. They're Jotun spies.'

Dallan whisked the reins and Zippy began to move again. His agitation was evident as he insisted, 'You must show us the entrance to the old englacial stream.'

Candle was silent.

'We can't go over the Pass,' Madmerry pointed out. 'The Belt of Veracity will attract every evil thing in the mountains.'

The cart had reached the top of the hill. Zippy was struggling out onto a flat narrow ridge in the teeth of a sudden wind. In front of them, the road petered out. Beyond a steep valley was the white expanse of a glacier; behind them, the gentle foothills sloped back along the road into the vales of Auberon.

'This can't be.' Madmerry shook her head in such agitation that feathers fell from her mask as it tinkled and jingled.

'What is it?' Dallan asked.

'We never turned off the road, so how can this be the wrong way?'

Hector rested his leather-cuffed paws on Fern's shoulder as he looked over it at Ginevra. He flicked his tail around Fern's neck to get Boody's attention. 'Council of war, girls. If the land's folding in on itself, can we be on the wrong road even when we're on the right road?'

'Some roads could be close to merging.' Boody's whisper was audible to everyone in the sudden silence. 'In the dark, it would be very difficult to tell.'

'Where are we?' Dallan asked.

Candle looked around in astonishment. 'We're on Mistmurk Height. It's exactly where it shouldn't be.'

ven before Fern could see any visible signs of agitation, she knew Dallan was about to go into meltdown. *If he is autistic, it's important that the world stay stable. That the rules be unchangeable and perfectly knowable.*

'I'm sure it's where it's always been,' she said. 'We must have taken the wrong turn in the dark.' *Better to tell him there's a mistake than to risk driving him over the edge.* She knew they had to block his panic before it started. 'We could go back in the morning. We just need to find some shelter for the night.'

'We can't make it back before twilight is over,' Madmerry said. 'Not even to find a farm. And we can't descend these cliffs in the dark. There's a chasm between us and where we need to be.'

'You can camp there.' Candle pointed to a group of rocks and lone tree on the ridge. Bent crooked by the wind it was shaped like a finger pointing towards the glacier. 'It's not ideal but…'

'*You*? Don't you mean "*we* can camp there"?' Madmerry asked. 'Or are you suggesting that you're about to leave us?'

'A bad choice of words,' Candle said. 'I am in your debt and I am aware of the seriousness of that. As I was saying, *we* can camp there. It's not ideal but apart from the wind, it's safe enough.'

Dallan threw back his head and laughed. Fern could hear the bitter, tormented edge to it. *He's losing it.*

'Safe enough?' he spat at Candle. 'There'll be wolves here within the hour and Jotuns, too, if you're right about those ravens.'

'Wolves don't come this far.' Candle dismissed the thought with a shake of his red curls.

But 'this far' isn't as far as it used to be. Fern didn't dare voice her thoughts.

'I'd be more concerned about manticores.' There was an almost contemptuous edge to Candle's voice. 'If that idea of yours about Barbizca setting them on Ansey is true. But even if it is, it'll take several days for her to set it in motion. She'll have to borrow some from Rogin first.' He turned a smile on each of them in turn. 'As for the Jotuns, my dears—why would they be interested in a party of children?'

Dallan nudged him. 'You've got the Belt of Veracity.'

'I've had it for years. It's no more danger to anyone here than in Auberon.'

'True. But, speaking hypothetically of course, what if we had another one of the seven Powers with us?'

Candle's laugh came out as a snort. 'In that unlikely and, as you point out, purely hypothetical event, we could be in considerable peril. We might even be a magnet for trouble.'

'What do you mean: *magnet for trouble*?' Hector asked.

'There's a theory the Powers are seeking to be reunited. That one will draw another to it. But I've been wearing this Belt for three hundred years and I've yet to see the slightest evidence of it.' Candle grinned, a gold-capped tooth appearing in the corner of his mouth. 'You had me going for a while there with your talk of the end of the world and anomalous dualities. But it's all a clever ruse, isn't it, to get me to let you take a short-cut through the Deeps of the Nardelf?' His grin faded. 'Where are you running off to?'

'You don't believe in the Powers.' Madmerry's statement was flat, as if she was struggling with a new idea. Her mask bobbed as she put her hand under her chin to consider it.

'I do,' Hector announced. 'And I've got the gist of this conversation.' He turned to Boody and Ginevra. 'Point to note for our Council of War, girls. We are in a cart with persons wearing two of the Seven Powers. I hate to say I told you so—but we should have stayed at our Tree.'

'Dallan said *hypothetical*,' Ginevra said. 'That means it's not actual fact.'

'Read between the lines, girlie.' Hector slid off Fern's shoulder and slumped into her lap. 'He just said that not to scare us.'

'It never occurred to Madmerry or me you'd be persuaded by gold.' Dallan glanced at Candle as he whisked the reins once. Zippy set off towards the lone tree near the rocks. 'We know dwarves can't be bought and we know the stories that they lust after gold are wild exaggerations. But we did think that the secret of the englacial stream in exchange for the Helmet of Providence was a good bargain.'

'By dark earth and bright fire, you have the Helmet of Providence?' He looked up and stared at Dallan, then at Madmerry. 'A good bargain?' His hand flew to his waist. '*Good?* My kingdom would be the greatest force to reckon with between the mountains and the sea.'

'I thought you didn't believe in the Powers.'

Candle ignored Dallan's comment. He pulled up his jerkin to reveal a thin white belt around his sturdy waist. He stood up on the seat so they could all see. As the cart reached the rocks, he jumped from one to another until he was at the top. The belt gave off a faint light, making it visible in the darkness. Candle himself was almost invisible against the night and the belt seemed to float, sparkling and alive, against a fine veil of petalled stars.

Fern could see it was encrusted with jewels and tooled with fine gold. There were words on it but she couldn't make them out.

'Two of The Powers.' Candle's voice had taken on a strange tone. 'Together for the very first time since they were fashioned in the Time of Misted Memory. So that's what drew the Jotun to us at the fairground.' He nodded down at Dallan and Madmerry. 'I see now why you felt you had to flee Auberon. You were right to fear that the long arm of the frost giants would reach out for you. That's what the ravens are seeking.'

'We weren't worried about the frost giants,' Madmerry said.

Candle shook his head, as if in disbelief. 'You should have been.

I see it now. There may even have been Three of The Powers at the fairground. Rumour has it that the Knights of Renown possess the Shield of the Daystar. Which should be in the possession of the Kingdom of Vicontium. Ysgarde denies knowing anything about it, of course. And the Vircontians would challenge it but they aren't ready to dispute the tradition that those silver shields always reveal the integrity of their bearers.'

'The silver shields have been compromised?' Madmerry craned her neck to peer up at him.

'It's said the shields aren't what they were—that they're just metal. Metal polished so it always shines whether its bearer is honourable or not.' Candle snorted. 'I don't know if Quystein has the Shield of the Daystar but, if he did, it would explain why the Jotun was in Auberon—it would have felt such a gathering of The Powers.'

His tone changed again. 'Imagine! Three of The Powers! And Two of them here with us at this very moment? We could rule the world! The Kingdom of the Dwarves would no longer be the edge of the world, but the centre, the pinnacle, the dazzling zenith of the greatest civilisation ever known.' He raised his arm.

Fern felt her lip curling. He didn't know it, she was sure, but he'd just reproduced a Nazi salute.

He dropped his arm. 'Why are you looking at me like that?' he asked her.

She hesitated. 'In my world, we have a saying: power corrupts and absolute power corrupts absolutely.'

'You really are from another world?' He jumped back down the rocks until he was on a level with the cart.

His eyes bored into hers for a moment. She watched his face as he caught his dream of domination and strangled it.

'Thank you.' He bowed. 'I am in your debt, as well, now.'

'Don't anyone move.' Hector raised his face just a fraction from Fern's lap. 'Don't turn around and don't make any sudden gestures. There's something coming up from the bog through the trees. I saw it dodge behind some rocks.'

Boody took to the air.

'Why does everyone ignore me?' Hector sighed. 'What's ambiguous about "Don't anyone move"?'

'Wolves, you say?' Candle turned to Dallan. 'Get a fire going. Quickly! You wouldn't happen to have a sword handy, do you? I seem to have lost my blade. Tell me you've got a sword.'

'No.' Dallan shook his head. A moment later, he pulled a long dagger out of a hidden sheath at his belt. 'I only have a knife for chopping herbs.'

'Perfect!' Candle grabbed it, to Dallan's obvious perplexity. He ran an expert finger along its sharp edge. 'Dwarf size, finely honed.' Leaping from the rocks onto the cart, he jumped down and sped off after Boody.

Dallan looked even more disconcerted.

'We've no wood for a fire,' Madmerry told him. 'Get some quickly.'

'The cart.' Dallan turned at once to Fern. 'It was your gift. You must say if we use it.'

'It is a gift and I no longer have a say.' She began helping him to pull out one of the smaller slats from the tumbrel. It splintered as they prised it loose. Dallan put his foot on the sections and broke them into smaller pieces.

'Good work, Dallan. Keep going.' Madmerry ripped out grasses and feathers from her head–dress. She gestured to Fern as she went to stand over the woodpile Dallan was creating. 'Shield me from the wind.'

As Fern covered her, Dallan yanked an adjoining section off, threw it to the ground and reached for another.

Fern watched as Madmerry pulled two stones from a pouch, knelt down and struck them together above the tiny heap of dried grass and feathers. Almost at once, the grass bloomed into firestrands and leapt with flame.

Fern stared. *I'd never be able to do that with a pair of stones.*

Madmerry jumped back. The feathers began to smoke but some wood splinters from the cart had already caught fire and began to crackle. Madmerry fanned them and called to Dallan. 'As soon as they've caught fully, take a stick each. We will go together down the hill to help Candle.'

Fern felt just a little put out by Madmerry's commanding tone. There was no hint of a request or a 'please' attached. *I suppose it's got to be that way for Dallan. You can't be subtle around him.*

Madmerry handed a firetorch to Fern, then to Dallan. Holding them up, they advanced down the ridge.

What am I doing? Fern stared at the firestick in front of her. Then she realised that watching the stick was a bad idea. She could only see its scarlet flames, not the enemy ahead. *Can we beat off a wolf with nothing more than a burning stick?*

It was a comfort not to be alone. She could feel Ginevra and Hector close behind her. Candle was up ahead, crouched in ambush behind a wedge–shaped boulder.

A long shadowy shape was loping up the slope just below his hiding place. As he signalled to them, the shadow darted for cover.

I think it's just tangled itself in a thornbush. Are we scaring it off? Maybe it's just a scout for a bigger pack. Fern felt sick. *That means we can't afford to scare it—we've got to kill it.*

She realised Candle must have had exactly the same thought. With a yell, he rushed out of hiding and, brandishing the knife, threw himself onto the shadow. The wolf fell to the ground and Candle struck blow after blow at its dark throat.

His grunts turned into a wild, unexpected shriek. 'No! It can't be.' The intensity of his cry shocked Fern.

She froze. So did Dallan.

Madmerry took off. She hurtled down the hillside, her torch flaming behind her as she slid to a halt beside Candle.

'I've killed him!' Candle fell to his knees and began keening.

'Oww, I'm dented.' The shadow struggled to its feet. 'Oow, seriously dented.'

Fern recognised the voice. It was Ansey. She began to run.

'Did he crink your neck?' Hector called out as Dallan thundered behind her. 'He's good at that.'

'No.' Ansey staggered around, moving with awkward steps. 'Though I think I'm going to have serious bruises.'

'I slit your throat.' Candle got up from his knees and stared. 'I stabbed you.'

Ansey patted a collar at his neck. 'You'll have to try harder. What are you doing here, Candle? This is Mistmurk Height.'

Candle took a deep breath. 'It's a long story. But I guess the essence of it is that we took a wrong road. And somehow it's turned out right.'

'I'm so glad.'

Fern could tell by his tone Candle was seriously shaken. And probably not by nearly killing Ansey. He sounded as if his beliefs in the way things worked were being seriously rattled.

He's not the only one. She shook her head as Boody winged down to land on her shoulder. She could hardly take her eyes off the watersilver collar around Ansey's neck. *It goes with my whistle.* She didn't know why she was so sure, but she knew they should be partnered.

'How did *you* get here, Your Highness?' Madmerry asked.

Ansey shook himself. 'The Jotun took me into the Mistmurk. I was only coming this way so I could get my bearings.'

'Just so you could get your bearings?' Candle took a deep breath.

'You escaped from a Jotun?' Madmerry's tone was one of disbelief.

'Actually, it let me go. Though it did say it would kill me if ever we meet again.'

'Peculiar.' Candle sounded suspicious. He pointed to the sword at Ansey's side. 'What's this?'

Ansey withdrew the sword from its sheath. Candle took one look at the blade, threw up his hands, turned around and huffed back up the hillside. 'No.' He shook his head. 'No! This is wrong. This is outrageous. The world does not work like this. Even if it's ending. The Powers are not real.'

Dallan stared after him. 'You know,' he confided to Madmerry, 'I don't think he's entirely sane. One minute he doesn't believe in the Powers and the next he says he can rule the world with them and now he says they're not real.'

'You're a fine one to talk, crazy boy,' Candle flung over his shoulder. 'There is no inconsistency in what I said. It is possible to rule the world with the Powers, even if they are not real. People respond to the idea, regardless of whether it's true or not.'

Hector bounded up the hill after him. 'You have one seriously warped mind, even for a dwarf. How can you consider such a deception? I'd hate to think what you'd be like if you hadn't been wearing the Belt of Veracity for the last three hundred years.'

Ansey trudged up the slope after Hector, the others trailing just behind him. 'Candle, are you three hundred years old?'

'No!' Candle snapped. 'Do you have any idea what that Sword is?'

Ansey's voice was mild, almost timid. 'By your reaction, I'm guessing you think it's one of the Powers. But I don't think it can be. The Jotun would not have forgotten it, if it was.'

'Forgotten it?' Candle turned, put his hands on his hips and roared. '*Forgotten* it?'

Fern could see he'd lost his temper. Dallan didn't quite cower against her but he moved closer. Madmerry put her arm around him.

'Children! Not a warrior, not a mage, not a sage! No strength of arm or might of mind between the lot of you!' His gaze moved past Ansey and fixed itself on Dallan. 'Not even sight of eye! And yet between you, you have two of The Powers.'

'Don't correct him!' Hector turned to glare at Ginevra and Boody. 'I'm telling you, do not ignore me this time, girls.' His voice dropped to a hissing whisper. 'Say one word about the third Power and venison steak with owl–sauce will be on my next dinner menu.'

Fern was astonished. *Did Hector have one of the Powers? Or was he talking about something Boody or Ginevra had?*

She could see Dallan and Madmerry were just as surprised.

Candle thumped his way back up the hillside towards the fire. 'Pick the Sword up, Buttercup,' he yelled over his shoulder. 'We'd better have a Council of War.'

'*Buttercup?!*' Both Hector and Dallan turned to Ansey, their voices raised in almost identical tones of disbelief.

'That's bullying,' Dallan said.

'I wouldn't go that far.' Hector shook his head. 'Mild teasing, perhaps. How do you put up with it? No, don't tell me. I understand.' He trotted up the hill. 'The things we tolerate in the name of friendship.'

'I'm glad you're beginning to appreciate what I have to put up with,' Ginevra said to him.

Hector scowled. 'I don't suppose there's the slightest hope of being back to the White Tree tonight.'

Dallan seemed to regain some equilibrium with the knowledge that Candle called Ansey 'Buttercup'. 'I wouldn't like a nickname like that.'

'It was the only thing about Candle that irritated me.' Ansey started back up the hill. 'I'm seeing a whole new side to him, though.'

They reached the tumbrel to discover Candle was pulling at the sides of the cart and throwing the wood onto the bonfire.

'Wolves, he said.' Candle pointed at Dallan. 'And Jotuns. They already know we're here. So, we may as well be warm.' He seemed calmer as Ansey went to help him. 'If we can build the fire up, I may be able to signal to Fastness Height. Bramble will be here on the double.' He stomped to the front of the cart. 'Where's food? You did think to bring food, didn't you? A Council of War is always better on a full stomach.'

'What are you so angry about?' Ansey asked.

There was a long silence. 'I'm angry because I'm afraid. I've never been afraid in my life before. And it's not fear for myself—it's for you. I don't know how to defend seven children against what is likely to come against us.'

Ginevra sniffed. 'No strength of arm or might of mind, you said.' She planted her front legs and stomped a dainty hoof. 'But didn't you forget power of spirit? We may be children, but you'd still be in Auberon if it weren't for us.'

Fern watched her in the firelight as her long eyelashes blinked slowly up and down. *Ginevra's so gentle you'd think she'd never stand up to anyone, then she comes out with something like this.*

'You're right, little one.' Candle's voice was low as he bowed to the group. 'Let's sit down.' He faced Dallan. 'I think that before any decision can be made about future action, I need to know how you come to have the Helmet of Providence.'

'On one condition.' Madmerry took hold of Dallan's hand.

'Condition?'

'First you tell us why the King of Dwarves is playing at companion to the Heir of Auberon.'

Candle shrugged and sat down in front of the fire. 'It's simple.' He glanced at Ansey a they joined him. 'There was concern Queen Barbizca might be a Jotun skinchanger and I came to Auberon as a representative of the Council of Wynterbrydge to assess that possibility.'

'Jotun skinchanger?' Ansey's mouth dropped open.

'A shapeshifter. A Mistress of Illusion.'

'She's a frost giant?'

''Fraid not.' Candle shook his head. 'No, Your Highness, she's just an extremely ambitious woman who, tragically, is insanely jealous of your father's continuing love for your mother and for you.'

'I could have told you that.'

Candle sighed. 'But what you can't tell me is why, though she pours unrelenting poison into his ear, it keeps backfiring. Instead of your father banishing you, as she keeps reminding him Rogin of Fyrzentsuu tried to do with Prince Emyr, he's become obsessed with protecting you.'

'Protecting me?'

'Even from yourself. Ansey, your father has a terribly warped way of showing it, but he loves you very much.'

Fern watched Ansey's face. A movement by her side distracted her and she noticed Madmerry squeezing Dallan's hand.

'How long did it take you to figure out Barbizca wasn't a Jotun?' Madmerry asked.

'It took a month to be entirely sure,' Candle said.

'A month?' Ansey asked.

'I was about to leave, mission accomplished, when I was ambushed by a small boy.' He began to poke together a heap of coals from the fire. 'I don't know how the small boy had worked out I was leaving, because I certainly gave no hint of it, but as I was picking up my journey roll, I realised it had been opened. I wasn't worried about it being searched, but I was concerned something incriminating might have been placed in it. I checked inside and found, of all things, a "thank you" note from Prince Ancelin, wishing me a safe trip and asking me to drop in and say "hello" when next I was in Auberon.' Candle glared at Ansey.

'Sorry.'

'How often do I have to tell you that you apologise far too much? Dwarves don't cry, but I came very close. It was the most moving, desperate expression of loneliness I've encountered in the last eight hundred years. I figured I could stay another few days. My Kingdom wasn't going to fall apart just for the sake of a week or so.'

'A *week* or so?' Ansey held up his hands. 'Candle, it's been *years*.'

'Truly, it was on the very tip of my tongue to tell you I was about to depart—remember that day in the stables I'd saddled a horse while you were secretly meeting Jens?—when I looked up and there was Gratian, being shown around.'

Ansey leaned back.

'Gratian…' Candle sighed. 'He's just one of the best spies who ever walked into Auberon. As soon as he joined the King's Shield, he had the commander's ear and was able to come and go wherever he liked in the castle.'

'Gratian?' Ansey's face fell. 'A spy?'

'From the moment I saw him, I knew I couldn't leave. I had to find out what he was up to.'

'And what was he up to?'

'He was looking for a copy of a prophecy.'

'I know, I know.' Hector held up his paw. '*The King Who Guards The Gate*?'

'Correct.'

'Did he find it?' Dallan asked.

'Not that I know of.' Candle shook his head. 'And before you ask, no, I didn't find it either. And believe me, I tried. I talked my young charge, Prince Ancelin, into studying all sorts of esoteric lore so I had excuses to poke into every book, scroll and parchment in the castle on his behalf. The Council of Wynterbrydge even sent some of its finest mage–scholars to help me: Old Greywhiskers, assisted by Harper, took the castle library apart from top to bottom. With Callum's help, they even went to the march–forts and searched every one of them from dungeon to tower.'

'The tutors were in on it? They're all spies?' Ansey's face registered his dismay. 'And March Lord Callum? What's this prophecy? And why's it so important?'

'We've no idea. All we know is that the Jotuns have poured all their resources into finding the king who guards the gate. They're not even making a secret of it anymore.' He steepled his hands together and looked at Dallan. 'And this is why the King of Dwarves was playing companion to the Heir of Auberon. Looking for clues as to how the Jotuns are planning to bring on the end of the world. Now you tell me how a blind boy happens to be hiding the Helmet of Providence.'

'Actually I'm the one hiding it,' Madmerry said.

'Where?'

'In plain sight.'

Candle clicked his fingers. 'Under the mask. But how did you get it?'

'That's simple.' Dallan clutched his hands together and began talking very fast. 'I was sheep–herding on the high pasture near the Wreathwatch Pass. A snow–storm came up without warning. I stumbled through the blizzard and got lost. I was disoriented and freezing. The snow was so heavy I couldn't see. All I could do was put one foot after another and hope I didn't fall down in a drift. I was looking for a sheepfold and its hut. After a while the mist began to lift and I saw the turrets of a castle, positioned between two small peaks and swathed in glittering ice. I thought it was a hallucination. Or maybe snow–blindness. It disappeared and the mist began to dance with sparkling lights. I went towards the castle. I was stupid. I should have run as fast as I could in the opposite direction.'

All jerky sentences and nervous twitching. Fern stared as Dallan finally took a breath. *He doesn't even like thinking about this.*

'You found the Court of the Snow–demons?' Hector's eyes were like huge coins. 'And you've lived to tell the tale? Wow!'

'Ector…' Tears sparked in Dallan's eyes. '…you make me feel heroic, rather than ashamed.'

Fern sensed what a huge admission that was.

'Bad scene, huh? Listen, Boy Wonder, the snow–demon special of the day is guilt with a special remorse sauce. And it's backed up with a lavish side–dish of undivided attention, all served to the accompaniment of background songs which begin: "Oh, you poor child, come warm yourself and stay with us and be comforted by the only folk who understand your pain." You were got, weren't you, right where you most condemned yourself?'

Dallan began to shake.

Don't melt down, Dallan. You're doing great. Fern copied Madmerry and squeezed his hand.

'I don't know how I got away. I was the adoring thrall of the Wreathwatch Woman. I had almost forgotten who I was. I was enslaved by her image of me as an innocent victim of my father's malice and my mother's abandonment. She fed off that anger and resentment. And when I felt ashamed of thinking that way, she changed tactics and piled on the guilt and fed on that instead. There was a storm—it might even have been the same storm. I've got no idea if it was hours or months I spent in the hall of the White Mother—and when she went out, seeking, as she said, to save other lost travellers, I heard a voice, like a sigh from the centre of the storm, speaking to me. "Rise up and go, for the moment is ordained. If you do not grasp it, you will be lost forever. You will not even remember your name to use its power to save yourself. Do not forget to take the Helmet of Time with you." So I ran out into the storm, taking the Helmet with me. She knew at once I'd gone and she sent her wolves and snow–leopards after me. She called curses down from the sky, promising me my heart's desire if I would return. I tried not to listen, but I knew she had already begun to be part of me when I felt her despair at my going and I knew that same desolation and loneliness in myself. I thought I would be torn apart by the pain as I went down the Pass, unable to see anything. I wasn't just snow–blind, I'd lost my sight. I could hear the wolves howling, gaining on me. I couldn't see anything. I just ran. I was certain I would die.'

He stopped and took a deep breath.

To Fern's surprise, Madmerry took up the story. 'When Dallan rushed through the door of our cottage, I thought at first he was another of the robbers. They were terrible men who had just killed my family. They tried to make my father reveal where our treasure was by torturing me. They sliced my face.' She touched her mask so it tinkled. 'But there was no treasure. They killed my father when they realised we really were just farmers scratching out a living on some of the worst land in the Kingdoms. They were turning to have more vicious fun with me when Dallan burst in. I'd been praying for deliverance and it seemed like it wasn't coming when a pack of wolves leapt in right behind him. The robbers attacked the wolves. They weren't doing all that badly until the snow leopards arrived and, after them, the…' She broke off. 'I crawled into the storeroom and made it outside. I was mounting one of the robber's horses when Dallan called out, "I can't see. Please help me." So I did. And we've been together ever since.'

There was silence. Candle poked the coals and eyed Dallan. 'If it wasn't so obviously true, I wouldn't believe a word of it. A mysterious voice described one of the Powers to you as the Helmet of Time? And you escaped from a snow–demon who's clearly going to take revenge the moment you set foot once more anywhere near Wreathwatch Pass? How long ago did this happen?'

'Nearly two years,' Madmerry said.

'And you went to Auberon but never thought to seek help there? You had one of the Powers and did nothing about it.'

Dallan seemed uncomfortable. 'We didn't know who to trust.'

Candle scratched his temple. 'Assuming I would have revealed to you the secret of the englacial stream so you could get through the Wreathwatch safely, what were your plans?'

Dallan's face was almost concealed in firelight and shadow. 'The Vircontium stadiums always have need of good herbalists. And we're very good.'

Fern could see Candle was suspicious but she couldn't understand why.

'All right, children. I see nothing for it but to put the tent up, have dinner and get a good night's sleep.' He raised his hands. 'What else can we do? It's dark. We can't go on further, we can't go back down the track with the pony and it's pointless trying to descend the cliff-face behind us or the slope down to the Mistmurk in front of us. I'll stand first watch with…'

'Me.' Boody volunteered straight away. 'I'm not a day person.'

'I think Candle's right.' Madmerry turned to Dallan. 'The White Mother would surely wait until you're closer to send the wolves—and, as for the ravens, we don't know how far they have to go to report to the Jotuns.'

'Ravens?' Ansey asked. 'Two of them?'

'Yes,' Candle said.

Ansey scratched his head. 'That'll be Munin and Huginn. Uller's ravens.'

'Uller?' Candle asked. 'Uller Princekiller? And he let you go? You, of all people? With the Speaking Sword?' He stroked his jaw for almost a minute.

'It speaks?' Ansey looked at it in awe.

'They're trying to force the prophecy.' Candle nodded to himself. 'They're trying to create a gathering of the Powers to compel The King Who Guards the Gate to appear.' He paused. 'On the other hand, Uller's one of the few frost giants who travels alone. We might not have to contend with a whole band of them.'

'Well, it ain't good news,' Hector said, 'but it's hopeful. Let's eat and sleep. The sooner we're on our way in the morning, the sooner I'm back at my Tree.'

'How good it is to know someone here has no doubt we will win through.' Madmerry said. 'There's bread, cheese and apples in the cart. Dallan and I will put up the tent.'

Ansey smiled at Fern. 'Let's help.'

ern began to set up the rag tent with Ansey's help. Madmerry directed them while Dallan roasted apples on the coals. *I should go help him make cheese toasties.* But she didn't.

She needed time to think. *This is not a dream. Or an hallucination. This morning I was worrying about how to stay invisible, so I'd have a place to stay. Here no one has a place to stay. Here people need me.* She pulled at the silver whistle around her neck. *Even if I'm the wrong person.*

Ansey kept giving her sidelong looks. She liked him. She wasn't sure whether it was because she didn't have to think about every word she said before she opened her mouth, or whether it was just sympathy.

Don't start thinking of him as a potential friend. Remember you're in another dimension on the brink of annihilation. She was inside the tent, helping Madmerry screw together the central tent pole, when her mobile phone fell out of her pocket. She'd forgotten it. *There's sure to be zero reception but…* She turned it on.

No signal.

But I wonder if the flashlight app works. This darkness is getting to me.

She opened the app and blinked as a shaft of bluish light hit her eyes.

'What's that?' Madmerry had finished screwing the main tent pole together and was hoisting the roof up. The drooping centre of the tent began to rise.

'It's one of the functions I've got on my phone,' Fern said. 'I don't know how long it will last, though. But we could have light for a while.'

Ansey's silverscale collar rippled like water as he stepped closer. 'It's not witchlight?'

Fern shook her head. 'No, it's not magic.'

'Don't let Candle see it then. He'll probably steal it and try to copy it. Dwarves are like that.'

'He couldn't replicate this technology.'

'Don't be too sure.' Ansey turned to help Madmerry fix the central pole in place. Then they both went out to tighten the ropes.

Fern sat the phonelight against the central pole and left it on while she spread out Madmerry's blankets. *We're short. I guess I sleep in this cloak.* She grimaced to herself. *I guess I share this cloak.* She smiled. *Stop being negative*, she told herself. *This is the best sleepover ever.*

Dallan flipped open the rag door and carried in a cloth bundle of roasted apples and cheese toasties. *Guess I didn't need to teach him that one.*

She was surprised he said nothing about the phonelight. But perhaps Ansey and Madmerry had explained it to him. They came in a moment later, followed by Hector and Ginevra.

Tail up, Hector nosed his way towards the phone. 'Is it alive? Is it a firepetal fallen from a star?'

Fern turned to him. 'So stars are flowers in this world?'

'Aren't they everywhere?' Hector, daring, reached out to touch the screen with his leather–cuffed paw. The light disappeared. 'Eeek! I've killed it!'

Fern laughed. 'It's okay. I'll fix it.'

'Come and eat before it's all cold...' Madmerry was arranging places in a circle and she pointed to a vacant spot for Fern.

'...or there's nothing left...' Ansey added. He dropped onto the edge of a blanket, put his sword on his knees and reached into the bundle for a cheese toastie.

Fern crawled forward and activated the app again. Hector watched, wide–eyed, while everyone else reached for the cloth bundle. He was far more interested in her phone than the food. 'So stars are not fireflowers in your world. What are they?'

'Massive balls of hydrogen gas where the atoms are fusing and letting off incredible heat.' Fern grabbed a toastie before they all disappeared.

'Wow! What a divine thought!' Hector seemed mesmerised by the phone. 'The sun here is only a wildflower that slowly turns on its axis and closes at night.'

Fern negotiated a gooey strand of cheese into her mouth while the others started on the roasted apples. 'Is that poetry,' she asked, 'or science?'

Hector's paw was creeping towards the phone again. 'Is there a difference?'

'In our world there is.' Fern took off her cloak, rolled it up and settled back on it like a pillow. She ran her hands through her hair. 'At least some things are the same. Like gravity. That's good. I'd hate to be stuck in zero gravity.'

Ginevra curled up beside her. 'What's gravity?'

'It's what Isaac Newton discovered when an apple fell on his head.' Fern laughed as Dallan took the last of the roasted apples and held it up above his head.

'Is gravity a thump on the head?' Dallan turned his face up to inspect the apple. 'Urrgh! Or juice in the eye?' He blinked as a dribble of fluid fell on his face.

'It's a force that pulls you towards the centre of the world. It keeps your feet on the ground. It makes things fall from the sky.' Fern was disconcerted as, one by one, the others exchanged odd glances.

'I don't think she means the same as the centripetal here,' Hector announced after several seconds. 'How can the world have a centre that's not in the sky?'

'A centre in the sky?' Fern took a deep breath. *Would that pull things up, not down? Then how come they weren't floating in the air?*

'Of course the centre's in the sky. It's on one edge of the sun, skipping from petal to petal as the sun spins. It's been that way since the Englobing. All of the seven kingdoms are on the inside of a globe, facing the wildrose sun.'

A wildrose sun. Now that's a divine thought, Hector. I don't care what you think about hydrogen atoms fusing.

'It's not really seven.' Ginevra nibbled at an apple skin. 'There's a lost kingdom. It collapsed into the waves a few hundred years after the Englobing. There's only six left.'

'It still makes seven.' Dallan glowered as if Ginevra couldn't add up.

Fern felt a wave of drowsiness come over her. The smell of apple and the warm comfort of the food combined with the cosy atmosphere to make her sleepy. 'What's the Englobing?'

'It's when our dimension was created.' Madmerry yawned then took a silk scarf from one of her pockets and wrapped it around her face. As she took off her mask, she pulled the scarf up to hide the top of her head.

'We're in a bubble siphoned off from another dimension in a time of turmoil millennia ago.' Hector's eyes never left the mobile phone as he spoke. 'The stories are conflicting: some say it was done by a great mage to trap a powerful rival and our ancestors were caught in the backlash. Our entire cosmos sits like an ornament on the mage's desk. In it, the mage's rival is trapped in enchanted sleep.'

That's one mighty cool creation story. But too much like a fairytale to be real...

Ginevra stretched one dainty hoof across Fern's legs and yawned. 'But others say our dimension was a refuge that the rival built to escape the mage. Here he sleeps, awaiting the death of the mage so he can burst out of his prison.' She turned her pink almond eyes on Fern. 'How was your world created?'

Fern shrugged. 'There are conflicting stories in my world too. Some say God created it out of nothing in six days. And then He rested. But others say a Big Bang started it all and life has been evolving for billions of years.'

Ansey took the sword from his knees. 'I'd like to visit your world.'

And I'd like to get back to it...

'Lights out in here!' Candle poked his head inside the tent flap, his face scowling in the phonelight. 'Stop talking, children! You need to get some sleep before it's your turn on watch.' He spotted the mobile phone at the base of the tentpole.

His eyes gleamed and Fern began to wonder if Ansey had been right about him. *Would he steal it, if he got a chance?*

He shook his head and tutted. 'Don't waste the battery, girlie. There's no recharger here.'

And then he was gone.

Fern turned the phone off and the tent was plunged into darkness. As everyone fumbled around getting ready for sleep, she had just one thought in her mind. *How on earth did Candle know about mobile phones?*

runting to himself, Ansey stretched and yawned. *Oww, I'm stiff. Oww, I'm cold.* Frost tingled his toes as he crawled past the tangle of warm bodies inside the tent.

Through the doorway, he could see dawn painting the sky with a wash of rose tints. As he pulled the flap wide and looked back, he could just make out Madmerry's face. Her mask was by her side and her scarf had fallen off to reveal a lattice of puckered scars.

It was freezing outside even though the wind had dropped. He picked his way across the stony ground. Candle was sitting on one of the high rocks, blowing white puffs into his hands. Ansey glared up at him. 'You were supposed to wake me.'

'You needed rest and I needed to think.'

'About what you could do with two of the Powers?'

Candle winked down at him. 'You know me well, Buttercup. Though it may come as a surprise to know most of my thoughts were about our new friend, Dallan.'

'What?' Ansey didn't like the way Candle's tone had dropped to a whisper.

'It took me most of the night to work out what's wrong with his story. I couldn't quite put my finger on it but something didn't add up.'

Ansey's gaze darted back to the tent where the others were sleeping.

'Then it hit me.' Candle blew a long white spiral of mist into the frosty air. 'If the Wreathwatch Woman ever had the Helmet of

Providence in her possession for more than five minutes, snow–demons would be the current rulers of the world.'

'So they would.'

'Since manifestly they were still confined to the icy heights of the Scimitar Mountains, it therefore followed Dallan didn't steal it from the White Mother.'

'He didn't?' Ansey started to feel uncomfortable. *Last night I was beginning to feel like I belonged. That I'd found the friends I'd always hoped for. But have I escaped from Uller Princekiller only to fall into the hands of a different enemy?*

'No, he didn't.' Candle held up a finger. 'Instead she tried to steal it from him. Dallan must have already had it before ever he got lost on the Wreathwatch Pass. It's as simple as that.'

'Simple?'

Candle shrugged. 'Of course the very fact he was carrying it around while sheep–herding raises serious questions. How did he get it? What was he doing with it at the Wreathwatch Pass?' He tapped Ansey's shoulder. 'And, think on this, Buttercup, which side of the Pass? Was it Auberon? Or Fyrzentsou? I admit crossing from Rogin's kingdom would be a miracle, but it's no more extraordinary than escaping from the White Mother or having the Helmet in the first place.'

'We should question him.'

'No. We don't want him to know we know he's hiding something. You know, having that Helmet would have drawn the pitiless Mother inexorably to him.' Candle shivered. Ansey realised it wasn't with cold, but unease. 'She must have succeeded in unleashing its temporal flux at least partially, otherwise he'd have known he'd been in her clutches only minutes. It would never have crossed his mind to think he was captive for months.'

'So you believe some of his story?'

'I have to. He's got the Helmet. Or rather Madmerry has. I can feel the Belt responding to it. And to your Sword. I've never had a sensation like this before. In addition, I've no trouble understanding the fox, the fawn or the owl.'

Ansey was baffled. 'Don't you have the Flair? You understand the finches.'

Candle ignored the comment. 'Why hasn't there been hue and cry at the loss of one of the Powers? The Helmet was in the treasury of Rogin of Fyrzentsou.'

'Could he have stolen…?' Ansey watched the first firepetal of the sun lick the eastern horizon.

'You lied to me.'

Ansey slewed in surprise as Dallan came out of the tent, rubbing his eyes at the dawn. Behind him came a sound of muted singing. 'I did?'

Dallan scowled. 'Not you. The dwarf. He said he'd wake me for my watch. I might be nearly blind, but I can tell the difference between night and day.'

'You're up?' Candle sounded thrilled. 'What excellent timing! It's only another minute until you're due on second watch! Ancelin's just joined me.' He signalled Boody to come down.

'You didn't tell me first watch was all night long,' Dallan said. 'No wolves? No frost giants?'

Candle shook his head. 'Only a dragon I had to fight with my bare hands. I'm surprised the noise didn't wake you. It was a ferocious tussle. After I'd wrestled it and thrown it off the cliff, I had to put out the blaze its flame–throwing breath had started. I battled raging winds and an encroaching firestorm half the night. I'm surprised that noise didn't wake you either. And then…'

'The dragon's mother arrived.' Boody fluttered in, clearly exhausted, and settled on Candle's shoulder.

Ansey laughed. 'Thank you.'

Dallan stared at him and pulled fretfully at his forelock of hair. 'It does not seem a thing to laugh about.'

'But he's joking.'

Dallan frowned. 'Is it a joke, Boody?'

Boody stretched one wing. 'Of course it is.'

'Oh.' He looked perplexed for a moment. 'Then thank you both for letting us all sleep.' He turned aside to the cart, then with an abrupt motion, swivelled back. 'What's the proper way to address a dwarf king?'

Candle held his hands wide and grinned. 'Well, now, that depends on whether you're speaking to one of the petty chiefs of the stone villages to the south that style themselves monarchs, or whether you're speaking to the anointed High King, Lord of The Nardelf, Enthroned Serenity on the Rock of Time, Master of The Deeping Ways, Warden of the Scimitar Mountains, Well–Builder of the Stars, Son of Earth and Child of Ancient Dream.'

Ansey blew a white cloud of surprise. 'Those are all your titles?'

Candle's grin became wider as he turned to Dallan. 'The proper way to thank a dwarf king is to use a precise formula. It's exceptionally tricky, so you might want to repeat it after me.' The grin became wider. 'Are you ready?'

Dallan nodded. 'Yes.'

'Thank you, Candle.'

'Is that all?'

'I knew you'd get it wrong.' Candle turned to the owl on his shoulder. 'Didn't I say that he needed to repeat after me? I told him it was tricky, didn't I?'

'You'd think three words wouldn't be that difficult.' Boody tutted.

'Thank you, Candle.' Dallan dropped to his knees and bowed. 'I'm so sorry I got it wrong.'

Candle looked at him. 'I honestly think you're sincere. And that won't do at all.'

Dallan looked up. 'Why not?'

'I've decided to teach you to be a Master of Intrigue. Unlike Prince Ancelin, you have some natural skill. As you proved yesterday.' He cocked an eyebrow. 'If you were running away from home to become a knight, you wouldn't leave a note, would you?'

'No. I certainly wouldn't.' Dallan paused. 'Well, I might, but I'd make sure it pointed away from where I was heading.'

'Exactly, lad. Just what I'd expect from an Apprentice in Intrigue.'

Ansey realised that Candle's smile was too broad. *If he didn't trust Dallan, why was he offering to teach him?* He sighed. *But maybe he didn't do much different with me.* He thought about what Candle had asked and then realised what he'd been fishing for: *Dallan can write. He's a blind sheep–herder who can write. Another mystery.*

Dallan was still on his knees. As he got up, he squinted, shielding his eyes. 'What's that?'

Ansey turned. He could see nothing. 'What's what?'

'That bright thing.'

Ansey realised his reaction wasn't feigned.

'Quick,' Candle said. 'Get everyone up. I don't know what he's seeing but let's be ready for it.'

Boody dived up through the branches of the crooked tree and skimmed low along the ridge. A few seconds later she wheeled and sped towards them like an arrow.

Dallan was already taking down the tent as Madmerry stumbled out of it, putting her mask on.

Boody went straight to her shoulder as she moved out of Fern's way. 'There's a stairway across the valley and a man coming over it.'

'Impossible.' Candle hurried. 'You're seeing things, Boudicca's Chariot.'

'There's a stairway,' Boody repeated, 'and a man coming across it.'

'A stairway?' The rag tent dropped to the ground. Ansey helped Dallan extract the central pole as Hector and Ginevra fumbled their way out. 'What's it made of? Stone? Metal?'

'It looks like it's made of air,' Boody said. 'Air and light.'

Candle took a deep breath as he stared at Madmerry's mask, then at the sword hanging from Ansey's belt. 'Helmet of Time. I wonder if, together, they are capable of switching time…' He looked troubled. 'Seven thousand years ago, a span of the Airbridge of the Osiirians was footed on this ridge.'

Dallan nodded. 'True. It connected the ancient territories of Auberon and Zamberg.'

'Two thousand years ago, long after the Osiirians had vanished, only one of the spans was still intact. The one crossing the valley between here and Fyrzentsou. A thousand years ago, there was nothing left of that span.' Candle pushed Ansey towards the cart. Its sides were gone, burnt in the fire, but the floor was still intact. 'Turn it around and everyone on. *Now!* I'd rather face an entire battalion of frost giants in alliance with the White Mother than even chance a meeting with a single green Osiirian.'

Ansey was gathering Zippy's reins when a voice called: 'Hello there, Your Highness. I've brought you all some breakfast.'

Ansey hesitated. 'Is it an Osiirian?'

'Let's not wait to find out.' Candle grabbed hold of Fern and hoisted on the cart. 'Let's go. Quickly!'

Dallan helped Madmerry on.

'Good morning, Ancelin Bedwyr Cai!' the man called. 'I've brought fish. Fresh from Fyrzentsou.'

'He knows who we are and I don't think we're going to get far.' Ansey took a deep breath and dropped the reins. 'Let's try politeness. It worked with Uller.' He ignored Candle's groan and raised his hand in greeting. 'Hello there. What news from Fyrzentsou?'

'Famine.' The man carried a string of fish in his left hand and a leather box in his right. He was wearing a flared morning coat that seemed more suited to a court audience than a walk in the wilderness. And that, apart from the longest nose Ansey could ever remember seeing on anyone, was the only really unusual thing about him. He was surrounded by a cloud of finches.

Ansey didn't know whether to be relieved or not at the sight. At least it was obvious how the man knew who he was. The birds had told him.

'The crops have failed for the second year.' The man inclined his head to Candle. 'Hail to thee, Lord of The Nardelf.'

'I knew it wasn't "Thank you." I'll bet "Hail to thee, Lord of The Nardelf" is the proper way to address a dwarf king.' Dallan's words were a bare murmur but, to Ansey, the air seemed strange and sensitive, transmitting sounds with unusual clarity.

'It's only the correct form if you're not the dwarf king's friend.' The man smiled as he held up his string of fish. 'If you are, Dallan, then you simply say, "Hello, Candle."'

Dallan stepped back, wary. 'Do I know you? Your voice sounds familiar.'

'Only my friends recognise my voice.' The man headed over to the ashes of the fire. The finches followed as he placed the fish there and covered them with coals. 'You were considering retracing your steps and trying again to reach the Wreathwatch Way? I wouldn't advise it. Manticore riders have been sent into the Mistmurk after Prince Ancelin.'

'Oh, come on.' Candle shook his head in disbelief.

'They are back–up in case Uller failed to fulfil his contract. Which he has chosen to do. I will speak to him soon.'

'The frost giant is irrelevant. Where would Barbizca get them so quickly?'

'She has them on loan from Rogin. He kept a pair, even after they failed to track Emyr, and bred several packs. He uses them to hold onto power daily slipping further from his grasp. He is reduced to making his subjects fear him.'

'But they love him.' Dallan seemed agitated. 'Of all the rulers in these lands, he is the most respected and honoured.'

'Times have changed. The famines have caused discontent and there are murmurings of rebellion. The people blame Rogin for the crop failures.'

'How can they be his fault?'

'Sit down,' the man said. The finches twittered around him. 'The fish are ready and we have much to discuss.'

'Who are you?' Fern asked.

Ansey was startled. *Why didn't it occur to me to ask that? It seems so obvious and yet…*

The man smiled at her. 'Fern McDey, you're not supposed to be here, you know.'

'I'm not?' Fern seemed to bristle. 'Well, you look as out of place as I do. What's in that briefcase? Why are you wearing a suit and tie?'

What? Ansey was perplexed by Fern's questions. The man was dressed with a pale silk cloth around his neck and a morning coat of flaring amethyst. But there was nothing strange about it. Besides, his manners were impeccable, his voice as soft as a gentle breeze. *That nose, though. It was impossibly long.*

'He should not have given your step–sister the whistle.'

Fern paled as her hand went to the silver chain around her throat. 'I knew I wasn't the Perfect Helper.'

'No, indeed, that is not your calling. But you are fast filling the need.'

'Who are you?'

'I am the Song,' the man said. 'And I have been sung. I would not be here otherwise.'

Ansey felt unnerved. *I'm surrounded by crazy people. I used to think, when the Flair first manifested, that I was insane. But actually, compared to just about everyone here right now, I'm quite normal.*

'Ah, yes, the Flair, Ansey.' The finches twittered in obvious agitation around the man's head.

He read my thoughts?

'It would be a very good thing if you were to instruct the finches to inform your father you can converse with them.'

My father? I've been trying not to think about him. 'They don't seem to want that.'

'No, they don't. And I will not force them. But they would do it, if you asked.'

I'm starting to feel guilty and I'm not even sure why. 'My father wouldn't have a clue if a finch spoke to him.'

'He has the Flair.' The man's smile faded but his sea–blue eyes gleamed. 'And he has waited and watched for many years for any sign you have, too.'

'He's got the Flair? He can talk to birds and beasts?' Even in his surprise Ansey noted that Fern seemed suddenly disconcerted.

'Of course.' The man nodded and reached out to place a soothing hand on Fern's arm. 'It's one of the signs of the Heir to Auberon. The covenant on the bloodline first shows up in its oneness with other creatures.'

'What about Candle? He's got the Flair!'

Candle's crest of flame–coloured hair waved as he shook his head. 'No, I haven't. I've had over eight hundred years to study the language of birds and beasts. I've learned the hard way to speak their tongues, I have no natural talent.'

Ansey felt uncertain. *It's a relief to know I'm not crazy, but…* 'What about Dallan? He hasn't had eight hundred years.'

'We'll get to Dallan.' The man turned and held up a commanding finger. 'Stay, Dallan. Don't run. Don't be afraid.' He looked back at Ansey. 'You have not done well to hide this talent. You have terrified your father and played right into your step–mother's hands. She torments him with his secret fear: that you are not his son and your mother was unfaithful.'

Ansey felt as if his heart was being squeezed. Tears spilled out of his eyes. 'Was she?'

'Your father has decided it doesn't matter. He loves you anyway.'

Ansey had to know. 'Was she?'

'The answer lies with the Flair. Speak to the finches.'

Between sniffles, Ansey looked at the cloud of birds. 'Please tell King Maurtz you are my messengers and I'm sorry I didn't tell him about being able to talk to you little guys before.' He wiped his nose. 'And don't ask for a reward! Especially anything that involves owls or blackbirds.'

The man laughed as they twittered off. 'You know them well.'

'Is it like this in every Kingdom? That the Heir has the Flair?'

'All of the Kingdoms have covenanted bloodlines. But not all are the same kind. In Fyrzentsou, the line follows women, not men. The king should be the queen's consort, not a ruler in his own right.'

'That's not the case with Rogin,' Madmerry pointed out.

'No, it is not, Cindurrah. But then, he is a usurper.'

Cindurrah? Star–herder? Is that her real name? Ansey wiped his tears.

'Unlike other kingdoms, the queens of Fyrzentsou are the true rulers.' The man's full attention seemed to be on Madmerry but Ansey had the increasing sense he knew everything about them. 'The land–bond follows the line of queens. On her death, it is transferred to her Heir. On marriage, the land–bond is shared with the king. Have you not heard the saying: *The king is as the land, the land is as the king*?'

'Yes.' Madmerry's expression was wary. 'But I was under the impression it didn't mean anything.'

'It's a simplified statement of how the covenant works. There is drought and famine in Fyrzentsou because Rogin is not the true king.'

'He isn't?' Dallan jerked upright.

'He murdered Imri, the king nicknamed the Whirlwind. Then he tried to force Olethea into marriage and killed all her sisters except Olien. She was safe in her alpine monastery, having professed her vows as a servant of Ruēl.'

'Have I got it wrong?' Madmerry's lips disappeared as she pulled her mouth into a thoughtful expression. 'I thought Olien was Rogin's consort.'

'Yes, she was. Olethea died of a broken heart the week before Rogin's lavish planned wedding to her. He wasn't going to have his plans spoiled so he forced her sister Olien from the monastery and compelled her to go through with the marriage.'

'That's what I hate about humans.' Hector sighed and shook his head. 'They're the only creatures capable of turning into monsters.'

The man raised his hand and wagged his finger. 'Ahh, Ector, but remember they are also capable of becoming greater than angels.'

Hector squinted at the man. 'So Queen Olien's sickness is responsible for the famine in Fyrzentsou.'

'Not at all. Olien had relinquished her bloodline inheritance when she professed her vows. She was never able to be the Heir after that. So, because Rogin had killed almost the entire royal family, there was only one place for the land–bond to light.'

There was? Ansey felt his brow wrinkling in a frown. *I don't see how there could be. All the women were dead.*

'On Emyr!' Madmerry breathed, her mouth dropping open. 'On the baby.'

But he's the wrong gender.

The man nodded to Madmerry. 'Yes, on a child too small to understand or control it. A child who should have grown up and watched a younger sister being taught to master it over many decades.'

Ansey felt a surge of pity for Emyr. *His home life would have been much worse than mine. The Flair is really quite fun, if a little freaky. But having the entire weight of the kingdom on your shoulders, pressing into your thoughts and dreams—that would be terrible.*

The man looked at him. 'Yes, Emyr suffered. As a tiny child he was frightened by surprises and he was desperate to restrain the chaos oppressing him. That's why he loves rules.'

'To be able to be sure things were just right?' Madmerry asked.

The man nodded. 'A natural consequence of the pressure of the land–bond.'

'Why are you telling us this?' Dallan blurted out. He seemed angry. 'Emyr is dead.'

How does he know that? Ansey scowled. *But he's got a good point. What do we all need to know this for?*

'You all need to understand why Emyr appeared to be an idiot. "Dopey" is how Ancelin here would put it. His apparent stupidity saved him. Although he was subjected to Rogin's violence, it was never the worst of it. Rogin thought him too feeble–minded to bother.'

'What changed?' Madmerry moved closer to the man, her mask tinkling as she tilted it to look up at him.

'A few drunken courtiers decided to have a bit of fun with Emyr the idiot. They threw him into a sword–pit against a Vircontium gladiator. He was so natural with a sword that Rogin, for the very first time, began to be concerned.'

'Didn't he ask Olien?'

The man shook his head. 'Olien escaped the court long ago. Rogin has lied about her illness.'

Ansey frowned. 'So Emyr didn't betray Rogin. It's all lies.' He pressed his lips together. 'But Rogin's chasing him. So is he still alive? Uller didn't seem to know. He even thought Tybold might be Emyr.'

'Oh, as Dallan said, Emyr's quite dead.' The man smiled and his sea–blue eyes twinkled. 'Quite, quite dead. But he's coming back to life.'

'The dead don't come back to life,' Candle said.

Coming back to life? Ansey was perplexed.

'Now before I go off to visit your father and check on those messenger finches, I'd like to ask a favour.' The man winked at Ansey.

Maybe I won't go to Ysgarde, after all. 'Can I come with you?'

'You're always with me. You're part of my song.'

Oh. For just a moment I forgot that he's crazy…

'I'd like you to deliver a message.' The man reached into a concealed pocket and pulled out a ring. Then he clicked open his box—*what had Fern called it? A briefcase?*—and out of it, took out an old shield. It was mud–encrusted and covered with barnacles. It stank and it seemed far too big to have come from the small box. 'This ring and shield belong to Lord Ancelin of Tariquhaven. I'd be very grateful if you'd give them to him and tell him I'm returning them with my compliments.'

'Lord Ancelin of Tariquhaven?' Ansey was reluctant but he took the shield and ring. 'Ancelin?'

'Yes, you're named after him. He was your father's best friend, long ago.'

How come I've never heard of him? Unless that's who Uller meant when he mentioned a knight named Ancelin who killed his brothers. 'Where would I find him?'

'On the other side of the Airbridge, in a hermit's hut, within the Bowl of the Field of Stars.'

'I was thinking of going back to Auberon.'

'I'll tell your father that. He'll be so pleased you want to return.'

His tone was odd. *As if what I want is not what I'm going to get.*

'What makes you think we're going across the Airbridge?' Candle put his hands on his hips and glared at the man.

There was an unearthly howl from the woods lower on the ridge. Ansey turned. *It's coming from the Mistmurk.* A violent, inhuman baying started up. Zippy let out a bray of unbridled terror.

'Manticores!' Candle clapped his hand on Ansey's shoulder. 'They've found your scent. They'll tear us apart. They'll show no mercy.'

'What should we do?' Ansey turned to ask the man for advice.

But there was no one there. No one at all. There was a moment's utter silence and then Zippy whimpered as another blood–curdling scream came from the woods below.

'The Airbridge,' Madmerry said. 'It's our only hope.'

Candle nodded. 'The Airbridge.'

Madmerry put Dallan's hand into Fern's. 'Run. As fast as you can. I'll unharness Zippy.'

'Follow me.' Boody soared into the air. Fern and Dallan, Hector and Ginevra ran after her.

Ansey grabbed the shield he'd been given and the sword Uller had left behind. Madmerry and Candle struggled with Zippy's harness. 'Hurry!' he urged them. He watched Fern dash ahead, his cloak streaming out behind her. *My scent's on it. She's in danger.*

He began to run.

The memory of Fern rolling up the cloak for a pillow, then later spreading it out to cover herself and Madmerry was fresh in his mind. He recalled Hector curling up at her feet and grumbling about not getting back to his Tree. *We were sleeping so close to keep warm, everyone will have my scent on them.* Everyone. *The manticores are going to kill us all.*

'Quick!' he shouted back at Candle and Madmerry.

'Go, child!' Candle bellowed. 'I'm coming.'

He ran. *Faster than I've ever done in my life before.* He held up the sword. *But not fast enough.* There was no sign of a bridge ahead—air or otherwise. He stumbled up a scree of flat rocks, terrified as he saw Dallan and Fern skylined ahead of him.

And there it was.

He reached the top of the hill and saw below him an arched staircase, shimmering with dewdrop light. It crossed the valley in one gigantic span. *It's massive.*

He fled down to it.

ncient and technologically sublime, the bridge was transparent. *It's giant's work.* Yet it looked insubstantial—like congealed mist. *Very thin mist.* Ansey slowed to draw a ragged breath. *Are we going to be able to set foot on it and not fall through?*

Candle overtook him. 'Don't dawdle, child.'

Ansey put on speed again and tore down the hill. Every stride seemed to take forever.

Dallan was waiting for him when he reached the Stairway. 'Where's Merry?'

'I thought she was just behind me.'

'Merry!' Dallan's voice was edged with panic. 'Where are you?'

The expanse of scree obscured their overnight campsite. Madmerry was nowhere to be seen. Ansey's heart was in his throat.

'Come on, don't stop.' Hector jumped onto the first step. 'We've got to hurry.'

Well, they carry the weight of a fox. But...

There was a yell. Madmerry, waving her mask, came leaping over the scree on the back of Zippy. Flat stones clattered down the slope in a rush. 'Go!' she screamed as Zippy raced ahead of the avalanche. 'Go! Onto the bridge!'

A dozen manticores lunged at Zippy's flying hooves, riding the avalanche down towards the bridge.

Candle pulled a knife from his belt. 'You and Prince Ancelin make your way over. I'll delay them. You make your escape.'

'Escape?' Dallan asked. 'We can't out–run them.'

'The Bridge isn't wide.' Candle folded his arms. 'A stout dwarf can defend it.'

'How wide?' Dallan held his arms out. 'This wide?'

'Not quite.' Ansey raised Lord Ancelin's barnacle–crusted shield higher. 'Just a little less.'

'How high are the sides?' Dallan asked.

'There aren't any.'

'Good.' Dallan smiled. 'Your sword,' he said in a tone of such command that Ansey didn't hesitate for a moment. He surrendered the Speaking Sword.

Dallan held it out, testing its balance.

Ansey could have sworn it had begun to murmur. It was like the finches, humming with appreciation.

'The best Vircontium swordmasters...' Dallan took a stride away from the bridge and held the blade before his face. '...teach you to fight blindfolded.'

Ansey could hardly keep the jealousy out of his voice. 'You've been taught by the best swordmasters?'

Dallan stood, one foot in front of the other, obviously listening to the roar of the manticores above the thunder of the stones. His hair floated around his face. 'It's fortunate you never took lessons from that second–rate swordsmaster Tybold had. You'd have to unlearn everything you'd been taught.'

Ansey stared in disbelief at Dallan's easy, assured stance. It was almost as if he'd become a different person.

Candle took up a position beside him. 'If we get out of this alive, you will tell me the true story of where you got The Powers from, *sheep–herder*.'

Dallan smiled. 'If we do and you ask again nicely, I will consider your request, *babysitter*.'

The slide of stones slowed, spreading out as it reached the flat where the Airbridge was footed. A few tinkled over the side of the cliff into the chasm below.

Zippy, eyes wide with terror, crashed past Candle and Dallan. Ansey leapt aside as it skittered onto the Stairway. It teetered. Ansey rushed forward to calm it before it threw Madmerry off and she fell. *Zippy… settle down, we'll protect you.* He felt the flow of the Flair, stronger than ever.

'Keep going, all of you!' Dallan yelled. 'Go over the bridge.'

Ansey glanced back as he engaged the first of the manticores. It had raged ahead, its slavering jaws wide. With a single stroke, he took off its head and punched it back into the manticore behind it.

And I thought he was dopey.

Candle struck his knife straight into another manticore's heart and pitched the beast over the cliff beside the Stairway. Its tail lashed as it fell, a killing reflex. Candle ducked and it did no more damage than ruin his hairstyle.

Boody winged past Dallan. He stepped aside as another manticore surged towards him, slashing down so swiftly as it reached him that he killed it with one blow and allowed its forward momentum to take it over the cliff. His pirouette to avoid the stinging tail was almost a dance move.

Ansey noticed two manticores converging to try to bring Dallan to the ground. He dashed back to help. Holding the mud–crusted shield in front of him, he was ready when one of them leapt over Dallan. It landed on the shield, knocking him down. Ansey's scrambling was enough to unbalance it as Dallan dispatched the other before turning to slash off its scorpion tail and sending it off the edge of the bridge.

How can he possibly do this without seeing? Ansey wondered. Dallan's words came back to him: *The best Vircontium swordmasters teach you to fight blindfolded.*

Candle had hacked the face of another manticore. Green blood was dripping into its slitted eyes. The beast howled, whipping its tail back and forward. Candle dropped down to avoid the sting and with a heave from below, dispatched it over the cliff.

'Fall back,' Dallan commanded.

Ansey saw Candle hesitate, then obey. It crossed his mind the Lord of the Nardelf was used to giving orders in battle, not receiving them.

'Retreat up the Stairs.' Dallan walked backwards, step by step, the sword out.

The manticores rushed forward once more. But shoulder to shoulder Dallan and Candle were now like a single unit. With the advantage of height as well as sword and knife, they sent two of them plunging to the valley below.

'Back.' Candle urged Ansey upwards. 'Keep going and take your companions with you.'

'We can defend the Bridge.' Dallan moved up a step. 'They won't try to rush us again.'

At least not until you get tired. Or relax your vigilance. Ansey realised he could do nothing to help and that Zippy was struggling with the stairs. Her hooves were sliding on the smooth surface.

He wanted to help but he left it to Madmerry. Although he hated the gruesome fight with the manticores, he was fascinated by it. *How can Dallan know just when to strike?*

Up they went, backwards. Step by step, slow tread by slow tread. Fighting all the way. The manticores were relentless and, as soon as one was gone, another filled the gap.

Dallan's sword was always moving, Candle's knife always slicing.

Ansey was surprised to hear singing. Strange and out of place, a song started up behind him. It took him a moment to realise it was Fern's voice. He could only make out a few words: *...my vision... my heart.* When the song started to repeat, Madmerry joined in. So did Ginevra.

Why are the girls singing?

But it seemed to make a difference. Dallan and Candle had a breather as the manticores pulled back. Their surge was no longer inexorable.

Minutes went by without another attack. The singing went on. The words were clearer. *Be thou my vision...*

The manticores shook off their sluggishness and appeared more purposeful. As they advanced, their blood–coloured man–faces slobbered in anticipation.

They followed Candle and Dallan, just out of reach, swinging their vicious tails with effortless ease. Every time a breath of wind brought a whiff of their rank scent towards him, Ansey felt like throwing up. He wondered about the wind. Apart from the occasional gentle puff, the air around the Stairway seemed unnaturally calm.

The singing was clearer still. *Be thou my vision, oh lord of my heart…* He glanced at the girls. *Is it calming them? Or giving them courage? Or a prayer to give Dallan sight? Or confusing the manticores?*

He saw an eagle, high above the dazzling icefield of the glacier, but apart from that, two ravens were the only sign of life. They looped the loop around the Airbridge and went back the way they'd come. *Munin and Huginn.*

He didn't think anyone else had seen them, so he said nothing. What was the point of worrying everyone about a prince–killing frost giant far off with manticores so close?

The sun rose higher.

The manticores came on.

What will happen when we reach the top of the Airbridge? When the manticores hold the high ground and we are below them?

The same questions had obviously occurred to Dallan and Candle.

'Get that pony moving, Buttercup.' Candle didn't even glance backwards as he issued his instructions. 'Keep increasing the gap between us and yourselves and, as soon as you get to the top, get on the pony and go. Straight down the other side. Don't look back. Ride for help as fast as you can. Once the manticores see that you are beyond their reach, I'm certain they'll give up.'

No chance, Ansey wanted to say, but he didn't. 'Yes, Candle.' He did not have the slightest intention of obeying the instructions. *If I get Madmerry and Fern on the pony, I'm sure they can get away. With luck, they'll even be able to hold onto Hector and Ginevra and take them too. Boody can take care of herself.*

He started to feel dizzy. He'd been careful not to make the mistake of looking over the side of the Stairway to the icefield underneath. But as he caught a glimpse of it far below, he began to feel shaky. After just a few seconds, it was so bad he couldn't even look at the steps.

He found if he concentrated on an individual, the shakes grew less. He focussed on Zippy and Madmerry.

'Increase the gap.' He gestured to Fern, Hector and Ginevra, urging them on. By the time they had reached the highest point of the Bridge, Dallan and Candle were fifty steps below them.

Ansey began to explain his plan. 'Fern, you and Madmerry should get on Zippy and just go. It's a straight run down. Hector and Ginevra…'

'No!' Madmerry folded her arms. 'I'm not leaving anyone behind.'

'Neither am I.' Both Fern and Ginevra spoke at the same moment. Ansey could see how terrified they were.

'C'mon girls,' Hector said. 'Don't make a hasty ill–advised decision.'

Zippy snorted an adamant refusal at him.

Hector shook his head. 'I guess I'll make the vote unanimous then, even though it's against my better judgment.' He glared at Ansey. 'No, we're not leaving anyone behind.'

Ansey turned back towards Dallan and Candle. He realised then that the manticores, rather than drawing closer to them, had slowed to a leisurely pace.

No longer attacking, they were pulling back. *Or…* He shouted the warning too late. 'They're leaping!'

With a run–up, the two leaders sprang over the heads of Dallan and Candle. They dropped into the wide gap separating them from Ansey and the others.

Slewing on their padded feet, the manticores whipped around. Dallan and Candle were caught between those at the front and at their rear. They turned back to back and fought on.

Ansey rushed back down the Stairway, Boody like an arrow ahead of him. He had no idea what to do to help but he knew he would be too late.

The attack began. Dallan's sword came down on a manticore, killing it. He moved forward, kicked it aside and sent it plunging over the side of the Stairway into the valley below.

But a second manticore was already on him. It leapt, forcing him down onto the steps. He thrust upwards with his sword, pushing it aside but a third manticore was already waiting.

Candle couldn't turn to help: he was also fighting for his life. The two manticores above him were using the higher ground to advantage.

Dallan's sword arm was pinned as a manticore pounced and sent the sword itself flying through the air. Growling, it opened its jaws, ready for the kill.

'Can't even give the damn thing away.' A voice rippled with laughter as two ravens swooped over the top of the bridge, their beaks like spearpoints as they dived on the manticores. 'Is it a Sword or a boomerang?'

A moment later, the manticore attacking Dallan was gone, tossed aside like a broken matchstick.

'Uller.' Ansey hardly dared breathe the word as the frost giant appeared and with one sweep of his huge hand dashed the entire troop of manticores over the edge of the bridge. Their ululating screams made a tangle of echoes as they fell.

With one massive stride, Uller came to stand over Dallan as he lay sprawled on the steps. Candle dispatched the last of the manticores as Dallan scrambled up.

Ansey had no idea what to expect.

Candle turned, bloodstained knife in hand.

Ansey could see that every line of his body was tensed for attack. But Dallan, his teeth chattering with cold, was between him and the frost giant.

And Uller just stood there, sword in hand with the point at Dallan's throat, watching him through narrowed eyes, staring at the hair floating around his face. 'It can't be.'

His gaze lifted and he smiled at Ansey. 'Give me the Powers.'

Ansey heard the tinkle of Madmerry's mask and sensed Fern, Hector and Ginevra hurrying down to him. Out of the corner of his eye, he could see Boody was harassed by the two circling ravens. Each of her attempts to move in and help Dallan was frustrated by their stabbing beaks.

'Give me the Powers.' Uller moved the point of his sword to Dallan's heart. 'I know you've got them.' He glanced from Ansey to Candle. 'Give them to me or the boy dies.'

'N–n–no.' Dallan was shivering but he scrambled to his feet, facing Uller. 'You shouldn't take what's not yours.'

Without a sword in his hand, he sounds just dopey again. Like a child repeating rules. Dallan, don't aggravate Uller.

'So you left the Sword for Ansey, hoping it would draw The Powers to it or him to The Powers.' Candle's lip curled as he glared at Uller. 'But it didn't work.'

'Don't try to deceive me, runt.' Uller held up the sword. 'I have the Speaking Sword back and now, at last, it actually does speak. Ansey's collar is really the Mailcoat of Justice. I know the Belt never leaves your waist. And together they've drawn the Helmet to them.' He pointed to Madmerry's mask.

That's what he wanted. The Helmet. He'll kill us.

Dallan glared at Uller. 'You set this up to get the Helmet, but you're not going to.'

'And what's to stop me?' The Jotun took a step back and sneered. 'One of you?' He shook his head and snowflakes dropped onto Dallan's shoulders. 'All I see is a dwarf, a pony and seven children, none of whom is even remotely capable of resisting the might of Uller Princekiller.' He took a deep breath and laughed.

It echoed across the chasm.

But as it did, the taunting smile on his face turned to a frown. 'Seven children.'

A shadow flickered across his eyes. 'Seven.'

'And now the Sword speaks.' He took a step forward and pressed the swordpoint against Dallan's throat once more. 'What day of the week were you born, boy?'

For a moment Dallan didn't answer. Then: 'Saturday.'

'You, owl child.' Uller pointed at Boody. 'What day of the week were you born?'

'Thursday.'

'Prince Ancelin I already know.' Uller flicked his gaze towards Ansey for a moment. 'Sunday.'

His face was grim as he looked along the Stairway, scrutinising the group. 'Who is Friday's child?'

Madmerry raised her hand without a word.

Ansey could see a frown deepening on Fern's face. How could she not know the day she was born?

'You.' Uller pointed with his free hand at her. 'What day were you born?'

She shrugged. 'I'm not sure.'

Uller sneered. 'Yes, in your world, date is more important than day. What do you think?'

'Monday…' She sounded uncertain.

Uller just nodded. 'And Wednesday's child?'

'I am,' Ginevra said.

'Which by a system of elimination leaves the fox for Tuesday.' Uller raised an eyebrow at Hector. 'Is that correct?'

Hector pouted. 'I'd love to ruin this, whatever it is…' He bared his teeth at Uller. '…but yes, that's right.'

'When the Days come,' Uller murmured, 'assuming Their Power, then is the time unchancy late. Awake! It is the Daystar's hour; he brings *The King Who Guards The Gate*.' With a deep bow, he tipped the sword over and extended the hilt to Dallan.

Dallan seemed nonplussed. Unsteady, he took the Sword and placed it behind him.

A moment later Uller was gone, heading back down the Airbridge in a swirl of misty cloak, his ravens behind him.

'What happened just then?' Dallan held up the Sword and swallowed, gulping. 'We were dead. Why did he change his mind about killing us?'

There was silence.

When the Days come, assuming their Power, then is the time unchancy late… Ansey wasn't sure what it meant, but it didn't sound good.

After several seconds, Candle spoke. 'I don't think we should waste time wondering what Uller's up to. Let's get off this Bridge and figure it out later. The Caverns of the Nardelf are not far off and I offer you all my protection.'

'Thank you.' Ansey dropped the shield by his side. 'We accept.' Turning, he led the way over the top of the Airbridge towards Fyrzentsou.

e thou my vision. Fern had woken up with the song in her mind. She'd dreamt she was in a choir with Ansey and Ginevra. Mrs Ashe had been conducting and Hector had been her page–turner. She hadn't been able to get it out of her mind.

Even now, aching all over, hurrying after Ansey, the tune was stuck in her thoughts. She glanced behind her. Dallan and Candle were following. They were slow but it was a wonder they even managed to stand up.

They've been fighting and all I've been doing was helping Zippy up the stairs. That had been so nerve–racking. She was afraid of being pushed off the edge every time Zippy's hooves started to skate.

That's why I was singing. She remembered now. *To calm myself.* She'd been surprised how quickly Madmerry and Ginevra had picked up the words.

Zippy stopped.

'C'mon, girl,' Fern urged.

Zippy whimpered and tried to turn around.

'Something's wrong,' Madmerry said.

That has to be the understatement of all time. Zippy hated every single one of the steps as they slipped beneath her hooves so it could only mean trouble ahead.

Fern looked past the end of the bridge to some shale flats and beyond that a dusty hill. Nothing unusual. She tried to coax Zippy forward. However, even with Madmerry helping at the reins, nothing would budge the pony.

Candle tried to push but Zippy brayed with terror. Dallan sidled past, holding his sword. He was just behind Hector and Ansey.

Madmerry signalled to Boody. 'Can you see anything?'

Boody rose higher, banked in a semicircle and, swooping down over Ansey's head, disappeared behind a rock column. It was a dark colour, like deep veined copper and jutted up like a broken hand.

There was a sudden thud.

Ansey ran forward. Hector darted through his feet, almost tripping him as he reached the end of the bridge. 'No one move. I'm just going for a quick reconnoitre.' Flicking his tail, he turned for a moment to grin up at Ansey and Dallan. 'Of course, guys, if I'm not back in ten seconds, send out search parties.' Like a white arrow, he darted across the flat embankment towards the strange outcropping where Boody had vanished. A moment later, he streaked back.

He was so fast that Fern was stunned. *What could he possibly have seen?*

'It's…' Before he could finish, a floating shape, as gossamer fine as mist, as delicate as drifting snowflakes, appeared between Dallan and Ansey. Its writhing, swaying limbs swathed themselves around the two boys and lifted them into the air.

'…*her*,' Hector finished.

Zippy squealed and, bolting, dragged Madmerry and Fern underneath the mist body and off the bridge.

The motion of the floating shape was a lingering caress. Slowly the mist solidified into a tall queenly woman who bent to kiss Dallan. 'You're back, my love.' Her voice was a husky whisper. 'And you've brought a friend, darling! How thoughtful of you, my precious, my sweetling, my own dear child!'

'Are you his mother?' Candle glowered as the woman laid a line of kisses on Dallan's forehead. 'Mighty affectionate, if you're not.'

'A dwarf!' The woman clapped her hands. 'A sturdy, honest, no–nonsense dwarf! Oh, it's been an age since I was visited by someone so refreshingly direct and open!'

Hector pulled at Fern's cloak. *C'mon*, he mouthed.

'Don't try your blandishments on me, missy,' Candle snapped. 'I'm a dwarf, through and true, and I'm immune to your seductions.'

Fern winced. *Don't challenge it!* Zippy tried to pull her away. *Immune to its seductions! It hasn't even tried to get you yet, Candle. You take one good look at Dallan gazing rapturously up into its ugly face and you'll know what you're up against.* She only realised Madmerry had left when she saw her coming back.

'Don't go on!' The visible half of Madmerry's face was pasty as she emerged from behind the rock column. 'Don't.' She looked as if she wanted to be sick.

'Boody?' *She can't be dead.*

Madmerry held out her hands. The little owl was cupped in them. 'Just knocked out.'

Fern took a step forward but Madmerry wrenched her back. 'I said *don't.*'

'What's there?'

'The Wreathwatch Woman's loom. Skulls for weights and entrails for woof.'

Fern shuddered. She smelt something decaying. Trying not to throw up, she pointed to the mist queen. 'That's the Wreathwatch Woman?' Dallan, Ansey and Candle were still on the steps. Ginevra tip–toed off the moment the mist–woman was distracted.

'Yes,' Madmerry said.

'The White Mother? The snow–demon?'

'All of those. It's said her name is Solveigra and she was once a great queen who desired immortality. She's thousands of years old. She's a legend: an example of the dangers of wishing unwisely.'

'She'd have been better off asking for beauty. I've never seen anyone so repulsive.'

'Actually she's quite attractive,' Madmerry protested.

'She's revolting. Don't take this the wrong way, Merry, but you're not the prettiest sight with your mask off. Still believe me, you are the fairest of the fair, compared to …' Fern pointed at the Wreathwatch Mother. '…that *thing* there.'

Her weakness is the desire for beauty.

'What are we going to do?' Hector wailed under his breath. 'They're ensnared by her beauty and love.'

'*Love?*' Fern tried not to sneer. 'The only thing she loves is herself.'

'They're trapped, doomed.' Ginevra reached them with obvious relief.

'Is she really that ugly?' Madmerry seemed puzzled. 'I wonder if those glasses of yours defend you from her illusions. When she wished for eternal life a thousand years ago, she forgot to ask for eternal youth to go with it.'

'She wants The Powers,' Hector said, 'to get that eternal youth.'

Her weakness is the desire for beauty.

A fragment of conversation echoed across to Fern. 'Why, yes, Master Dwarf, indeed this was indeed the Airbridge of the Osiirians, but now it is Solveigra's Stair. And I extract a toll from all strangers…' The mist–woman's writhing arm danced lightly in the breeze. 'I have enough swords at the moment, so a Helmet would be sweet.'

'She knows we've got the Helmet of Providence over here,' Ginevra said. 'And she's not satisfied with the Sword Dallan has, the Belt Candle's wearing or the Mailcoat Ansey has.'

Her weakness is the desire for beauty. The thought kept recurring.

'We've got to get the guys away from her,' Hector said.

'How?' Madmerry asked.

'We've got to think of something.' Hector stomped his leather–cuffed paws. 'Oh no, she's taken the Mailcoat!'

Fern watched the Wreathwatch Woman fling it over the top of the finger–shaped rocks.

'If we have to wait for a voice coming out of the heart of a storm like Dallan heard…' Ginevra glanced up at the clear sky. '…we're going to be here a long time. Should we just rush her?'

Her weakness is the desire for beauty.

'No.' Fern gulped, terrified. 'I've got an idea. We don't have to wait for a storm. I know what her weakness is.'

Hector smiled in relief. 'I knew all along you were the perfect helper.'

'Well, the perfect helper needs help, Hector.' Fern felt her heart thumping against her ribcage. Not even the manticores had scared her this much. 'And you're it.'

'Me?' the fox squeaked.

'You and I are going to distract the mist–woman.' Fern decided to move before she changed her mind.

'And?' Hector hurried after her. 'What's going to happen once we've distracted her? I think you've forgotten about the wolves and snow–leopards she has on call… not to mention…' They were almost at the bridge. 'Okay, I'm in. C'mon, what's the plan?'

'I'm making this up as I go.' Fern realised the Wreathwatch Mother had entirely encircled Dallan, Ansey and Candle in her pearl–white swirling garments. Dallan was gazing at her as if she were a divine vision. 'Just play along.'

'Oh, you poor child.' The White Mother ran her hand through Ansey's hair. 'Come warm yourself in my palace. It's not far. You can rest your weary heart and body. Oh, you must stay with me and be comforted. I do understand your pain.'

'And I thought you were exaggerating.' Fern raised her voice as they reached the Bridge. 'No, no, Hector, you don't understand beauty, if that's all you can say. Helen of Troy would be insanely jealous? Snow White a mere pimply teenager by comparison? Sleeping Beauty an Ugly Duckling?' She pointed to the White Mother. 'See? She doesn't have traditional beauty, but that's not the point, is it? The point is elegance. And poise, of course. What's a mere pretty face? It's the whole package, Hector.'

Hector clearly wasn't quite sure what response was wanted. 'Hmmm.' He took a moment to inspect the Wreathwatch Woman. 'I may have been understated, I suppose. Or was I overstated?'

'Oh, Hector!' Fern took off her glasses and crouched down to place them on his snout. 'Try these glasses. They're not rose–coloured, but they're very powerful.' She nodded. 'Very *powerful*.'

'Oh.' Hector caught on. 'Full of *power*? And their function when it comes to beauty?'

Out of the corner of her eye, Fern could see that the White Mother had taken a step towards them. 'Oh Hector!' She tried to sound cross. 'I should have realised. What would foxes know? Beauty is in the eye of the beholder, don't you know?' She took the glasses from his snout and stood up. 'But how is beauty defined? Answer me that!'

'Beauty is truth,' Hector said. 'And truth is beauty.'

'Is that a practical definition?'

'Probably not!' Hector's gaze darted left and right as the White Mother took another step towards them. 'I stole it from a dwarf poet.'

Fern sighed and waved her glasses. 'You know, Hector, in some times and civilisations, fat is lovely and attractive, slim and willowy is disgusting. Some cultures insist on luscious curves as their ideal of beauty, while in others supermodels are booed from the catwalk unless they have figures like teenage boys. I need a more discerning judge than you. Why, you're not even human!' She tried not to shudder as she reached across the Wreathwatch Woman towards Dallan. 'Here, Dallan! Try on these glasses for me, will you? Hector needs a male to put it in the right perspective for him. I can't get through to him. He's being really obtuse today! He's so out of date in the way he views things.' She put her glasses on Dallan's face and lifted the hair out of his eyes.

His eyes really are two different colours. She tried to pinch him without being noticed. 'How's that? Cleared up your vision?'

Vision. Be thou my vision. She began to hum the tune.

Dallan just stared. His eyes behind the lenses grew wider as he turned from her to the Wreathwatch Woman. His mouth fell open.

Fern hadn't expected him to see anything different. She realised by his reaction she might have made a mistake. 'I know they're powerful, incredibly powerful, as a matter of fact—maybe they're too much for you. I'll just take them…'

But before she could remove the glasses, the Wreathwatch Woman reached out with a curl of misty finger and swiped them from her. 'Now, just a minute!' Fern whirled. 'You give those back! Don't you put those on! They're my glasses. Mine!'

The White Mother put them on.

'Take them off!' Fern shouted and took a step backward into Dallan. 'Thief!'

Dallan was agitated. 'You shouldn't take what doesn't belong to you.'

The Wreathwatch Woman stood there, peering through the glasses, looking around. Turning her face to the sky, she looked up towards the sun high above. And, with a swirl of white vapour and a hiss like steam, she disappeared. The glasses dropped, clattering, to the steps.

There was a moment of silence.

Fern heaved a deep sigh of relief.

Hector stared. 'What happened?'

'She was mist. We got her to focus a bit of strong light on herself. She couldn't take it.'

'*We?!*' Hector asked. '*We?!* What you mean 'we', girlie?'

'I couldn't have done it without you, Hector.' Fern started to shake as she realised what she'd accomplished. 'I'm sorry for that crack about foxes not knowing anything. I didn't mean it. I was so scared, sometimes I wasn't sure what I was saying.'

'For someone who didn't know what they were saying, you were outstanding.' Ansey patted her shoulder. 'I couldn't even open my mouth.'

'Is she gone?' Dallan reached out to put his hands in hers. He seemed as shaky as she was. Tears were running down his face. 'How did you know she was mist?'

I don't know. Just as I'm not sure if there was a voice in my mind telling me her weakness or whether I thought it myself.

'That was brilliant!' Candle slapped her on the back. 'You dissipated her and until she can get back together, she won't be able to call up her wolves and leopards.' His grin was enormous. 'We're safe for quite a while. We'll be long gone by the time she reconstitutes herself. Can I look at these magic glasses of yours?'

Fern recovered from her stumble. 'They're not magic.' She handed them to Candle and watched as he examined the lenses. *He knows about mobile phones but not about spectacles?* 'They're just ordinary glasses. Boody desperately wants a tinted pair, you know, to keep out the glare.'

Thinking of the tiny owl, she turned towards Madmerry. Boody seemed to be sitting up on her shoulder but, without her glasses, Fern wasn't sure.

'Now that we've reached Fyrzentsou,' Madmerry called out, 'anybody for breakfast?'

'*Breakfast*?!' Hector's tone conveyed his complete disbelief. 'Where would we get breakfast? Besides it's lunch time.'

'We've got baked fish.' Madmerry patted a pouch hanging over Zippy's side. 'You don't think I'd have left them for the manticores, do you?'

'Fish?' Hector's snout creased in dismay. 'I'm all for new and exciting culinary adventures, but *fish*! I suppose it's a step up from cheese toasties.' Leaping from the steps, he trotted off across the shale towards a dusty hill. Zippy followed him. Hector scouted as far as the top of the hill. 'Seems safe enough!' He scampered back past Zippy. 'And the danger–sniffing pony approves!' He sat up, his tail wagging like a dog.

'What more could anyone ask?' Candle said.

'A white Tree.' Hector's tail–wagging stopped and he glared. 'A white canopy. That's what more!'

'If you don't mind me saying, Hector, I've had enough excitement for one lifetime.' Ginevra skipped over to him. 'If I were you, I'd give up on the prince. If this is the training exercise for your future adventure, imagine what the real deal is going to be like.'

Chewing a corner of bread she'd torn off, Fern took two pieces of fish from Madmerry. *We need to rest.*

'Don't go far.' Candle wagged his finger at Dallan as he trudged up the hill. 'You owe me a story, sheep–herder.'

'I only said I'd *consider* telling you, babysitter,' Dallan called back. 'I didn't say I would.'

Candle rose up in obvious indignation but Fern put up her hands before he could move. 'Let me try!' She hurried up the hill. 'Here.' She sat down next to Dallan and wondered what he could see as he looked out over the dustbowl on the far side of the hill. 'I've brought you something to eat.'

'Thank you, Lady Fern.' Dallan took the fish from her. 'Is it really as dead as it feels?'

'The fish? Of course.' She looked at him in concern. His eyes were rimmed with coal–smudges and his face was tired and lined. His head lolled with exhaustion. Fern realised he was ready to drop with fatigue. *The battle with the manticores really took it out of him.*

'No, not the fish.' Dallan raised a listless hand. 'I meant Fyrzentsou.'

Fyrzentsou? Fern chewed on the hunk of bread. She gazed at the flat dusty grasslands and the brown hills. 'It's dry. Nothing's growing.'

'May I borrow your glasses?'

'Sure.' Fern licked her fingers before taking them off. She flicked aside his fringe and positioned them squarely on his nose. *One blue eye. One hazel–green.*

Dallan was silent as he looked out on the woods and grasslands. It was several minutes before he spoke. 'You're right.' His voice was so low, it would barely have stirred a feather. 'Nothing's growing. It's a wasteland. There's nothing but withered grass and dying trees, dry plains, barren mountains… Famine, wasn't that what the man on Mistmurk Height said?' He leaned back and gazed up at a cloud high above. 'I should have stayed… I should have stayed. But truly I didn't know…' He fell back with a sob.

Fern felt helpless. He was sprawled out, half–crumpled, and breathing in erratic gulps. 'What's wrong, Dallan? Please talk about it.'

His eyes rolled backwards. He stopped moving.

'Dallan!' Fern stared. *It's more than emotional stress.* She reached for his pulse. It was hardly there. His face was pale and blue–tinged. '*Help!*

A moment later, Ansey was running towards her. Candle was behind him, knife drawn. 'What's wrong?'

'Dallan…,' Fern pointed. 'He's…'

Ansey slid to a halt and crouched down next to him.

'C'mon, sheep–herder! Stop faking it. I'm waiting to hear how you got the Helmet.' Candle leaned over and shook Dallan. 'And Prince Buttercup wants a lesson in sword–fighting.' He shook him again. 'He's not pretending.'

Madmerry arrived with Boody above her, Ginevra and Hector by her side. She knelt down beside Dallan, took Fern's glasses off and pulled back his eyelids. Only the whites were showing. 'Maybe he got stung by a manticore tail and we didn't realise.' She pulled at the pouch on her belt. 'None of the herbs I have will help against that sort of poison.'

'Put him on Zippy and let's get him to The Nardelf,' Candle said. 'There are dwarf wives who have potions for everything.'

'How long will it take to get there?' Ansey asked.

'There's an easy route from here through the upfells of Fyrzentsou. We'll be there in less than an hour. The worst danger we're likely to encounter the whole way is a couple of suspicious sheep–herders.'

'He's hardly breathing.' Madmerry held a feather from her mask to Dallan's blue mouth. 'His heartbeat is almost non–existent.'

'I'll get Zippy.' Ansey hurried for the pony. Hector dashed off back to the rock outcropping on the shale flat. 'Where are you going?' Ansey called.

'Won't be a tick.' Hector disappeared behind the rock.

Fern stood up. *What are you doing, Hector?* But he wasn't gone long. A few seconds later he came back into view, holding one paw against his chest as he loped along on three legs. There was something in his mouth. *He's hurt himself.*

Hector held out the Mailcoat to Ansey. Then he let something drop from his mouth at Ansey's feet. 'This ought to slow her up. Even when she gets herself back together.'

'What is it?' Fern stared at the leaf–shaped block of ivory.

'It's a weaver's shuttle.' Hector looked exceptionally pleased with himself. 'She's a Fateweaver. Unless she can get that back, she won't be making mischief for a very long time.' Hector's expression was miserable. 'I should have thought of it before. That might be what's affecting Dallan. She will have woven her fate with his.' His tail drooped as Candle hoisted Dallan onto Zippy. He sat on the flower–dotted patch of green where Dallan had been lying, his face glum and despondent. 'It's my fault.'

Candle set a cracking pace with Zippy. Fern was hard put to keep up and let Ansey and the others forge ahead while she lagged behind with Hector.

He was silent and upset and trailed so far behind that Ginevra trotted back twice to be sure they weren't lost. 'I can follow your trail,' he grumped at her. 'I don't need to keep you in sight.'

Half an hour passed. As they tramped along the windswept mountain track, Fern noticed several people coming towards them. A man and two women.

'They don't look like a couple of suspicious sheep–herders.' Fern took in their fine white cloaks and sturdy boots as they stopped to pick up some stones. *Are they sniffing them?*

She watched them cast distrustful glances at Zippy and the others. They threw the stones aside and kept on coming without a word.

'It looks like half a town to me.' Hector pointed further down the trail. There were dozens—*no, hundreds*—of people swarming up the mountain.

Fern followed Hector as he darted behind a cairn of rocks to watch the procession. The people weren't moving very fast. They would walk several paces, pick up a stone, smell it, then throw it aside. 'What's with the stones?'

'No idea.' Hector frowned. 'Now why does a whole town come up into the mountains?' His frown became a glower. 'We could be in real trouble. There are still places where superstition reigns and people offer annual sacrifices to spirits like the White Mother.'

'Human sacrifices?' Fern was appalled.

'It's the White Mother, so I'd say they would prefer to appease her with white creatures.'

Fern stared in horror at his snow–coloured fur. *His tone is so casual, so unafraid.* Her gaze was drawn down the mountain to where Ginevra, dainty and milk–white, was trotting behind Zippy.

The people seemed disinterested in them. Their stone–sniffing seemed to consume all their attention.

Maybe it's a trick. Maybe they'll suddenly turn and take us all prisoner. But it doesn't seem like an ambush. Fern watched the rich in fine silk jostling the poor in torn, unkempt rags. For the most part, they moved in silence, only pointing from time to time at something high above.

Bigger stones, maybe. All she could see in that direction were empty mountain meadows where the wind whipped through the snowgrass and battered the delicate alpine flowers.

Hector suddenly hit his snout with his paw. 'Oh, sheep poop! I'm an idiot.' He swatted Fern's knee. 'Hurry!'

He tore down the track at breakneck speed. He hurtled past a few straggling townsfolk and sped towards Zippy. Fern was breathless by the time she caught up with them and it was obvious a heated argument was raging.

'Stop being evasive.' Hector was on his back-legs, thrusting his paws at Candle. 'We've gotta get outta here *now*.'

'It's pointless. The englacial stream will take us in the wrong direction.'

'That's not important. It's outside Fyrzentsou, isn't it?' Hector pointed back along the mountain track. 'Open your eyes and look! Get it?'

Candle gazed back along the Upfells Track where groups of people were picking flowers in the upland meadows.

'Remember the Legend of the Scented Stones of Fyrzentsou?' Hector asked.

Candle hit his forehead with his open palm. 'Of course! It's been staring me in the face all along! That's how Dallan got the Helmet!' He grabbed Zippy's reins and swung himself up on the pony's back behind Dallan's limp form. 'Follow me!'

'Run!' Hector swatted Fern's leg. 'They've realised!' He charged off.

Fern stared. *Realised what?* All she could see was that the people had turned around and were hurrying back towards them. They weren't stopping anymore to sniff at stones.

'Realised what?' Ansey looked as perplexed as Fern felt. But he just turned and darted after Zippy.

Fern ran. Madmerry was already ahead of Ansey, Boody winging by her side.

What's going on? What are the Scented Stones? Fern raced after them, Ginevra by her side. Hector led them across the mountain, down crevasses and across tiny watercourses. He used every available cover to hide from pursuit.

It's not working. There's too many of us. Fern could tell the crowd was gaining on them. She wasn't sure she could keep up the pace. *Why are we running?* There was no sign of Candle and Zippy.

Hector was waiting for them at the edge of the glacier. 'They can't have brought him this way,' Ansey panted.

'They didn't,' Hector admitted. 'I lost their trail back at one of the streams we crossed.'

Fern stared at the glacier. It was full of cracks and folds. She dreaded the thought of trying to tackle it. They were sure to be overtaken on the ice. *Why are they after us?* Looking ahead, she could see a high ridge on the side of the glacier. Hector was heading that way. It was so steep she knew that, if they had to climb it, the pursuit would catch them at once. *This is madness.*

Boody disappeared into a narrow rock fissure, Hector close behind. If she wasn't so exhausted, she would have cried with relief. *We don't have to climb it.*

'Down here!' Ansey jumped after them, Ginevra leaping at his heels.

Madmerry waited for her. She skinned her shins on the jagged rocks at the entrance. Madmerry followed her in. The yelling of the crowd grew louder. Hector was scrabbling along the length of the fissure. It was difficult even for him.

We're going to be trapped here. Fern followed Ansey as he scrambled into the dim recesses of the fissure. She was surprised it wasn't becoming darker. There was an opening ahead. *We're going through the ridge, not over it. But we're still not moving fast enough.*

She could hear voices—gruff and menacing—closing in as she crawled out, faltering with exhaustion, into the light.

No sooner had she stumbled into the open than a boulder crashed down from above. Ansey grabbed her and yanked her aside. Madmerry leapt out of the boulder's way.

She looked up, shuddering as the dust settled, wondering if the townsfolk were about to cause an avalanche.

How had they got to the top so quickly?

But there were no townsfolk. An unknown dwarf stood on top of the ridge above them. He held a tiny banner, black and patterned with an eagle. It flapped heavily in the stiff breeze. On his helmet he wore a wolf's tail.

'The Fifth Dwarf Legion at your service, Prince Ancelin.' He bowed to Ansey.

A moment later, there were hundreds of dwarves on the ridge

beside him. Their dark banners were held high, their small spears glinted, their wolves' helmets gleamed. As Fern stared, she realised that the boulder had—ever so neatly—blocked the passage through the fissure so that no pursuit could follow.

azed and catching his breath, Ansey took a step towards the dwarf commander. There was thunderous yelling from over the ridge.

'We'll contain this pack of jackals for you.' The dwarf saluted. 'Find your friend.'

'Thank you.' Ansey saluted. Turning, he realised Hector had already taken off, scampering down the rocky incline with Ginevra at his heels. He looked down at Boody, winging her way above them. Madmerry and Fern hurried after them.

He looked around in astonishment. He'd expected the ridge to be an ice–filled extension to the glacier or an expanse of harshly weathered rock. *It's a cirque. A bowl scooped out by ancient ice.* But instead of cold scraped stone, a lush green lawn spread out in front of him. More strange still, an avenue of interlocking stones led towards an airy spreading tree at the centre of a garden.

He drew the filthy shield closer to him as he noticed two hooded figures walking up the avenue on the far side of the tree. A movement caught his eye and he realised Zippy was munching away on the grass, right under the tree.

They're here. They're safe. I hope.

Ansey took a deep breath then headed down towards the hooded figures. They were making their slow dignified way to the tree and he caught up with them easily. 'Have you seen a boy? He was with a dwarf…' He found himself looking at bronze–gold features, set with one emerald and one sapphire eye.

Green and blue. Just like Emyr's supposed to have.

Fern came up, puffing. 'Yes, he's with a dwarf…and our pony.' She pointed to Zippy.

'No dwarves here.' The woman with the strange eyes smiled, her lips moving in a slow, placid curve.

No dwarves? 'But Zippy…' Ansey pointed to the pony too. 'The dwarf was with Zippy.' He could see the woman didn't understand. 'That's our pony—Zippy. The dwarf is Candle, he's a king.'

'No kings here, either.' The other hooded figure spoke. It was a man with a gruff, terse voice.

No dwarves? No kings? Ansey gestured with his thumb over his shoulder. 'But the dwarf legion. It's just back…' He stopped, realising that Zippy had no pack. *The Sword. And when was the last time I saw the Mailcoat? When Hector dropped the White Mother's shuttle at my feet, just before Dallan collapsed.* He couldn't remember anything about it after that. But he was sure Candle had it. *There's no way he'd have left it behind.*

For the first time, his trust in Candle began to waver. *Three of the Powers. The Belt makes three. Candle said that with Three of the Powers he could rule the world.* He turned to see a look of suspicion in Madmerry and Fern's eyes. *They're thinking exactly the same.*

'No dwarves came through here?' Madmerry asked.

'Of course not,' the woman said. 'No dwarves here. Ever.'

'Nor ever will be,' the hooded man said. 'Not unless they want to find themselves strung up by their toes and left to swing in the wind until they're nothing but bleached bones.'

Hector backed up past Zippy and positioned himself against the tree. 'You'd do that to them, just for trespassing?'

'Of course not,' the woman said. 'I've no objection to dwarves. Cheery little chaps, most of them. And their wives are as wise as they come. No, it's dwarf law that forbids them to come here. And dwarf law that prescribes the most horrific penalties if they disobey.'

She's got the Flair. She not only understood Hector, she showed no surprise at it. I don't get it. How come everyone's got the Flair suddenly?

Or did they always have it and just pretend not to?

'Dwarves come as far as the top of the bowl,' the man said, 'but no further.'

If dwarves don't come here, there's got to be a reason why. Ansey tried to catch Hector's eye. *Maybe we should surround this pair.*

'Candle wouldn't kidnap Dallan, would he?' Madmerry asked.

'What reason would he have?' Ansey asked.

Hector banged his head against the trunk of the tree. 'Because I told him who Dallan is.' He thumped his head once more. 'Oh, they were right! The den was right to expel me. I'm a total jinx.'

'You told him?' Madmerry asked. 'But how did you...?' She stopped.

'Told him what?' Ansey asked.

'Scented stones. Flowers blooming in the wasteland. It was obvious.' Hector groaned. 'I'm so stupid. I didn't think. But there was no reason not to trust Candle...'

Scented stones? There's some ancient legend of Fyrzentsou... but I don't recall...

Ginevra walked around the tree. '*Dallan!*'

Ansey ran at her shriek. On the far side of the tree, under its dappled canopy, was a bed. On it, stretched out as if he were fast asleep, was Dallan. His skin was pale as parchment and his closed eyes had sunk into coal–blue hollows.

'He's dead?'

'No.' The woman came to join them by the side of the bed. She stared at the still form. 'Though what ails him, I cannot tell. This is your friend Dallan?'

Ansey nodded.

'We didn't know his name but we placed him out here under the greenwood for the fresh air and sunlight.' She looked at the dish she was carrying. 'I've been feeding him a special broth. It's so potent it'd be enough to restore a giant with a spear in his belly, a sword through his heart and an axe in his skull to perfect health in an hour. It should have cured a boy like this in moments. I can't understand it.'

Ansey could hardly believe how thin Dallan had grown since they last saw him. He was almost wraith–like.

'I've some herb–skill,' Madmerry said. 'Could I look at your broth?'

The woman obliged and held the dish out so she could sniff it. Madmerry raised her eyebrows and stuck her finger in the broth. 'Wonderbloom.' She licked the finger. 'Perhaps it just needs time to work.'

'It's had over a week.'

'A week!' Madmerry exclaimed.

'That's not possible,' Ansey said. 'We were with Dallan less than an hour ago.'

'When you crossed the threshold of The Basin of The Field of Stars, you passed into a time eddy,' the man informed him.

'This is the Basin of the Field of Stars?' *Hold on. That was the name the man on Mistmurk Height used. How had he known we would come this way?* Ansey felt in his pocket for the ring he was to deliver.

He looked at the shield in his hand and the man's words came back to him. They were so vivid in his mind it was almost as if they'd just been spoken: *This ring and shield belong to Lord Ancelin of Tariquhaven. I'd be very grateful if you'd give them to him and tell him I'm returning them with my compliments.*

'What's a time eddy?' Hector's features had curled in dismay. 'I'm getting that same bad feeling I got when I first heard the words "anomalous duality".'

'It's where time doesn't flow at the same rate as the rest of the world,' the woman said. 'Though whether the time here is fast or slow, comparatively speaking, depends on how and where you disturbed the eddy when you entered.' She smiled. 'If you happen to land right in the middle of the eddy, no time passes at all in the outside world, however long you spend in the Field of Stars.'

'Oh,' said Fern, 'like the wardrobe into Narnia?'

'Is there a wardrobe into Narnia now? The only way I've ever heard to get there was using rings.'

Ansey wondered what they were talking about. He felt the ring in his pocket. *Will it help us get out of here?*

'What about Dallan?' Madmerry brought his attention back to the biggest problem. *The irritating, dopey, incomparably skilful Dallan. How can I be so jealous of a sheep-herder?*

'What other remedies have you tried?' she asked the woman.

'We've tried everything we know, haven't we, Lance?' The woman waited for the man's answer.

He nodded. 'Olien and I have tried everything for Sleeping Beauty except kissing him. We had to draw the line somewhere, you know.'

Olien? Could she be the queen of Fyrzentsou? Ansey shook his head. *No, must be heaps of women with that name.* Still, he felt as if he were missing some joke as a wink passed between her and Lance.

There was silence.

Ansey took a deep breath and held up the ring and the mud-crusted shield. 'I was told to deliver these to Lord Ancelin of Tariquhaven. He's here, isn't he?'

All colour drained from Lance's face as he stared at the ring and shield. 'Where in heaven above and earth below did you get those?'

'A man gave them to me and told me to say they are returned with compliments. Are you Lord Ancelin?'

'Who are you?' Lance's expression was wary, his tone almost aggressive.

Ansey felt awkward. 'Just a messenger.'

'Who sent you? How did you get these things?'

'There was this man. He didn't give his name—just these things…' Ansey hesitated as a contemptuous sneer crossed Lance's face. '…and some fish.'

'And what if I refuse to take them?' Lance's colour turned pasty.

Ansey felt foolish holding out the ring and the shield.

'Lance, stop making things difficult for the boy,' Olien said. 'It's hardly his fault. If by some miracle of heaven, your shield and ring have…'

'Miracle?' Lance spat as red dots appeared in his pale cheeks and violent anger seemed to consume him. 'When I left Ysgarde, I made it clear I would be true to myself and myself alone. I would accept no man's bidding but my own.'

Ansey took a step back as Lance raised a fist.

'Any message from heaven must come from the hand of Ancelin, by the word of Ancelin, in the power and the strength of Ancelin.' Lance almost shouted the last words.

There was silence.

Ginevra kicked Ansey's shin lightly.

Hector nudged his knee.

Ansey tried not to look in any particular direction. He just gave a vigorous shake of his head.

'If you're shy about this, buddy,' Hector stage–whispered, 'I could tell him for you.'

'This isn't the right moment.'

'Not the right moment?' Olien peered from one to the other. 'Is there something more?'

'More?' Hector drew himself up. 'Is there something more?' He raised his paw and glared at Lance. 'So you won't accept anything but by the hand and word of Ancelin, eh?' He turned with a swish of his tail. 'Well, may I introduce…' He paused dramatically and extended his paw in a formal gesture towards Ansey. '…my pal, Ancelin Bedwyr Cai, Prince of Auberon.'

'*Ancelin?*'

For a moment, Ansey thought Lord Ancelin was going to explode. His face turned a vivid shade of purplish red. He yanked the ring and the shield from Ansey's hands, pushed him backwards and stormed off. 'I'm sorry,' Ansey called after him.

'Do you always apologise for things that aren't your fault?' Olien asked.

'He does,' said Madmerry, Ginevra and Hector in one voice.

'I'll take the ring and the shield back, if it'll help,' Ansey offered.

Olien shook her head. 'It's not that easy. Lance not only lost all belief in the goodness of heaven but he cursed it and flung his ring of fealty and shield of faith off a cliff into a raging sea. I'm sure he never expected to see them again. He wandered the world, seeking peace, until he came here.'

'Did he find peace?' Fern asked.

'What do you think? He might say he trusts no one but himself, but in fact he trusts himself least of all. And now he thinks a dirty trick's being played on him.' Olien turned her one blue eye and one green eye on Ansey, sizing him up. 'Here you come, swaggering into his sanctuary, bearing his name: are you a herald of forgiveness or of judgment? What does the Ancient of Days mean by sending you?'

'It sounds like a second chance to me,' said Boody.

'The Ancient of Days?' Hector asked. 'That guy on Mistmurk Height? He didn't look ancient. He did look odd, though.' He thumped his paw. 'Fact is, I thought he was a fisherman. All those fish, you know. I haven't changed my mind now you tell us Lord Ancelin flung these things into the sea. Who else is likely to find them except a fisherman?'

'What kind of fisherman comes across an Airbridge that hasn't existed for a thousand years?' Fern asked.

'A very *old* fisherman.'

'Very old as in "ancient of days"?' Madmerry said.

'What do you mean by Ancient of Days?' Fern asked.

'Speaking of Days,' Hector interrupted, 'you wouldn't happen to know a prophecy, by any chance, would you?' He tried to sound casual as he addressed Olien. 'About Days coming and assuming their Powers?'

'Where would a fox like you hear a prophecy like that? From the fisherman?'

'Oh, just around.' Hector held up his paws in a nonchalant gesture. 'Around. A prophecy about Sunday's child and Monday's child and so on and Power thingies. I'm particularly interested in any verse about Tuesday's child.'

Olien was quiet for several seconds. 'There's never been any prophecy about the Days being children.' She drew back, wonder dawning on her face. She began counting the group. She finished with Dallan, lying as still as death on the bed. 'Seven.'

'It'd be really helpful…' Hector's voice deepened as he cleared his throat. '…if we could get some information on this prophecy.'

'Prophecies are notoriously ambiguous.' Olien's gaze drifted in the direction Lance had taken. 'You mentioned a dwarf. Did a dwarf tell you this prophecy?'

'It was a frost giant, actually,' Madmerry said.

Olien took a step back. 'The Jotuns know?' Her soft voice took on a note of alarm. 'The Jotuns know the Days are already gathered? And that they're children? There's no safety here, then. We must get you all to Ysgarde immediately. Lance is just going to have to leave his high–principled pride behind.' Her face took on a faraway look. 'Until Ysgarde falls at the end of all days, then no place on earth could be safer…'

'Ysgarde falls at the end of all days?' Hector swatted her long tunic. 'Is that days with a little "d" or Days with a capital "D"?' He turned to Ginevra and Boody. 'Girls, let's go home right now. I'll escort you.'

Ansey frowned at Olien. 'You don't have to come to Ysgarde. Just point us in the right direction.'

'Of course I'm coming,' Olien said. 'And so's Lance.'

'Lord Ancelin didn't sound happy about Ysgarde. Was he a Knight of Renown?'

'Yes. All that's stopping him from going back now is stubborn pride. He's got his ring and shield again.'

'But if he left there when he lost faith in everything, then it's understandable he wouldn't want to go back. So it's best if we find our own way.' Ansey made an effort to relax his frown. He smiled down at Hector. 'Thanks for coming this far.'

'Hold on, hold on, I didn't say I was leaving,' Hector said.

'Yes, you did.'

'No, I didn't. Just that I was thinking about it.'

'You're getting like Dallan.' Ansey put his hands on his hips.

'I admit to learning a trick or two from Boy Wonder.' Hector flicked his tail and turned to face Olien. 'Now back up in this conversation. Return to "prophecies are notoriously ambiguous" and give us some specific details on wording. What are the Days? And how are they connected to The Powers?'

'As you don't have The Powers,' Olien said, 'it's not a concern.'

'But we *did* have some of the Powers.' Ansey wasn't sure how much to tell her. *Probably best to keep the Helmet secret.* 'They were with Zippy.'

'And now they're with the missing dwarf?' Olien took a deep breath. 'This gets more complex by the moment.'

'What about Dallan?' Fern asked.

'Yes.' Madmerry folded her arms and her mask jingled as she nodded. 'How are we going to take him with us? If the dwarves aren't on our side, what're we going to do? We can't fight them.'

There was silence for several seconds.

Hector raised a paw to attract Olien's attention. 'I know this is the Basin of the Field of Stars, but are we in Fyrzentsou?'

Olien shook her head. 'No, this is the border between the kingdoms of Auberon and Fyrzentsou, the dwarf realm of The Nardelf and the Snow Citadel of the Wreathwatch Wraiths. We are independent: claims of sovereignty mean nothing here. Even time holds no constant sway.'

'Well, that kills that idea.' Hector scowled as he gazed at Dallan's waxen features. 'I thought his problem was Fyrzentsou itself but I guess it isn't.'

'I'll get Lance.' Olien gestured to Madmerry and Fern. 'Round up the pony and we'll work out some way to move Dallan.'

As she left, Ansey realised what he had to do. It required determination and bravery, but he knew he had no other option. He had to get to Ysgarde by himself. Alone.

Fern's right: there's no point in trying to retrieve the Powers from the Nardelf. What can any of us do, even together, against the might of a dwarf legion? And why should Lord Ancelin have to go to Ysgarde if he doesn't want to?

As soon as everyone was distracted by Dallan, he sauntered off, as if taking a casual look around. The moment he was sure he was out of sight, he ran as fast as he could. Back up the avenue of stones and up the incline towards the top of the cirque.

Risking a glance over his shoulder, he relaxed when he realised there was no pursuit. No one had seen him. Only a few seconds more and he'd be out of the Basin and no one would be able to catch him.

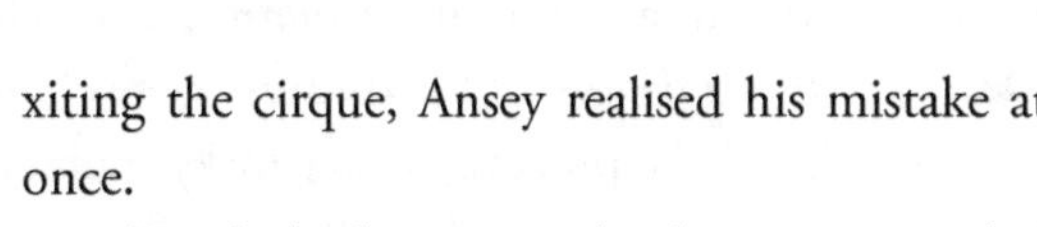

xiting the cirque, Ansey realised his mistake at once.

'Don't look surprised whatever you do.' Hector tapped his forepaw. 'You took your time.'

Ansey stepped across the top of the Basin. 'How did *you* get *here*? I…' He noticed half a dozen grim–looking dwarves standing several paces behind Hector.

'We've been waiting for you to get out of that time eddy for hours.'

Time eddy? I begin to understand why the dwarves have a rule about never entering the place.

'Mistress Olien and her charge have been sent ahead,' one of the dwarves said. 'Your friends, however, were reluctant to be parted from you.'

Ansey bent down to pat Hector. 'Thank you.' He dropped his voice. 'What happened?'

They were waiting for us, Hector mouthed. His cheerful grin belied the worry in his eyes. *We didn't stand a chance.*

'I'm Nibble.' The dwarf bowed. 'Commander of the Eagle Legion. The Lord of The Nardelf, Enthroned Serenity on the Rock of Time, Master of The Deeping Ways, Warden of the Scimitar Mountains, Well–Builder of the Stars, Son of Ancient Earth and Child of Eternal Dream bids you follow us on the Wreathwatch Way.' He saluted. 'May I welcome you, Your Highness, all in the name of the Cavern Kin?'

Oh great. Once Candle's got what he wants, he's all courtesy and charm. 'Thank you, Nibble.' He saluted back. Hector at his heels, he allowed himself to be led away by the dwarf. Boody was perched on Fern's shoulder and Madmerry held Lord Ancelin's shield as Ginevra walked by her side. The Lord of Tariquhaven himself was dressed in a tunic of golden brocade. His expression was grim as the marching dwarves came down the slope with Ansey and Hector.

Ansey didn't know much dwarfish. It was a language Candle had been reluctant to teach him. But he could pick up isolated words from the conversations around him. *Children... the Days... the Ancient of Days... with the Powers...* The dwarves were clearly astonished.

Nibble led the procession over rocky moraine to the foot of the glacier. They hopped across furrowed, sometimes jagged, creases most of the way. *This is wrong. Glacial ice carves smooth and sharp, not in folds.*

At the glacier's edge, Nibble opened a door that looked like a block of fissured ice. Ansey followed him into the darkness beyond. The walls and ceiling closed in around him. 'Dark in here, isn't it?' Hector's voice drifted up from his feet.

'Yes.' Boody flew in. 'Isn't it wonderful?'

'Don't push.' Madmerry sidled past two dwarf sentries as she stepped in. Fern was behind her and Lord Ancelin at the rear. The darkness disappeared as another door opened and a light–filled tunnel appeared.

We're inside the ice. Ansey felt a shiver pass up his spine. Shadowed blue and green, the ice had a translucence seeming to gleam with ancient secrets.

Nibble presented them with heavy furs. 'We'll leave these at the other end,' he whispered to Lord Ancelin. 'Keep your voices down. Everything resonates in here. Our sound engineers are working on the problem, but I swear they're making it worse, not better.' He stepped into the tunnel. Even the tread of his feet echoed thunderously.

Ansey stared up at the ice, awed by the way it glowed with a pale green luminescence. The ceiling was intricately and meticulously carved with various scenes: battles with giants and men, dwarf coronations, spectacular feasts and the making of alliances.

It's all perfect. Not a crease, wrinkle or furrow anywhere. They've put a lot of effort into keeping it intact. Just like Father with his marble rollers, I guess.

'We lose three arrow–lengths a year off the end of the glacier.' Nibble pointed back at the entrance. 'Just breaks off.'

They reached a stairway carved of ice. 'I don't understand,' Fern said. 'Why don't you make something so wonderful out of something permanent?'

'Nothing is permanent,' Nibble said. 'Not even stone.'

So they don't protect this place against Time. I guess that tells us that whatever is causing the distortion of the land isn't Time. 'I'm going to have frostbite shortly.' Ansey began to mount the ice stairs. 'My feet are freezing.'

'Me too,' Fern said.

Moments later, they were swept off their feet by two robust dwarves. Ansey stared at the face next to his own. It smiled so cheekily he couldn't even think of a protest. He watched as Boody, dislodged from Fern's shoulder, fluttered on ahead.

The two of them were carried up the ice stairs. They went past peepholes of lilac and pink crystals. 'Rubbishy stuff,' the smiling dwarves informed them. They seemed unable to stop talking, despite Nibble's instruction to keep quiet. 'Look at that! Amethyst and rose quartz. Nice twinkle but cheap as chips.' They even chattered on through the detours of glittering limestone, where cone–shaped stalactites inched their way decade by decade towards the floor. 'See that baby one dripping there?' The dwarves pointed together to one of the smaller stalactites. 'Born about the same time as Khufu laid the first stone for his Great Pyramid.'

'You have Pyramids in this world too?' Fern asked them. 'And the Pharoah Khufu?'

The dwarves clammed up and went back to smiling. They pointed out ice statues built into niches in the walls, but they didn't say another word.

They said too much. Ansey was sure of it. *Pyramids and the Pharoah Khufu—I've got to ask Fern later.*

'They are the Subtle Gentles.' Nibble whispered as he pointed to the ice statues. 'Artists whose works and achievements are their lives. Truly great art is not in sculpture or paint, word or music. The greatest artists are those who spend their lives in helping and serving others. You'll notice there aren't many of them.' He indicated the last statue at the top of the Way. 'This is Puddle. Few of the Kin knew her during her lifetime but, when she died, her obituary revealed she was an artist of the highest calibre.'

Nothing prepared Ansey for his first sight of The Nardelf. He was stunned. Beyond the silvered arched entrance set with gemstones was an immense hall. The massive iridescent columns, lit from the inside with a blue light, gleamed as they soared to an impossible height. *They shouldn't be able to support their own weight, let alone the mountain above.*

The two dwarves set Ansey and Fern on their feet and allowed them to move forward. Ansey couldn't stop marvelling at the black marble floor, the gleaming columns and the colossal space.

'Serious over–compensation.' Hector gazed up in awe.

'What for?' Ginevra whispered.

'Clearly a complex about their short stature.'

Lord Ancelin took a deep breath. 'You may have something there.'

Ansey realised the hall they were in was a throneroom. He realised that meant he needed to behave less like a gawking peasant and hold himself with dignity.

A table was set at the far side of the room and behind it was a throne whose back went almost to the ceiling. It was made of black alabaster and adorned with parallel lines of pure gold. Light shafted down from high above on the figure seated on the throne. There, in full ceremonial armour, wearing a back–crested crown of finest gold, was Candle.

The first thing that crossed Ansey's mind was an incident a year previously when Candle had wiped up the mess after he'd had food poisoning. He felt small, awkward and embarrassed. *A king acting as a servant—it wasn't right.*

But it was.

It was exactly what the argument with his father had been about: *what is the nature of true kingship?*

Lord Ancelin stepped forward, but Ansey pulled him back. *I have to do this.* He knew it was his duty and his alone. He guessed that no outsiders had been inside the Nardelf for more than a thousand years. He bowed, dropping his head as he raised his hand in salute. 'Hail to thee, Lord of The Nardelf.'

'Oh, cut it out, Ansey.' Candle stood up, his hair gleaming with jewels inside the crested crown.

He looked up to find a reassuring twinkle in Candle's eye. *You didn't take the Powers to use them. Whatever you took them for, it wasn't that.* He smiled. *And we're still friends.* 'Is Dallan recovered?'

Candle winked. 'I regret to tell you the poor boy died only a few moments ago.'

Ansey was baffled. The wink and Candle's smile didn't match the statement. He heard a sob behind him and realised Madmerry had burst into tears.

'Oh, quit with the melodrama!' Hector swatted Madmerry's legs. 'You knew all along this had to happen soon.'

'Melodrama?' Ansey couldn't make out why both Candle and Hector seemed so heartless. 'Hector, stop it! If you can't have any sympathy, at least behave responsibly.'

'Oh, but he's very responsible.' Olien's voice came from the shadows near the throne. Moving into the light, she smiled at Hector. 'If it wasn't for the wits of the fox, Dallan would have died in Fyrzentsou.'

'But he died here anyway.' Tears were streaming down Fern's cheeks. 'Didn't he?'

'No, not in quite the same way,' another voice said. 'So Hector really does deserve thanks for saving me.'

'It was nothing much.' Hector shrugged and assumed a modest expression.

A black figure emerged from the darkness. '*Dallan!*' Fern and Madmerry squealed together.

Ansey was stunned. The transformation was even greater than Candle's. Dallan's blonde fringe had been trimmed, he was wearing brand new glasses and the silver–embroidered tunic he had on sported the royal arms of Fyrzentsou. 'You're alive!'

'No, Dallan's dead. He died on the way here.' Hector batted his snout with one of his paws. 'Don't you get it?'

Ansey shook his head.

'You're as stupid as I am and that's saying something.' Hector sighed. 'This is one seriously dumb fox. So caught up in the idea of a canopy as a tree, couldn't see that it could be a rag tent. This, folks, is my day of destiny.' He beamed and did a little jig. 'Actually it was a day or so ago, but let's not be pedantic. May I introduce you all to Emyr, rightful King of Fyrzentsou.'

'King?' Fern sounded as baffled as Ansey felt.

Then he thought back to Uller's reaction on the Airbridge as he'd looked at Dallan. *One blue eye, one green eye. That's what the long fringe was meant to hide. So why hadn't Uller carried out his assignment when he'd had the chance?*

Candle was scowling at Madmerry. 'If you'd told us who he was from the start, wildling, I'd have realised straight away it was the land–bond caused his collapse. It was only when Hector mentioned the Scented Stones…'

'I'd forgotten the legend.' Hector looked so pleased with himself. 'But then I remembered the coronation song of Fyrzentsou about the mountains rejoicing, the flowers budding, the stones turning perfumed.'

Ansey still couldn't quite believe it. He stared at Dallan. '*You're the rightful king of Fyrzentsou?*'

'Of course he is,' Hector said. 'That's what caused his illness. Fyrzentsou was sucking him dry. And that's why the people went up the mountain—because it was blooming. Their wasteland was coming alive. They would have taken Boy Wonder from us, you know, and let Fyrzentsou kill him.'

'The land–bond's not like that.' Olien spoke up. 'But it would have driven him crazy. He's never been taught how to shield it.'

It took Ansey a moment to work it out. 'You're his aunt.'

Emyr's glasses winked as he slewed round to her. 'Why didn't you say something? Can you take this from me?' He sounded desperate.

'Emyr, Emyr.' Olien shook her head. 'I didn't want to surprise you too soon. And no, I can't take it from you. But I can teach you about it.'

Emyr nodded. He turned to Fern, a smile gentling his lips. 'Thank you.'

Fern seemed surprised. 'What for?'

'The idea of glasses.' He turned to look at each of them in turn. His eyes seemed to plead with Ansey. 'I'm not crowned, you know. I'm only an ordinary prince really, no different to you.'

'No different?' Candle asked. 'Hold on now. Ansey is Sunday's child and you're Saturday's child.'

Ansey whirled to face him. 'You know what the Jotun meant by that?'

Candle's smile was thin and grim. 'It means a slap in the face for every sibyl and soothsayer of the last millennium. No one's predicted you lot. Not even close. No one's foreseen…' He paused, scowling as he looked around each of the seven in turn.

'Children?' Hector supplied.

'Children.' Olien patted Emyr on the shoulder.

'Which is an even bigger slap in the face,' Candle went on, 'for anyone who predicted the Coming of The Days meant the advent of mighty warriors or great mages.'

'I'm not sure I want to be a Day,' Hector said. 'What does it entail?'

'It means you save the world,' Candle said.

'Is that all?' Hector clapped his paws together and turned to Ginevra and Boody. 'Girls, I was right before—let's go now before this adventure gets more out of hand.' He waved to Emyr. 'Been nice knowing you, kid.'

'Or if you don't save the world,' Candle said, 'everything and everybody is destroyed. This is the greatest threat to this dimension since the Englobing itself.'

'I knew there'd be a catch.'

'Stop grumbling, Hector,' Ansey said. 'I think of all of us, you're the one enjoying this the most. Quit saying you're going home all the time when you have no intention of it.'

Hector glared. 'This is one seriously scared fox.' His voice was a wail. 'The rest of you seem to have been born without fear, but I don't mind admitting I'm a coward.'

Ansey squatted down beside him. 'I'm petrified too.'

Candle clapped his hands. 'Come, come, all of you. Sit down.'

Doors on either side of the hall opened wide and lines of dwarves came scurrying, first with chairs, and then with food. 'There's gifts on the table for each of you.' Candle pointed to a velvet pouch. 'Let's start with yours, Boudicca's Chariot.'

Madmerry loosened the drawstring for Boody.

'*Sunglasses!*' Boody soared up into the air, looped around the high back of Candle's throne, sped to the ceiling and came down again like a bullet. '*Sunglasses!*' she shrilled again, landing on the table in front of Madmerry and lifting her face up to be fitted with the spectacles. 'Oooh! I'm dreaming.'

'After that,' Candle said, 'I fear my other gifts will be an anti–climax.'

Ansey lifted the lid of the box in front of him. There was a sword inside. 'For when you take lessons from Emyr.' Candle winked at him. 'It's got a couple of special features I think you'll enjoy. It's specially programmed never to lose to anyone named Tybold.'

There was a gold–plated *No Visitors or Relatives Except By Appointment* sign for Hector. 'If we survive whatever cataclysm is looming,' Candle said, 'I assure you, you'll need that. It also has special features, but I'd like them to be a surprise.'

For Ginevra there was a necklace of berry–shaped gemstones.

'Sorry, very unimaginative of me, falling back on jewellery.' Candle grinned. 'If ever you're hunted and can't lose the pack, drop one of the berries behind you.'

For Madmerry there was a book of herb lore. 'So ancient and comprehensive,' Candle informed her, 'that some of the plants in it are extinct.'

For Fern, there was a ring which fitted her smallest finger. 'It's a Finder,' Candle said. 'If you lose something, you just whisper its name to the ring and it will assist you.'

He turned to Emyr. 'The last is for you, rightful king of Fyrzentsou.'

Emyr shook his head and pointed to the glasses on his face. 'These ground lenses, Lord of The Nardelf, are already the greatest imaginable gift. I need no other.'

'Then just humour me, lad, by accepting my generosity.'

Emyr came forward and opened the box, drawing out a tiny silvermetal branch from which bloomed a perfect daisy. He stared at the delicate tints of the petals as the scent of the bloom wafted through the air. 'Is it living?' His voice was reverent. 'Or a work of art?'

'It's living and it's also artificial, a crafted thing. It is The Flower of Heart's Desire.'

Odd choice for a boy, even if he is a king. Ansey couldn't help but wonder at Candle's choice. Then he realised: *daisy* means *day's eye. He's given it to the Day he thinks needs eyes or maybe extra–special vision. No wonder he chose Emyr.*

'The Wreathwatch Woman tried to deceive you,' Candle said. 'True heart's desire is not that which you get, it's that which you give. Be careful where you bestow it.'

'Thank you. If you did not already have my eternal friendship, I would swear it readily.'

'A good neighbour policy never goes astray.' Candle winked. 'And now, before we sort out this business of the Powers, we're going to dine.' He put his hands on his hips. 'No arguments, no dissension. Am I not Lord of The Nardelf? And shall not what I command in my own hall be instantly obeyed? We are going to eat ourselves to a standstill!'

Ansey was nonplussed by the choice as the servants lifted the high lids off the dishes. There were three kinds of baked meat and four kinds of roast fowl, seven different sauces, hot steaming vegetables and warm mint–drenched fruit, golden cheeses and butter pastries, blackberry wines and amber cider, rich bubbly cordials and silk–sieved water. 'Mercy!' Hector cried half way through.

'Intermission!' Candle agreed.

'Intermission?' Ansey held his stomach and groaned.

'Be grateful this is not one of Nero's banquets,' Candle said, 'or we'd all be going out for a good purge at the vomitorium before we started again.'

'Nero?' Fern asked. 'The mad Emperor? Who fiddled while Rome burned?'

'What's an emperor?' Ansey put the word in his mind, along with pyramids and Pharoah Khufu.

'What's a vomitorium?' Hector asked. 'It's not what it sounds like, is it?'

'Time enough for questions later,' Candle said. 'We're going to begin our discussion about the Powers. So far, we have five of them.'

'Five?' Emyr looked to the far side of the feasting table where the Powers were laid out: the Belt, the Mailcoat and the Sword. 'Looks like three to me. Four with the Helmet Madmerry has on.'

'And five with the Messenger Shoes Hector is wearing.'

Hector looked shocked and crestfallen, all at once. 'How did you guess?'

'So I was right?' Candle looked pleased with himself.

Ansey stared down at the dark leather cuffs around Hector's ankles. He would never have called them 'shoes'.

'Only the last two Powers are needed now. One is a Shield and the other's nature has been hidden since before time began.'

Ansey looked at Lord Ancelin's shield. *Was that it?*

'The time of the end must be near.' Candle folded his arms. 'The giants are preparing to attack the Knights of Renown in their fortress of Ysgarde. The Jotuns are not the only ones with prophecies: *The world is well while Ysgarde stands, when Ysgarde falls then woe's at hand.'* He nodded. 'But have no fear: you are all safe here. And I know you will all want to bathe and rest, so I have assigned you each rooms.'

I don't want to rest. I want to discuss this further.

Emyr obviously agreed with him. 'You don't need to go to any trouble, Lord of the Nardelf.'

'I assure you it's no trouble.' Candle clapped his hands and lines of dwarves appeared once more. 'Ask my servants for whatever you need.' He pointed to the Powers. 'Would you like me to put these under lock and key or would you like to take them with you?'

After a moment's hesitation, Ansey held up his hands. 'They might be better off locked up safely.' And with a low bow, he went out, preceded by a dwarf attendant.

In complete silence, he was led through white marble hallways. Even when he tried to talk to the dwarf, there was no response. *He's been told to keep his mouth shut.*

His room was bigger than the banqueting hall at Auberon. It was gilded in costly metals. The bed in the middle was draped with cloth–of–gold. 'I'll just rest now.' He dismissed the dwarf with a wave. 'I'll call you when I need you.' He lay down on the brocade, closed his eyes and pretended to sleep.

or the first hour Ansey stayed alert, straining his ears to hear any sounds nearby. He found it very hard to stay awake after that. He realised he must have dozed because he woke up to whispering outside his door. He waited again. Another hour went by. And another. He knew he was drifting in and out of sleep. But he woke up with a jerk the moment he felt a wriggle at the back of his bed.

'Hi!' Hector pushed his snout out between the two largest pillows in the nest he'd pushed to the side. 'Sorry I took so long.'

'Actually, I'm surprised you made it before morning.'

'Being white's never been much of an advantage before, except in winter. But then the whole den was white so it wasn't much of an advantage then, either. But it's great camouflage in these marble hallways.' He held up his paws. They were bare. 'Fern took my Messenger Shoes off so I could do some discreet spying.'

'What's going on?' Ansey didn't expect good news.

'We're the only ones here, except for a contingent they've left to guard us.'

'They're all gone?' Ansey was surprised by the speed of their departure.

Hector nodded. 'Candle made a stirring speech about the time of the end along with now is the hour the dwarves will emerge as champions of the Light. He's gone to take command of the legions and assist Ysgarde when the Jotuns attack. Lord Ancelin and Olien both left with him. I think it was against their better judgment.' He scowled. 'But even their doubts were swept away when Candle said that, in this case, Seven Days do not make One Week, they simply are weak.'

'What!' Ansey sat up bolt upright. 'Who does he think he is?'

'Exactly!' Hector was obviously angry about the comment. 'It was all I could do to remain in hiding and not give him a piece of my mind.'

'Just because we're children! They think we can't contribute anything. They think we'd only get in the way.' His eyes narrowed as he fumed. 'And Candle tried to deceive us about the Powers.'

'That wasn't half obvious,' Hector said.

'You realised they were copies?'

'We all did!' A smirk appeared on Hector's face. 'Candle wouldn't have offered them to us if they were the real deal.'

Ansey felt wretched. 'I trusted him.'

Hector crawled out from between the pillows and sat up, a snow–white speck in the middle of a vast cloth–of–gold counterpane. 'I don't think he wants them for himself. If things go badly, as I suspect he thinks they will, he wants us and the Powers here for a couple of reasons: firstly, because deep–down, despite the prophecy, he believes it's safer here than in Ysgarde and secondly, if the whole earth does fall, he wants the Powers here to protect the Nardelf. If only one place in all our world survives, his little coal–black heart wants this to be it.'

'I'm sure we can help,' Ansey said. 'It can't be coincidence all seven of us suddenly meet each other and then happen across so many of the Powers. If only we can figure out how to use them.' He was silent a moment. 'Can we get out of here unseen?'

'I'd leave something here to make it look like you're asleep,' Hector said.

Ansey plumped up one of the pillows and, hopping off the bed, stuffed it under the covers. He wrinkled, folded and disturbed the brocade to make it look as if a restless sleeper were underneath.

Hector stood back to observe the counterpane. 'All those folds and wrinkles remind me of Auberon. Not of the Castle, of course, but everywhere else that hasn't been flattened.'

Ansey stared at the brocade with its crumples and creases. He thought back to the day he'd tried to escape to Ysgarde, remembering the soldiers' talk Gratian had tried to quell. 'It does, doesn't it? Wrinkles in the landscape.' He remembered the men saying that it wasn't as far to the Mistmurk as it had been. *It isn't. Something's changing the world.* 'I wonder what sleeper's been disturbed.' He tried to brush off the fear he felt.

Hector froze. 'Now why didn't I think of the Sleeper waking before this?'

'What Sleeper waking?' Ansey tip–toed to the door.

Hector padded up beside him. 'It's a nursery story vixens scare fox cubs with. If the cubs are naughty and don't go to bed, the vixens say it's just the sort of behaviour that will wake the Dark Sleeper and bring about the end of the world. Bad behaviour, they say, will break the mage's enchantment and allow the Sleeper to wake and shatter the ornament that is our dimension.'

There was no one in the hallway. Hector padded across the marble floor, as much skating as walking.

'If that's so…' Ansey folded his arms. '…what does Candle think he's doing? The clash of armies isn't going to put a Dark Sleeper back to sleep.' He looked down at Hector. 'You know, maybe the reason warriors or mages or soothsayers haven't been chosen as the Days is because it's not that kind of job.' Taking a deep breath, he felt a weight lift off his shoulders. 'Maybe it's not even that hard.'

Hector stopped at a junction, turned and scowled. 'Not that hard? With the Dark Sleeper?' He shook his head. 'Well, count me out. I'd prefer to fight the Jotun Armies of Night, thank you very much. We'd only be outnumbered ten thousand to one.'

'Hector, there might be a Dark Sleeper but it's not going to be the one trapped by the Englobing. Don't be scared because of a nursery story.'

Hector disappeared through a side doorway. Ansey hurried

after him, following as he bounded up a small flight of stairs. Hector stopped and swivelled as he reached the top. 'Let me tell you this, Your Highness. There is nothing in the entire universe, absolutely nothing, more terrifying than a nursery bogeyman that's even partly real.'

They locked eyes. Ansey nodded. *He's right. We are in deep trouble. And if there is a Dark Sleeper, we're doomed and the whole world with us.*

Hector turned, whisked his tail in the air and set off once more. He went down a stairwell, through a narrow hall, up a winding walkway, down a spiral stair, across a vast cavernous kitchen and into a silver chute. 'Press the fourth button from the top.'

'This one?' Ansey peered at a small rectangular plate. 'For maintenance, contact Ajax Lift Co.'

'No. The one that says *Gym and Pool.*'

Ansey pressed the button and jumped as the door closed. 'Wha…?' He grabbed the wall as the silver chute began to move. 'What is this?'

Hector crinkled his snout. 'Don't know. It doesn't have the least smell of magic about it, but it doesn't look dwarfish either, does it?'

Ansey shook his head. The silver chute stopped. The door opened. 'Ground floor,' a mellifluous voice intoned. 'Hotel reception, restaurants, gymnasium and pool. Have a nice day.'

Ansey fled out the door. Hector whisked his tail up. 'Thank you.' He minced out. 'This way. We're almost there.'

Ansey looked over his shoulder towards the silver chute, suspicious thoughts unsettling his mind. *I bet the dwarves know a way through the dimensions. To Fern's world. Candle knew what her phone thing witchlight was. And he knew about glasses too. Even back in Auberon he knew.*

Fern's world has got to be their plan of last resort: to escape there if this dimension is destroyed.

As Hector turned into a room, the heavy oak door opened just as mysteriously as the silver chute had done. Ansey hesitated. 'Come in!' Emyr poked his head out of the room. 'Don't stand there.'

Ansey hurried in. 'Where is everyone?'

'Boody's gone looking for where the Powers are hidden. Madmerry, Fern and Ginevra have gone to look for a way out, other than the englacial stream.'

'What did you let them do that for?' Ansey asked. 'Why didn't you go with them?'

'Too risky. Everyone would expect it of you or me, but the girls think they can get away with it.' Emyr scratched his forehead near his glasses. 'They're wandering around, giggling about a party.' At that moment, laughter echoed along the hall outside. 'They're here.' Emyr looked at Ansey and Hector. 'You hide just in case they got caught.'

Ansey ducked behind a small suit of armour. Hector was still out in the open when a pair of dwarves came into the room ahead of the girls. He dived for the floor and tried to imitate a fur foot rug.

'Look who found us and brought us back, Dallan!' Madmerry laughed. 'These nice dwarves!'

Ansey peeked at the girls. Fern had brushed her hair and changed into a white gown with a braided green vest. She no longer looked otherworldly.

The girls' escort were the same two dwarves who had carried him and Fern up the stairway inside the glacier. *And who clammed up when Fern had asked about the pyramids and Pharoah Khufu.* 'This is Wobble…' Madmerry introduced the dwarves to Emyr. '…and this is Nobble.'

'We got so lost!' Ginevra giggled airily. Her act was brilliant.

Fern threw herself onto the bed. 'But we couldn't find the kitchen.'

The two dwarves exchanged glances. 'Good try, ladies.' Wobble kicked Hector.

'You can't fool me.' He kicked again. As Hector yelped, Wobble turned towards the suit of armour. 'If you want to play your little games, boys and girls, it's fine by us. But don't expect us to turn a blind eye.'

Ansey scrambled out from behind the armour. He tried not to look as sheepish as he felt. 'So you're in charge of keeping us here.'

'What a boring duty!' Emyr looked to be sizing up the dwarves' rigid posture and scowling countenances. 'What've you done to deserve it? Or is this just your turn in the rotation?'

He's so different with a new set of clothes, a good scrub and some glasses. I've got to get him to teach me swordplay.

Emyr's sudden smile was so bright it seemed supremely calculating. 'I don't suppose either of you play fletch?' he asked the dwarves.

I'm an idiot. I should have thought of it. Dwarves might not be as big on gold as rumoured but they love games. They love wagers.

Both dwarves brightened, grins splitting their faces. 'You play fletch?'

'Beginning…' Emyr's smile turned diffident. 'Not advanced.'

'Get a board,' Wobble ordered. Nobble was out the door in an instant. 'Care for a wager?' he asked Emyr.

'Wager?' Emyr looked doubtful. 'I don't have anything worth… Oh, I suppose we could play for the usual stakes: half my kingdom and my daughter's hand in marriage.'

Ansey hoped the dwarf didn't notice the looks of sudden stunned surprise and raised eyebrows around the room. But he must have missed them.

'Done. Is she good–looking?'

Emyr didn't answer. 'What can you offer me in return?'

Nobble bounded in and began to set up the board.

'Gold,' Wobble said.

Emyr shook his head.

'Jewels,' Wobble offered.

Emyr shook his head again.

'A map to the world of pyramids and lift maintenance men,' Nobble suggested.

They really do know a way to another dimension. Ansey felt an urge to strangle Candle.

Emyr looked tempted by this offer. But, after a moment's hesitation, he shook his head once more. 'The key to the treasury.' He scooped the raven pieces into his hand.

Half an hour later, he pushed his new glasses up his nose and turned on Fern. 'You didn't tell me that wearing glasses causes headaches. I don't know if they're worth it.'

'The headaches go quickly.' She patted his shoulder. 'You're just getting used to the glasses.'

The dwarves were also complaining. 'You said you were a beginner.'

'I am.' Emyr folded his arms. 'No one will play with me.'

'Rightly so,' Nobble stated. 'So where'd you learn these last couple of moves?'

'I made it up. It's my own strategy. I call it Emyr's Enclosure. I wasn't sure how well it would work—I've never had a chance to try it for real before. I've only ever played against myself. And it's hard to trick yourself.'

'*We've* been tricked.' Wobble folded his arms and glared.

'You concede defeat?' Emyr asked.

'We can't give you the key to the treasury,' Nobble said.

'His Enthroned Serenity's got it,' Wobble added.

Emyr scowled. Boody hooted from Fern's shoulder. She looked much younger with dark glasses on. 'If you think The Powers are locked in the Treasury, think again. They're encased in crystal, hidden in the King's Quarters.'

'*What!?*' Wobble and Nobble almost shrieked the word together. 'In his travelling case?' Nobble spat. 'The scoundrel! The thief! After all his fine words! We must seize the Day, he said, because the Seven Days are not One Week, they are…' He broke off, clearly unwilling to repeat the insult.

Wobble glared at Emyr. 'In his travelling case! All ready to take off and leave if worst comes to worst!'

Ansey sized up the outraged dwarves. *They hate being stuck here.* 'If you escorted us to Ysgarde, with the Powers, you could help us save the Day. We realise we need help and we think you're the ones. You're so obviously noble, brave and heroic…' He could see Hector signalling him not to overdo the fulsome praise. '…and I know Candle doesn't like competition. Especially in those areas.'

It worked. The dwarves puffed out their chests. Nobble scooted off and was back in less than a minute with Candle's crystal travelling case. It looked remarkably like a long thin version of the briefcase belonging to the man who had appeared on Mistmurk Height.

Without delay, they were on their way.

Wobble took the lead. 'Let's take the lift.' He exchanged glances with Nobble. 'Any luck, if we go across the top of the Pass, we'll beat everyone to Ysgarde.'

'Why wouldn't they use this same route then?' Madmerry asked.

'Jotuns might see 'em.' Wobble shrugged. 'Which would spoil the surprise attack. Even if the giants do see us, it won't matter much. A small party of travellers moving across the high pass. Not worth troubling themselves with when the Armies of Night are on the march.'

'What's a lift?' Ansey asked, just as they reached the silver chute.

Wobble just smiled and pointed. 'We're going to the penthouse.'

There was plenty of room in the lift, even with Emyr holding out the Speaking Sword. He had persuaded Nobble to open the travelling case and give it to him.

Ansey was puzzled by the lift's fittings. 'What's this?' He pointed to a strange grey object set in a recess.

'Emergency phone.' Fern's gaze met his, as Wobble stood on tip–toe to press the top button. 'You use it to call for help if the lift breaks down.'

'Isn't it magic?' Emyr asked her, twirling the sword.

Fern shook her head. 'It's just a lift. An elevator.' She looked at the sword. 'I'd point that at the ground.' She hit herself. 'I mean— Dallan, I mean, Emyr. Please point the sword at the ground. The lift is about to…'

As the lift jolted to life, Emyr jumped. So did Madmerry.

We're going up. Ansey was pleased he hadn't looked surprised. *This device proves beyond doubt the dwarves have a way to move between dimensions.* A minute later, there was a slight shudder as the lift halted. A bell sounded and the doors whooshed open. 'Penthouse suite to your right,' the lift said. 'Have a nice day.'

'Have a nice day yourself.' Hector scurried out. 'Whoa!' His voice had an eerie echo. 'This is not what I expected by a penthouse.'

Ansey was only a step behind him. He came out almost at the top of a mountain. A bleak landscape stretched out in front of him.

'And I thought Fyrzentsou was in a bad way.' Emyr came to stare, open–mouthed, beside him.

Uprooted, shattered trees lay strewn in radial lines, slag heaps of tumbled rock teetered and rumbled as their summits fell into lifeless valleys, oily trickles meandered in gleaming murky strands between the ravaged hillocks. A cold tremulous mist rising up the mountain brought a rotting stench with it.

'What is this place?' Ansey was appalled. As far as his eye could see, to the dark hills of the distant horizon, there was no sign of life.

'Jotun country,' the dwarves said together.

'Well,' said Hector, 'that explains everything. It's obvious why they're attacking Ysgarde.'

'It is?' Fern asked.

Hector nodded. 'I wouldn't want to live here either.'

Ansey felt a sick fascination with the grotesque forms in the ruined landscape. *That's not something I'm likely to disagree with any time soon.*

The dwarves sniffed. 'This is an old outpost, a sentry lookout,' Nobble said. 'If ever we saw anything untoward happening, we'd light a beacon so Ysgarde would be warned.'

'That,' Wobble said, 'was, of course, in the days before the land started to contract. When Ysgarde was a distant peak at the far end of the Scimitar Mountains, not our next–door neighbour.'

'Come on,' Nobble said. 'I don't want to miss the big fight.'

azing at the top of the mountain, Ansey could see tattered clouds ringing the fortress of Ysgarde. Its lilac turrets rose above the narrow windswept pass. Immense and beautiful, towering above the nearer peaks, Ysgarde was a titanic stronghold with battlements that sparkled in the frosty air like snowflakes in sunlight.

'Look!' Ansey pointed beyond the fortress, across the peaks of the Scimitar Mountains. His gaze reached over the dales of Fyrzentsou and Auberon to the distant plain of Vircontium. The unnatural upfolds of the landscape were obvious from this height. They radiated out from the pass of Ysgarde. 'And look!' He indicated the vale below. More great trees lay uprooted, snapped and twisted, their topmost branches all pointing back through the pass. 'Whatever's happening spreads from here.'

He stared at the dark knife edges of rock that were like tight pleating in the nearest peaks. The creases smoothed out to faint dimpled folds as they tapered off to the horizon.

'The Sleeper's tugging at his blanket.' Hector looked back at Jotun country.

Ansey's gaze travelled back to the lilac towers of Ysgarde and the circle of tall pines surrounding it. 'Why isn't the fortress affected?'

'Floats,' said Nobble.

'Top suspension job,' Wobble agreed. 'It's not really anchored in the rock face, it's riding on a pseudolithic cushion. It's got full Richter compensation, plus the latest in motive tectonic capability. The quiver–to–stack ratio is phenomenal. But despite that, hypostatic tests show it can survive a shake quotient of well over a billion cycles in the strata flux. Goes with the flow, it does, and thus is basically indestructible.'

There was silence. Ansey exchanged glances with Emyr and noticed Madmerry and Fern both turning to him as if hoping he'd explain. He realised that no one had the slightest clue what Wobble meant. They all began to laugh.

Wobble glared. 'It's an engineering masterpiece.' His tone was defensive. 'Architecture's nothing to write about—all vitreous and spindly, not to mention that pukesome shade of lilac. The whole effect's positively ugly. But that's what they wanted and that's what we gave 'em. There's no accounting for taste.'

'But it's impregnable,' Nobble said.

'Nothing's impregnable,' Wobble corrected. 'It only has one weakness—the entry gate. Let's face it, if it were truly impregnable, getting in and out would be a security nightmare. But the gate's guarded by enough wardspells to fry any Jotun who tries to overcome them.'

'Come on, folks.' Nobble pointed ahead of them. 'You can see the pass is choked with rock folds. There used to be a spectacular drop here: three leagues straight down. But now it's just an easy walkway to Ysgarde.'

Ansey hurried across the pass. At the top the stone folds were so tight and so close it was simple to negotiate. Not far down on either side, the folds fell away to a curtain of rubble and then to a high valley.

Ysgarde was straight ahead. *So close... at last*! The huge gate was open as they approached, the portcullis up and the drawbridge down. A lone sentinel accosted them as they reached the entry and demanded their names.

'Wobble, Nobble, Monday, Tuesday, Wednesday, Thursday, Friday, Saturday and Sunday,' Wobble said. 'Here to save the day. Which is obviously a brand new day, because the rest of the week is already accounted for.'

'Trying t' be funny, are ya?' The scarred grizzle–faced man lowered his pike.

Wobble shook his head. 'You didn't expect anyone's true name, did you?'

Ansey pushed him aside. 'Prince Ancelin of Auberon, with a party of friends, to see Lord Quystein.'

The sentinel cackled. 'Oh, you'll be as welcome as a plague germ at a love festival.' He snorted. 'Don't you know there's a war on?'

'What's this?' A knight from the inner courtyard came over. She was brandishing a sword, swinging it to and fro, then letting it twirl in her hands. Her surcoat was sky–blue and gold, blazoned diagonally with flame tongues, a dark blue rose in the golden fire. 'Who on earth are these children, Parment?'

'Delegation to see His Q–ness,' the old soldier said.

'Impossible.' The knight planted the sword in front of her. 'We're off any moment.' She glared at Ansey. 'Who are you?'

'No one.' Ansey took a step back, realising the impossibility of the situation. *How can we convince anyone of anything? They see us as kids, nothing else.* 'No one. We'll just be on our way.'

'Not so fast.' The old soldier grabbed Ansey's arm. He glanced at the knight. 'Boy says he's Maurtz's brat.'

'No!' The knight stared at Ansey with an expression of dismay on her face. 'Here, now?'

Hector tapped the knight's greaves, rat–a–tat rat–a–tat, to get her attention. 'Now, look, sweetie, I'm not blaming you for lacking the proper response to this extraordinary situation which should be, "Oh congratulations, Your Highness, on escaping the Jotuns without our help." Clearly you're under considerable stress. But you could at least conceal your irritation in the name of politeness, chivalry and diplomatic courtesy. You are insulting royalty.'

'Who on earth are you?' The knight looked down in disbelief. 'When did foxes start to talk?'

'I'm Hector. Protector of local Princes, of which we currently have somewhat of a surfeit…'

'Lady Ysanne!' came a bellow from the courtyard. 'What *is* going on? Why aren't you ready?' Lord Quystein stomped over. His face when he saw the group, with Ansey in front of them, drained of all colour. 'What are you all doing here?'

'We've come to help,' Ansey said.

'*Help*?!' Quystein's voice came out as a strangled choke.

'Perhaps they can help,' the old soldier said.

Quystein turned in obvious disbelief. 'What, Parment?'

'We need all the fighters we can get, right?' Parment's voice was earnest. 'All hands on deck, all shoulders to the plough, all feet at the ready, all that?'

'Them?' If Ysanne was trying to keep a note of derision out of her voice, she failed.

Parment's hands flew back and forward in a gesture of denial. 'No, no! This gate virtually guards itself and you could use *me*, right? It's a waste of a good seasoned fighter—namely Patricus Percival Parment—when we could have the little tykes here do the job. They look sensible enough. It's not a job requires brawn, nor even much brain.' His grizzled face was set in an expression not far removed from pleading. 'If you've said it once, Your Q–ness, sir, you've said a dozen times—the gate's so simple, a child could manage it.' He smiled, showing the gaps in his teeth. 'Oh, please let me go. You know the Commander would, if he was here…' Begging, he put a hand on Ansey's shoulder. 'The boy's bright—and, if, as you say, he's been in the hands of the Jotuns, he isn't going to fall for any of their tricks.'

Quystein looked torn. He looked at his importunate sentry, he stared at Ansey, seeing—Ansey suspected—an untried and inexperienced child. Then he made a decision. 'I must be mad. But we do need everyone.' He thumped Parment on the shoulder, but he didn't take his gaze from Ansey. 'Hurry, man,' he ordered the soldier. 'If you're not battle–kitted when we're ready to leave, you'll have to catch us up. The dwarves will attack once the Jotuns are in position, whether we're there to back them or not.'

Parment limped off in unabashed glee.

Quystein bent over so he was looking in Ansey's eyes. 'This is a highly responsible position. Normally a squire, in his last office before he becomes a knight, has the honour of a watch on the gate of Ysgarde. It is a sacred trust. Will you take an oath?'

Ansey felt awed and frightened. But he expected that's what Quystein intended him to feel. He nodded, unable to say a word.

'Good,' Quystein said. 'Now repeat after me: I will guard this gate…'

Ansey closed his eyes in the solemnity of the moment. 'I will guard this gate…'

'…faithfully carrying out this trust…'

'Faithfully carrying out this trust.'

'…defending it against all comers…'

'Defending it against all comers.'

'…allowing none entry…'

'Allowing none entry.'

'…until the Acting Commander returns at the head of the Knights of Renown…'

'Until you return at the head of the Knights of Renown.'

Quystein glared at him. 'There will always be an Acting Commander but it may not be me.'

'There will always be…' Ansey began, until Quystein gripped his shoulder. Ansey's eyes opened and he blinked.

Wobble was at his side. 'Control Z. Back up a sentence.'

'Oh.' Ansey shook his head to clear it. *I've just been as dopey and literal as Emyr. It must be rubbing off on me.* Every word of the oath was still clear in his mind. 'Until *the Acting Commander* returns at the head of the Knights of Renown.' He bowed.

Quystein patted him on the head. 'The Ancient of Days preserve you.' He raised his hand as if in benediction to the dwarves and all the Days. 'The Ancient of Days preserve you all.' He turned to Ysanne. 'Let's move. Would you lead us out, Lady?'

'Hey!' Wobble and Nobble exclaimed together.

Quystein turned back, obviously impatient.

'Two things,' Wobble said. 'One, we'd like to join you in this fight.'

'You'd be most welcome.' Quystein's tone was grateful.

'And two,' Nobble said, 'the security of any building is always partly physical and partly psychological. If you don't give the boy here a silver shield, he's not going to look like a real Knight of Renown.'

'Bluff,' Wobble added. 'The Jotuns know they can't get in without an invitation, but without a silver shield showing at the gateway, they might just get ideas in their big, fat skulls.'

'Find the boy a spare shield,' Nobble said. 'Let him at least look the part from a distance.'

'See to it,' Quystein ordered Ysanne as he turned to address Ansey once more. 'Obedience is the first hallmark of a true knight. Do not fail me. Keep the gate closed.' He strode off, Ysanne only a step behind him.

Nobble and Wobble turned to each other and slapped palms. They turned to Ansey, huge grins on their faces. 'Bet you don't know what we've done for you, kid. Hope you've always harboured a secret ambition to become a knight.'

Ansey looked at their beaming grins. 'It wasn't secret.'

Both Wobble and Nobble looked smug. They sobered at once as a shadow fell on them. Ansey turned with them and found himself looking up into the open visor of Lord Ancelin of Tariquhaven. His golden surcoat had a rampant red lion holding a black lance. It fluttered in a sudden breeze.

'The gate is simplicity itself to operate.' He smiled as he handed Ansey a silver shield. 'All you have to do is tell it loudly to close itself once we're gone and open up when we come riding back in triumph. Don't let anyone in. Under any circumstances.'

'Yes, sir.' Ansey tried to control the tremble in his hands as he took hold of the silver shield.

Lord Ancelin nodded. 'Good lad.' His voice dropped. 'I may not get another opportunity to thank you, so I want you to know I'm very grateful for this chance.'

'It's nothing to do with me.'

Lord Ancelin dropped his voice even lower. 'If we don't win this conflict and the Jotuns succeed in releasing the Sleeper from the Abyss, lock yourself in the castle with your friends, seal the gate and don't come out for anything.'

Ansey gulped. 'Yes, sir.'

With a bright golden whirl of surcoat, Lord Ancelin was gone. A deafening thunder of hooves in the courtyard preceded the departure of the Knights of Renown. Lady Ysanne, bearing a plain silver standard, rode out at their head. Beside her was a squire not much older than Ansey. He was carrying a yellow pennant with a dark blue rose. And after her, with their dazzling silver shields, rode the Knights of Renown on their warhorses, their plumes and pennons flying, their armour bright, their lances aloft, their swords by their sides.

Olien was there in her hood, riding between Lord Ancelin and a knight with a black hand on his white surcoat. Her horse was laden with panniers and baskets overstuffed with rolls of thin white linen. Wobble and Nobble fell in at the rear.

'Thank you.' Fern waved to them from the end of the drawbridge. A chorus of thanks from Hector, Ginevra, Boody, Madmerry and Emyr joined her a moment later as they all farewelled the troop. Then she turned to Emyr. 'Let's go into the castle. It's just like a fairytale…'

'I don't think that's possible…' Ansey turned to the gate as she frowned at him.

Emyr backed his doubts. 'Lord Quystein did not give us permission to go inside.'

'Stop being so pedantic, for once.' Fern's frown deepened to a scowl.

'This is a time when Emyr is quite right to be literal,' said Hector. 'We'd be asking for trouble if we even tried.'

Ansey walked back across the drawbridge and looked up, feeling awkward. 'Hello, gate. Please close.' There was an immediate rumble as the portcullis slammed down. 'And please, gate, please don't open again until I tell you.' The drawbridge shook for a moment as if in warning and then began to withdraw. 'Thank you, gate.'

He dashed to the end of the drawbridge while it has still moving. Gripping his silver shield, he jumped the moat, landing next to Emyr. He slewed around just in time to see three pairs of huge metal beams slot together, holding the drawbridge in. Then a second portcullis slammed down.

'Some gate!' Boody was on Fern's shoulder again. 'I'm going to take a quick reconnoitre.' She took to wing and soon disappeared from sight around a far wall.

'As soon as she gets back, we've got to have a council.' Hector plunked himself on the nearest piece of turf. 'About using the Powers.'

'Do you think I'm supposed to walk up and down like a sentry?' Ansey asked.

No one answered.

'I wonder how long they'll be?' Fern asked.

Ansey shrugged. He could still see the occasional wink of a silver shield as the knights pushed on through the forest below.

'Those shields are really one of the most stupid ideas I've ever seen.' Hector shook his head. 'Talk about advertising your presence.'

'In this instance, it's clever,' Emyr said. 'The Jotuns will be watching the silver shields, not looking out for an ambush by a dwarf legion.'

'I suppose so.' Hector sounded doubtful.

'Where's Boody?' Ginevra asked. 'This doesn't seem like a *quick* reconnoitre to me.'

'No, it's not.' Emyr held up his sword. 'I'll just take a walk around the castle. The rest of you, stay here, and help Ansey guard the gate.'

'I'll come.' Hector held up a paw. 'Don't argue. I may not be much in the line of protection, but I scream for help really well.'

Emyr laughed as they set off.

You know, I have a suspicion he hasn't laughed in years. This could turn out well. So long as I do a good job at guarding this gate, they might let me train as a knight.

Ansey paced up and down, trying to look like a sentry. Madmerry began to whistle, then stopped. It was more than half an hour before Emyr and Hector returned. 'Nice castle,' was all the little fox said.

'Boody back?' Emyr asked.

Ansey shook his head.

Emyr looked up at the battlements. 'I hope she didn't try to fly over.'

It was ten minutes before the little owl appeared, coming up slowly through the trees below them. There was blood on one of her wings. 'Idiots, idiots, idiots.' She made an unsteady landing on Madmerry's shoulder.

'You're wounded!' she cried.

'A flesh wound.'

'Where've you been?' Emyr asked.

'Jotun country. Went to have a close look at it.' Boody took a deep breath. 'Eternal mist, unending shadow, the abyss of darkness.' She looked up at the gate. 'And that, as Hector would say, is the better end of town.' Her breathing was better. 'I zipped back down the valley to have a look at what's cooking with the war—and spotted a couple of hundred frost giants and storm giants just sitting there watching the dwarves.'

'Eyeballing each other?' Hector asked.

'No! The dwarves are all holed up, waiting in ambush, watching the main Jotun force without the slightest idea they're under surveillance by what looks like a crack squad. So I zoomed down there to warn the idiots to watch their backs and their archers shot at me. *Shot* at me! I was lucky to get out of there alive. I couldn't get through their lines to Candle. They were stupidly convinced I was some sort of evil bird of darkness and a spy.'

Ginevra was incredulous. 'What made them think that?'

'These dark glasses!'

'So it's a trap,' Emyr said. 'The Knights of Renown and the dwarves will both be caught in it and annihilated. Unless somehow we can warn them.'

'How can we do that?' Hector asked. 'They're at least an hour ahead of us and on horses.'

'Horses… True—but that means they will have to keep to a trail. There's bound to be a short cut.' Emyr smiled. 'And it's not as if I actually have to catch up with them. Just get within hailing distance.'

'What's this "I" business?' Hector demanded. 'It's "we", Your Majesty. *We.*'

'A valley like this,' Fern said, 'should have an Echo Point. If we can find it, all we've got to do is stand there and yell "behind you".'

'That might work!' Madmerry nodded. 'If I heard "behind you" echoing down at me, I'd have a good look to see what's at my back.'

'You're a genius, sweetie.' Hector planted a huge slurpy kiss on Fern's knee. 'We don't have to be anywhere near any battle to do that.'

'It'll warn the Jotuns too,' Ginevra cautioned.

'Nothing we can do about that,' Emyr said. 'Right, now who's going to stay to help Ansey?'

Ansey threw up one hand. 'I don't need babysitting! I'll be fine. All I've got to do is look stubborn.' He grinned. 'I can do that.'

Emyr seemed unsure.

'If there was any real danger, Quystein wouldn't have left us by ourselves, would he?' Ansey asked.

'That's a good point.' Emyr smiled as he held out the Sword. 'Still, you hold on to this.' He lowered his voice. 'It really does talk. I wasn't that good against the manticores. It told me what to do.'

It talks? How come no one else hears it? Ansey could see Emyr was already far too attached to the Sword. *This is a huge act of friendship, as far as he's concerned. He thinks of it as his. Come to think of it, I think of it as his.*

Emyr's voice returned to normal. 'If we see anything headed your way, we'll be right back.'

'In a jiff.' Hector ran down the hill, heading off the path as he reached the treeline. Emyr and the others set off after him. Boody was sitting on Madmerry's shoulder.

Ansey took a deep breath. *What was that in the shadow of the forest?* He sighed with relief.

Just two birds.

nsey held the shield in one hand and the Sword in the other as he went back to the edge of the moat. He felt like a fraud. Just as he decided to prop the silver shield against a large rock, there were sounds of movement back at the treeline.

He thought at first it was Emyr and Madmerry squabbling as they returned for something they'd forgotten. But a wizened old man and an even more wizened old woman appeared, dragging a handcart up through the trees. 'Am I supposed to be a mindreader?' the man shouted. 'How was I to know you'd hidden it in the *other* teapot?'

'Well, why didn't you bring *all the teapots*?' the woman yelled.

'For the same reason I didn't bring the whole kitchen.' The man snorted and shook his white beard. He smiled abruptly as he spotted Ansey. 'Come and help me, young fella.'

Ansey went to help the old couple pull the cart forward.

'So The Q left you in charge?' the man asked. 'Don't think I've seen you 'round before. New recruit?'

'Not exactly.' Ansey eyed the old rocker, footstool and conglomeration of pans and canisters in the cart. 'I'm just minding the gate.'

'Good lad! No doubt His High and Mighty Q–ness has left instructions as to where we're to be given quarters for the duration. Not being as young as I used to be, it had better not be the stables this time.'

'No. He didn't say a word. He didn't even tell me you were coming.'

The old man shook his head. 'That'd be right! I'm telling you, lad, I'm holding out for the day the Commander's back and The Q's finally been put in his place. Fellow's got no manners. He'll expect a feast tonight, five courses to be sure, to celebrate victory. Who's to prepare it all? Lal and meself, no doubt. He'll have taken the squires, the pages and even the kitchenhands.' He turned to his wife. 'Wouldn't that be right, Lal?'

'It would, Van.' The woman eyed Ansey's hands with a critical look. 'How are you at peeling potatoes, youngster?'

'I can't let you through the gate,' Ansey blurted out.

'What nonsense is this?' The old man stopped hauling the cart and put his hands on his hips. 'That'd be right. His Q–ness forgot to tell you the entry code, didn't he? Got you to lock it up nice and tight and now you can't get it back open.' He turned to his wife. 'No doubt about it, lucky we're back so quick, eh Lal? This poor lad'd be fainting from lack of proper sustenance.'

'Today's code,' Lal said, 'is Seven Wednesday Seventeen.' She smiled. 'Go ahead and try it.'

'I can't let you in.' Ansey shook his head. 'My orders are very explicit.' *I will guard this gate…faithfully carrying out this trust…defending it against all comers…allowing none entry… until the Acting Commander returns at the head of the Knights of Renown…* 'Very explicit.'

'Of course,' the man said. 'But your orders apply to strangers, not to us.'

'I promised I wouldn't let anyone in.'

'We're not *anyone*,' the woman said. 'We're Lally and Van. Everyone at Ysgarde knows us.'

Ansey stepped back a pace. 'I can't let you in. No exceptions.'

'You'll be in trouble, boy,' Van warned.

'I can't let you in.'

The argument went on for several minutes before Ansey managed to convince the couple that he wasn't going to give in. After that, they went to their cart, rummaged in some canisters and brought out fruit and pastries which they ate in silence. At the end, they licked their lips before smiling at him with thin, gloating expressions.

He couldn't wait until the others returned. *Hurry, everyone! Please hurry. Why are you taking so long?*

He heard another sound on the trail. A young knight staggered up through the trees. White-faced and ashen, his green surcoat dusty and dishevelled, he was limping from a bad wound on his leg. His silver shield was dull and dented. 'Open up!' he called as he toiled up the trail. 'Open up!'

Ansey rushed to him. 'Are you all right?'

'Open up! It's a rout. The Jotuns are coming, we have to prepare the castle defences.'

Ansey let the knight lean on him and together they staggered towards the gate. He looked at the wide streak of blood on the knight's leg, hoping Madmerry would soon be back. She'd know what to do for the wound. *In the meantime, I'd better get him inside and comfortable.*

'Gate!' As he raised his hand to address the gate, he caught sight of the knight's shield. It was dull and becoming duller by the moment.

Behind him, he heard an exclamation from Van. 'Sense at last! Get the cart, Lal, he's seen the light! We're going in.'

'I'm afraid we can't do that.' Ansey looked the young knight straight in the eye. 'Perhaps it's best if I don't know your name.' He dropped his voice to a whisper. 'What I don't know, I can't tell. You haven't been in a battle. You've run away before it started. You've given yourself that wound. Is this your first combat?'

The knight wouldn't meet Ansey's eyes. 'I'm a coward.' He looked up abruptly, straight into Ansey's eyes. 'You go down to the battle. I'll stay and guard the gate.'

'No.'

'Coward,' the knight flung at him.

Ansey felt heat rising at the back of his neck. 'I'm not.'

'Oh?' The knight's upper lip curved in a sneer. 'Don't think you can hide behind duty as a shield. You're trying to make out you're better than I am, but you're not.'

'If I thought for one second that you'd guard the gate until Lord Quystein returns, I'd do it. But you won't. You'll open it as soon as I'm out of sight.'

'What if I gave you my word?' the young knight begged.

Ansey didn't answer. *'Yes'* was at the tip of his tongue, but it didn't come out. *Obedience is the first hallmark of a true knight. That's what Quystein had said. Which means I've failed. I could withstand the reasonable pleas of two old people, but not the whines of a young coward. What sort of person does that make me?* He stood there, agonising, for so long that, when he turned around, he was surprised to find the young knight was limping back along the trail into the trees. Ansey nearly called out after him, but he found there was a lump choking his throat.

He felt dejected. Sitting down next to his shield, he realised he wanted to talk to Emyr. *And I want to talk to him now.* Emyr would know what to do. *I don't know why he will, but I know he's got the answer. Where is he? And the others? They're taking such a dreadfully long time.*

And then he heard them trundling back up the trail. *Trundling? But they didn't have anything to trundle with.* A moment later, a small covered wagon came into view. It was being pulled by a sad, dejected pony. 'Zippy!'

The pony looked up warily, a tired, hopeless look in her eye. She caught sight of him and, with a sudden fling of her hooves, let out a squeal of rapturous delight. Bounding up the hill, dragging the wagon behind her, she screeched to a halt in front of the silver shield, leaned over it and began licking Ansey's face. 'Stop it!' He started to laugh. 'Stop it, girl!' So, obedient, Zippy did just as he asked. Instead she began to nuzzle his neck and nibble his ear instead. 'Where'd you come from, girl?' Ansey patted her between the ears. 'What are you doing here?'

'And who might you be?'

The gruff voice coming from behind the wagon startled Ansey. At first he couldn't see any one. Then a tiny sharp-faced man appeared, his curled ears keeping a floppy over-sized red cap in place. He carried a whip.

'I might ask you the same. Who are you? And what are you doing with Zippy?'

'Oh, "Zippy", is it?' the little man sneered. 'Zippy? First zip I've seen has been in the last half minute.'

'If you treat her right, she's the best and bravest pony in the world.' Ansey felt the heat rise at the back of his neck again as he stared at the whip.

'Ha!' said the little man.

'Who are you?' Ansey demanded.

'Xerxes Xenophon is the name, Human Resource Manager.' The little man pulled himself up to his full height, about as high as Ansey's chin. He flicked a white rectangle out of his pocket. 'My card.'

Ansey stared at it. 'Oh.'

'I had to take a detour,' Xerxes jerked his thumb back down the path. 'It's about to be a war zone down there, I tell you. Knights, dwarves, frost giants, storm giants.' He rolled his eyes. 'And me with perishable merchandise. And penalty rates for late delivery!'

Perishable merchandise? That means food. He had tried not to give a single thought to how hungry he was ever since Van and Lal had gleefully consumed their fruit and pastries in front of him. 'Is your merchandise for sale?' He tried to sound casual.

Xerxes' eyes gleamed. 'Of course! You're interested, I can tell!' He jerked a rope by the side of the wagon and flung up the canvas cover.

Ansey was dumbstruck. There was a cage underneath. He peered into the gloom behind the iron bars, but all he could see was a dozen luminous eyes. It took him several seconds to realise what the small half–naked bodies were. 'They're children!' He whirled on Xerxes. 'You're a slave trader.'

'Certainly not.' The little man sounded indignant. 'I'm a Human Resource Manager. Postgraduate degree in Business Economics.'

Ansey was aghast. 'You can't sell human beings.'

'You certainly can.' Xerxes sighed and looked doleful. 'It's not as lucrative as performing elephants but the market dropped out of that a while back. Diversification, that's the key.'

'You *can't* sell human beings,' Ansey repeated. 'It's *not right*.'

'Oh.' Xerxes pursed his lips and looked sidelong at him. 'Sit down a moment, youngster, while I do you a favour.'

Ansey was doubtful. Xerxes smiled, showing all his yellow fangs. 'Oh, all right. Free of charge.'

Still Ansey hesitated.

'You want to put me in a good mood with that pony, doncha?' Xerxes asked.

Ansey sat immediately.

'Now,' Xerxes went on, 'I can see you've been brought up with the old virtues—which have their natural outworking for you in knighthood: courtesy, obedience, honour. I can also see that you are courageous in action. But are you also fearless of thought?'

'I hope so.'

'Good! Then think about this: right and wrong are antiquated concepts, infantile ideas that true men fling aside to embrace destiny. You need to free your mind from these puerile restrictions, experience a liberty that few have the courage to seize. I can see the potential in you, young man, I can see the promise and aptitude that will one day be squandered, lost, ruined while your noble ideals are shattered and destroyed.'

Xerxes sighed and shook his head. His cap nearly fell off but, with a flick of his coiled ears, it was on again, at an even more jaunty angle. 'This is the real world, young man. Decisions in the real world are not made on the basis of right and wrong, but on the basis of profit. That is an implacable reality that you cannot right and that you will need to do wrong to change. Now if, to achieve right, you need to do wrong, you are a hypocrite. Where is your honour then?'

'I don't see how you necessarily need to do wrong to achieve right.'

'A degree in Business Economics would soon set you straight.' Xerxes waggled a long skinny finger. 'Let us take, as our example, the slave trade. Or any employment where there's a wage tier. Dwarves don't pay elves as much as they pay pixies, for instance, for cloud–minding. Dwarf mercenaries in Vircontium are paid less than sprite mercenaries who are paid less than the most dim–witted cyclops. Now, the plain fact is—as has been amply demonstrated over and over—if laws are put in place to outlaw slavery or pay the dwarves as much as the sprites and the sprites as much as the cyclops, the elves as much as the pixies, and so on, one thing is inevitable. And what is that?'

Ansey had a feeling it was a trick question. 'It'd be fair?'

Xerxes tutted. 'Untold hardship. That's what's inevitable. The dwarves and elves would be out of jobs, the vast majority of slaves would have nowhere to go. Freedom means starvation, equality means unemployment.' He clapped his hands and nodded at Ansey. 'It's only the privileged don't understand that.'

All through the speech, Ansey had been sizing Xerxes up. 'Profit. Let's cut through this complex morality to the bottom line. That's the greatest good, isn't it? At least for Xerxes Xenophon?'

Xerxes grinned. 'Ah, I knew you'd understand.'

'I think I do.' Ansey took a step back. 'I'd like to buy all your merchandise. Pony included.'

Xerxes snorted. 'You don't have the price.'

'Don't I?' Ansey held out the Speaking Sword, hilt extended. *I just hope Emyr understands. He might never speak to me again.*

Xerxes whistled. 'I couldn't get rid of that. Not and stay alive.'

'Of course you could. Melt down the metal and extract the gold.' *I can't believe I'm suggesting this.*

'Done.' Xerxes grabbed for the Sword in a single swift swipe, as if afraid Ansey would suddenly change his mind.

But Ansey was faster. He flicked the Sword up, high over his shoulder. 'Key to the cage first.' He was already wavering. *What if the Sword can't protect itself?*

As Xerxes took the key out of a filthy pocket, Ansey lowered the Sword again. The moment the exchange took place, Xerxes scampered off, as fast as he could, going back down the trail the way he came. Ansey blinked. For an instant—*for the merest fraction of a fraction of a second*—Xerxes' shadow had seemed far too long and broad for a small, thin trader. *But it can't have been.*

As Xerxes reached the trees, he called back, 'A pleasure doing business with you.' Then he disappeared.

Ansey fell to the ground and wept.

acking up behind the nearest tree, Xerxes Xenophon began to change shape. Two ravens fluttered down, one to each shoulder. The curled ears disappeared, the floppy red cap vanished, the thin shoulders bulged and, a moment later, Uller Princekiller appeared, his head in the branches, his boots in a puddle.

'Be ready,' he said to Munin and Huginn. 'I've muddied the water about what's right and wrong. He's wondering if he should keep his oath about not opening the gate. What's going to make the difference is that he's got to feed those starving mites I've left him. A social conscience is so wonderfully useful. The moment the gate comes up, I want you in among them and in there.'

'Right, boss.' Munin hopped over to a branch to watch the scene before the gate unfold. Ansey had already opened the cage and, with the help of Lal and Van, was helping the emaciated children down to the ground.

Uller threw the Sword on the ground and got into position. 'Shouldn't be long now.'

But it was. An hour later, Ansey had given the slave children a portion of bread and released Zippy from the wagon.

However he hadn't opened the gate. He hadn't even looked like it had crossed his mind.

Uller was surprised at his willpower. Lal and Van mentioned the possibility of proper food, sufficient water and appropriate shelter unfailingly every two minutes. They said that the children were dying.

And that's true. That's exactly why I picked them. Uller waited. *Maybe Prince Ancelin thinks they're exaggerating.* He noticed Ansey kept looking down the trail. *Did he see me? No… he's wishing that the king of Fyrzentsou would come back. Come to think of it: he has been gone a mighty long time.*

Uller looked up. A haze of smoke was visible above the trees. He thought he should be able to hear the din of battle, but very little sound penetrated the silence of the woods and trail.

He looked back at Ansey. *Surely the conflict in the kid's mind has got to be acute by this stage. Yeah, yeah, 'Do not fail me,' Quystein said. 'Keep the gate closed.' It's a duty and a charge that you should be finding more and more difficult to keep. By now, you should be thinking that you aren't even sure you should keep it.*

Uller scowled as he peered across the distance at Ansey, trying to penetrate his mind. He saw a bleak, desolate look when Ansey thought no one else was looking. *Yes, it's working. He'll crack. It might just take longer than most.*

A drizzle of light rain had begun to fall. The slave children had whimpered when Ansey suggested they get back in the wagon. After another round of the interminable argument with Lal and Van, he'd rigged up a shelter using the canvas from the wagon.

Come on, child, give in. Open the gate. This is just miserable weather.

Another half hour of surveillance went by. The ravens were cold, despondent and dripping. 'I've been thinking.' Huginn gave a watery sniff.

'I don't pay you to think.' Uller didn't mean to snap but he knew he was looking less like a giant and more like a snowman with every passing minute. The fine rain froze around him, turning his exterior to ice. 'I'm getting really irritated with that boy's ideals.'

'I've been thinking,' Huginn continued, 'that it's a pity he's a prince.'

Uller only just managed to bite back his annoyance and conceal his frustration. *Patience wins this war. Do not lose it, ever. Even with the bird.* 'Why's that?'

'Because if he were a king, the solution to all our problems is slap bang in front of us. In case you haven't noticed, he's guarding a gate.'

Frost crackled as Uller drew in his breath. 'So he is.' His eyes narrowed. 'Now, why didn't I notice that?'

'Sssshhh!' Munin flapped his wings. 'Company coming.'

We've waited too long.

A strange bell–like sound resonated through the forest. A shaft of sunlight pierced the rain–misted sky and, moments later, the huge arch of a rainbow appeared, its foot halfway up the trail to the castle. 'Who's that?' Huginn squawked as Zippy gave a whinny of delight.

A figure stepped off the rainbow.

'Stupid crow,' Uller hissed. 'Keep your voice down. Now that's one brilliant illusion. I must figure out how it's done.' He watched as the figure hailed Ansey and then strode towards him.

'Hello,' Ansey called back.

The relief in his voice was so great that Uller wanted to curse. *It was clear the boy had been ready to give in—he'd finally reached the complete end of his strength of will.*

'It's you! You've changed your clothes since Mistmurk Height.'

'Hello, Ansey,' the man said. 'Yes, the suit wasn't quite the right attire this time. This is a toga. What do you think?'

Ansey seemed unsure. 'It's different.'

'How are you?'

'Wet.' Ansey blinked as a dribble of water ran into his eye.

'Lovely day if you're a duck, utterly wretched if you're a frost giant.' The man turned towards the forest and looked straight at the tree where Uller was hiding. 'Frost giants, you see, absorb heat from the air around them—they keep their body temperature constant that way—which, of course, makes the air in their immediate vicinity seem exceedingly chilly. Which is how they got the name, "frost giants". On a day like today, that process of heat absorption will actually be turning them into big blocks of ice.'

Every word drifted down sharp and clear to the woods. Munin looked down at Uller. 'Illusion, huh? Oh yeah? Boss, that guy knows we're here. He knows you're turning into a snowman.'

'Impossible.' Uller's lips crackled with ice rime.

Ansey's voice echoed down to him. 'That might make a big difference in battle.'

'It *is* making a big difference,' the man said. 'Today's weather is turning the tide of war.'

'You didn't stay long in Auberon,' Ansey asked.

'I only ever intended a flying visit,' the man said. 'But it was successful. I talked to your father and so did the finches. He was so delighted to know they could talk to you. He's sent a messenger to you with an important letter.'

'Are you the messenger? To order me back?'

'Not in this instance. And your father will not order you back. His letter is simply to ask your forgiveness.'

'Oh.' Ansey's stiff attitude became softer. 'Where are you going? Why have you come this way?'

'I came because I was sung. Someone called for a Perfect Helper.'

Ansey smiled. 'I think Fern will be pleased to give up the title.'

'I'm sure she will. She was called by mistake—she fell into a set-up for someone else. I'm here to make the mistake turn out for good.' The man nodded. 'Just as I assured your father that his mistake in not allowing you to become a knight—a permission he has now granted, by the way—will be turned towards an immensely greater good.'

'Oh.' Ansey looked down. 'So you fix mistakes? Is that what you do? I gave your gifts to Lord Ancelin.'

'I know,' the man said. 'He's using them well.'

'How come I'd never heard of him before, if I'm named after him?'

'Well, Your Majesty, that's an interesting story, which you should have been told long ago.' The man put his arm around Ansey's shoulders. 'It's quite simple—Lord Ancelin was your father's best friend. But Lord Ancelin was also deeply in love with your mother and she with him. She was torn between her love for Ancelin and her duty to her husband and, through him, to the kingdom.'

Ancelin—Uller found he was grinding his teeth as the man spoke. *That same unchancy knight who killed my brothers.* He could see Ansey didn't want to ask about his mother, but also that he felt compelled. 'What did she do?'

'Lord Ancelin asked her to leave with him and, in terrible grief, she refused. She put duty before her own personal happiness. To her own surprise, she eventually found great joy being married to your father. The day you were born, she knew she'd made the right choice.' The man smiled at Ansey. 'Even though you were only a baby, you had the power to unite Auberon or destroy it. Your father loved you almost unreasoningly and would have stormed the gates of hell to get you back if your mother had left him for another man.'

'So my father's King Maurtz?'

'The Flair has finally put all his doubts at rest.'

'Doubts?'

'Oh yes,' the man said. 'But not at first. Not until long after Jénève died and he'd married Barbizca. By then, your father had forgotten Jénève had protested *his* decision to call you "Ancelin" after his best friend and, with Barbizca's help, remembered instead that it was *her* idea.'

Ansey stood there, rain dripping in rivulets through his hair. Uller could see he was trying to think.

Messy, messy. Now it's not just about opening the gate, it's about mothers and fathers and kingdoms and destinies.

'Who's going to win the war?' Ansey asked.

'It's in the balance.' The man turned his face to the valley where the smoke had almost disappeared, washed down from the sky by the rain. 'This battle is decided—but the war, that's an entirely different matter. The outcome of the war hangs on a knife edge. The choices of just two people can turn it either way. Two people. Both with the same name.'

'Ancelin.'

Uller could see Ansey was hardly able to do more than breathe the word.

'But how?' he asked the man.

'You are not chosen as Sunday's Child because you are a fine warrior, a mighty knight or the wisest of sages or mages.' He picked up the silver shield next to Ansey and scrutinised it closely. Touching the tip of his middle finger to his lips, he planted a kiss in the centre of the shield. 'Now why do you think you were chosen?'

Ansey frowned.

Come on, child. Uller sniffed. *I want to hear this. Why are you Sunday's Child?* He was curious. *Why are the Days children? And why does that knowledge not reduce me to despair? Why does it fan a hope I thought was long dead?*

'I don't know,' Ansey said.

'And why is it a good thing that your wish to become a knight has been delayed?'

'To teach me patience?'

The man smiled. 'If you learned patience, that was a bonus. But that was not the purpose. If you were a Knight today, you would choose the way of the warrior. You would not even consider the way of peace.'

Clear echoing laughter could be heard from the trail.

No! Uller couldn't believe the timing. He was sure it was Emyr and the others, returning at last. But he didn't allow himself to be distracted. He kept his eyes on the man as he moved away from Ansey towards the children. The man was bending down to the tent, touching the fevered forehead of two of the tiniest and sickliest of the slave children. His voice was a gentle whisper but Uller could hear it even at a distance: 'Would you like a great green giraffe to play with? I have one who would like to walk the clouds with you.'

'Ansey!' A chorus of happy voices drew Uller's attention away from the man.

'Where've you been?' Ansey called.

Uller was astonished at how utterly filthy they all were. Tuesday's child was no longer a white fox, he was streaked black. Wednesday's child had a single white spot left just below her tail. The rest of the Days were covered in grime so dark that their clothes, despite the rain, seemed to have been blackened by a chimney. The little owl, Thursday's child, was black as ebony, and almost invisible in Friday's pitch–coloured headdress.

It took Uller several seconds to realise what they were covered in—smoke and soot.

'What's happened?' Ansey asked.

'A stroke of genius.' Hector pointed to Fern.

'Green wood makes a lot of smoke,' Boody said.

'Yes.' Ansey nodded. 'Yes, it does.'

'I just mentioned that we could try smoke signals,' Fern said. 'Except then I realised it wouldn't be a good idea because we couldn't code a message and even if we could, how would the dwarves read it?'

'But it occurred to Madmerry and me,' Emyr said, 'that smoke would irritate the storm giants. Not all that much, but enough to make them misty and drizzly. And then I imagined what misty and drizzly would mean next to a frost giant.' His grin was huge. 'They're iced in, immobilised. We made enough smoke to thwart the surprise attack completely.' He began to laugh.

Uller wanted to kill him.

'In fact, we iced up the battlefield.' Emyr was clearly delighted with the outcome. 'It was lucky we were on the ridge, way out of range, because Candle's furious.'

'He's not at all grateful,' Boody added.

'He said he'd smack our bottoms.' Ginevra sounded miffed.

Uller decided that was putting it politely. The dwarves were foul-mouthed unless they really curbed their temper.

'Why?' Ansey asked.

It was Madmerry who answered. 'Because Lord Ancelin wouldn't let him attack the Jotuns once it was obvious what we'd done. Quystein thought it was a bit unsporting but was willing to let Candle go ahead anyway. However Lord Ancelin persuaded him they'd be condoning a massacre to let the dwarves sweep down on the Jotuns, seeing how helpless they were.'

Ansey turned. 'Was that the choice Lord Ancelin...?' He broke off.

Uller could see his consternation. He'd expected the man to still be there to answer his question. But he'd gone. Disappeared. Even Uller, watching the whole scene with concentrated intensity, had missed the moment when he vanished.

He tried to shake the snow off himself, but only managed to move a faint sprinkling.

'We've lost,' Huginn said. 'Hear that, boss? Freutim's attack has failed. Everything now depends on the goodwill of those unchancy knights.'

'*One* unchancy knight,' Uller groaned. 'The same one who killed my brothers.' He grimaced and pointed to the ravens. 'Get to Auberon.'

'Hey, boss,' Munin said, 'we're loyal. We don't cut and run. Not us.'

'We'll find some way of chiselling you out of there,' Huginn added.

'Get to Auberon and find out if Maurtz is still alive.'

'What?' Huginn asked. 'Boss, you're clutching at feathers.'

'I don't know who that man was up there,' Uller said. 'But I have my suspicions.'

'Me too,' Munin said. 'I don't understand how the likes of us, though, could overhear the Ancient of Days giving a word of encouragement to Sunday's child. Not a syllable of that little interchange should have been comprehensible to us. We ain't his buddies.'

'What makes you think that's the Ancient of Days?' Huginn asked. 'You're losing it, pal.'

Munin pecked at him. 'I think it was the clear signs of omnipotence and omniscience that gave it away. Or maybe it was the long nose.'

'All good points,' Uller said. 'Regardless of his identity, however, in the middle of that little tête à tête, he called our young friend, "Your Majesty".'

'Oh.' Huginn blinked. Uller could feel his raven brain put two and two together.

'Don't go away.' Munin spread his wings. 'We'll be back in a flash.'

'I'm not going anywhere.' Uller's teeth chattered as the ravens disappeared into the trees. 'Not until there's a thaw.' He turned his attention back to Ansey and his friends, wondering what he'd missed. *Children.* The thought was almost bitter. *I should never have underestimated them. They didn't even have the Powers with them and yet they routed the armies of darkness.* He smiled. *At least they managed to annoy those damnably pompous dwarves somewhat seriously in the process.*

Uller became still, utterly still. He could hear the sounds of a dozen or more horses coming up the trail through the trees. Much as he wanted to, he didn't turn his head. He waited to catch a view of the riders when they came up to Ysgarde.

He knew Quystein was coming, long before he saw the pennons and standards, long before he heard the voices of the riders. He knew it because he could see Lal and Van coming up out of the makeshift tent to shout complaints and to inform the Acting Commander there'd be no feast because Ansey had refused to let them in.

The drawbridge began to lower.

The Days all clustered together in a tight, protective little group as Quystein shouted savage insults at Ansey.

Take it out on someone your own size, why don't you? Quystein was clearly livid all his planning and preparations had gone to waste in an indecisive, inconclusive conflict.

Van and Lal went on with their whines: how the idiot boy had not only refused to let them in but he'd been wilful and stupid in ignoring their pleas for the poor slave children dying of fever.

Uller saw Quystein's temper reach boiling point. Calling Ansey to him, he spat in his face. 'Do you expect me to praise you?'

I doubt if he's been expecting anything of the kind. You haven't seen the torment he's been in as he's weighed up honour and integrity against the worth of a human life.

Ansey's face drained of all colour. He hung his head, apparently trying to work out what he'd done wrong. This was a mistake. A huge mailed hand hit the side of his face.

'Look at me when I speak to you, boy!' Quystein bellowed.

Shaking, Ansey looked up.

'You're a fool,' Quystein spat. 'You can't be trusted to do the simplest of jobs and get it right. Get out of my sight!'

Emyr took Ansey by the elbow and drew him backwards. That too was a mistake. 'You!' Quystein snarled at Emyr. 'Don't think of going anywhere! I'll want to talk to you shortly.'

With that, he rode into the castle.

Well, well, well. Uller felt a moment of surprise. *And I thought those shields were fakes. I thought they'd replaced the real deal with stainless steel replicas.*

Quystein's bright silver shield had been misting to a darker and darker grey the closer he got to the gate.

louds of misty blue veiled one horizon as the sunrose folded up the last of its petals. A moonleaf spiralled into a star–pricked twilight on the other. Ansey leaned against the stone wall of the highest, steepest battlement in all of Ysgarde.

He'd thought no one would come here and his guess proved correct. He'd had the tower to himself for hours. He stared, without seeing, into the silence. The rain had stopped and the night was fine and clear.

His face throbbed. The pain where Quystein's mailed gauntlet had met his jaw was getting worse. Still, that was nothing to the pain in his heart. The desolation he'd felt when he'd promised his father never to seek to become a knight was nothing to this aching emptiness. It was a hollow devastation. And it was circled relentlessly by humiliation, remorse and guilt.

Emyr had inadvertedly made it worse. 'I explained about the Smoke Squadron.' He was in a dark mood after an interview with Quystein. 'I let them know about the ambush too. They hadn't realised. But magnanimously, because we've saved them from a surprise attack, they're going to forgive us.' He'd shaken his head in disbelief. 'We're invited to the feast.'

But I'm not part of the Smoke Squadron, Ansey had thought in misery. *No one has forgiven me.* He didn't have a clue how to explain to Emyr about giving the Sword to Xerxes but he was about to broach the terrible subject when Candle arrived for the victory celebration. The Lord of the Nardelf had been in high, cheerful spirits. The dwarf bodyguard accompanying him broke into song at the slightest excuse.

'It took me a while to see the funny side of it, I'll admit.' Candle had ruffled Fern's hair and Hector's fur. 'But when I did, I realised that it's the finest joke in centuries.' He had slapped both Ansey and Emyr on the back. 'And to think I was ever worried about you lot.' His grin had been replaced by a solemn, stern expression. 'I apologise. Again.' A very thin smile touched his lips. 'I hope not to make it a habit.' It was clear Candle had heard about the whole saga of the episode at the gate. 'Next time,' he had advised, tousling Ansey's hair, 'use a bit of common sense.'

Common sense? Ansey's thoughts had been bleak. He'd smiled to hide the acute isolation he'd felt. Wandering around, he'd tried to find something useful to do. And so he had discovered Madmerry in a hall, tending the wounded. Two of the slave children had died.

He'd wanted to die too. Unable to bear the pain any longer, he had slipped away, looking for a solitary place. It wasn't hard to find. Ysgarde was in tremendous confusion. News of the war had spread with great rapidity. Apart from the wounded, there were troops needing billets and squadrons being briefed. Companies of soldiers and other orders of Knights were on the way from nearby Kingdoms, their volunteers eager to swell the ranks of Ysgarde's defenders.

Calls for aid had gone out even before the battle had begun, but it was only late in the day when help began to arrive. A temporary encampment had been established outside the walls and the noise of it drifted up to Ansey, high on the battlement. The laughter and camaraderie of the troops below made him feel even more alone.

'I thought I might find you here.'

Ansey couldn't believe it. 'Gratian!' He turned and there was the Captain of the King's Shield, his whip-scarred face in deep shadow. It truly was Gratian—Gratian, who had seen him humiliated and beaten in Auberon, Gratian who had ruined his own career to help his tutors escape the Queen's wrath.

A swirl of cloak suddenly enfolded him, strong arms were around him and it was all he could do not to break down and sob his heart out.

Still Gratian wasn't fooled. 'Tell me about it.'

'It's all my fault.' Ansey felt as if there were a stone lodged high in his throat. 'I'm stupid and now they're dead. If I'd just been sensible instead of trying to be a proper knight…'

'Proper knights aren't sensible?'

Ansey choked in his efforts to stifle a sob. Gratian held Ansey at arm's length and looked at his face. 'I thought you'd heard some bad news, but you haven't, have you? Tell me what this is about.'

'The gate.' Tears sparked at Ansey's eyes.

'The gate?' Gratian held up a shield. 'Is this yours then?'

Ansey, blur–eyed, looked at the silver shield. Except it wasn't just silver anymore. There was a golden star at its centre. *Where the man with the long nose had kissed it.*

Gratian peered at him. 'You haven't answered.' His eyes narrowed. 'Is it yours?'

'I don't know.' Ansey shook his head. 'It might be. That could be where the Song kissed it.'

'The Song kissed it?' Gratian sounded incredulous. 'Tell me about the Song… no, tell me about what happened at the gate.'

'He's part of the story.' Ansey trembled as he began to tell the disaster from beginning to end. He left nothing out. His self–criticism made Lal and Van's pale into insignificance.

'Sir Rhodri Harke,' Gratian said, when he came to the part about the knight in the green surcoat.

Ansey looked up at Gratian in fright. 'You won't tell on him, will you, sir?'

Gratian's gaze met his. 'No one tells on anyone around here.' His tone was gentle. 'Don't you understand that?' He patted Ansey's head. 'Their shields do it for them.' His mouth curved in a thin curious smile. 'Rhodri's been searching the castle for you, just to thank you, you know. You kicked his self–worth just enough to get him back to the battlefield in time to rescue good old Lance from a troll. Rhodri's covered himself in glory.'

'There were trolls down there?'

'Yes, there were trolls down there. Just a couple.' Gratian patted Ansey on the shoulder. 'But that's a tale for another time. Come on, keep going with this story of yours.'

Ansey told how he'd given the Sword to Xerxes and also how he hadn't dared tell anyone yet. 'I'm not sure Dallan and the others would understand why I think the Powers aren't any more important than the lives they are supposed to save.'

Gratian nodded. 'What an interesting perspective. How good to have sufficient innocence to see what grown–ups might miss.'

Ansey, encouraged by Gratian's approval, told of how he'd wanted to give in, so many times. He bit back a sob as he spoke of how hard it was to keep the trust Quystein had placed in him and how just as he was about the give in, the man from Mistmurk Height had arrived. 'The Ancient of Days, so Lord Ancelin said, but Hector says he's just a fisherman.'

'What did he call himself?' Gratian asked.

'The Song,' Ansey said. 'He said he's been sung and that's why he came.'

'Oh.' Gratian's breath caught in his throat. As he shivered, Ansey felt a tingle up his own spine.

'Go on,' Gratian whispered.

So he went on to relate what Quystein had said and everything that had happened after it was discovered he'd refused to open the gate to anyone. Not Lal and Van. Not Rhodri Harke. Not Xerxes Xenophon. Not the slave children.

He felt himself crumble inside when he had to speak of them. His whole face quivered.

When he couldn't go on, Gratian gave a deep sigh. 'I wish I had time to explain to you, Ansey, that the slave children would have died anyway. There was nothing could save them, they were so far gone. I also wish we had time for you to go down and offer your forgiveness to Quystein, but we don't. And I further wish we…'

'What do I need to forgive Quystein for? He didn't…'

'For taking out his anger on you.' Gratian urged Ansey forward. He picked up the star shield and pointed towards the stairwell entry. 'Come on, let's go. And let's hurry. It won't be long before the news is out. I may already have left your departure too late…'

'Late…? Departure? What do you…?' Ansey didn't finish the question, for at that moment, behind him, a blaze of light broke out in a ring around Ysgarde. A thousand torches had been lit. And then, seconds later, ten thousand. And then a million.

'They *know*,' Gratian breathed. 'How in the Nine Netherhells did they find out so quickly? I only realised two minutes ago.' He let fly with a muttered string of abuse. Ansey was surprised at how fluently and foully he could curse.

He watched Gratian stride over to the battlements and stare, grim-faced, at the ring of torchlight. There were the Jotun armies— frost giants, storm giants, fire giants, trolls, effreets and mara-mares. 'Get back.' Gratian pushed him aside. 'Keep your head down.'

'But…' Ansey pointed at the encircling hordes. 'They've got children with them. Giant children. And women.' He pointed again. 'And look—a flag of truce.' He blinked, recognising not so much the flagbearer as the two ravens on his shoulders. 'It's Uller!'

'How do you know a frost giant by name?' Gratian's eyes seemed to spark with fire. Then he shook his head. 'No, don't tell me.' He grabbed Ansey, almost wrenching his arm as he dragged him towards the stairwell. He propelled him down the dark steps to the courtyard, his curses increasing in creativity all the way. After damning his ancestry for a dozen generations, he began on his own personal deficiencies. He swept Ansey across the confusion of the courtyard straight into the hands of Rhodri Harke. Bundling up the star shield in his cloak, he thrust it at Rhodri and barked out an order. 'Keep this, and get this fine gatekeeper something to eat.'

'Yes, sir.' Rhodri bowed. 'But, sir, there's Jotuns—Jotuns at the gate.'

'Yes, I know,' Gratian said.

At that moment Lord Ancelin and Lord Quystein spotted Gratian. They rushed to him, looking harassed. 'Lord Commander!'

Ancelin was out of breath. 'There must be a million Jotuns out there!'

Lord Commander? Ansey's thoughts reeled. *Gratian is the Lord Commander of the Knights of Renown? But what was he doing in Auberon?* And then Ansey realised. *Whatever it was was so important he couldn't entrust the job to anyone else. No wonder when he arrived and got a job as a simple soldier, Candle stayed on.* He took a deep breath. *Was it the same thing Candle was looking for? The prophecy of The King Who Guards the Gate?*

'Don't exaggerate, Lance.' Torchlight flickered over Gratian's scarred face. 'It's probably only *half* a million.'

'So we're only outnumbered a hundred to one instead of two hundred to one,' Lord Ancelin retorted. 'Have you a plan?'

'I'm going to go out there and talk to them,' Gratian said. 'They've got a flag of truce.'

'You're going to see what they want?' Quystein sounded doubtful.

'I know what they want. The very same thing as they've always wanted—The King Who Guards The Gate.' He shook his head. 'They haven't changed. I'll speak to them—we need to play for time.'

'I'll come with you,' Lord Ancelin offered.

'No, you won't, Lance! I want you and Rhodri to check if the secret passage is safe, and if it is, to take our little gatekeeper here…' He patted Ansey on the shoulder. '…our royal gatekeeper is to be escorted out that way as quickly and quietly as possible.' In the shadowed half–light, a meaningful look passed from his eyes to Lord Ancelin's.

Ansey saw the look and frowned. He saw that Quystein had seen the look too and was looking aghast. 'I'm sorry.' He bowed to Ansey. 'Oh. I'm sorry.'

It didn't make sense. 'I'm not going. You can't make me!'

Gratian just looked at him. 'You want a thumping? It's a fine time to suddenly decide to be disobedient after all the times you have been so faithful and diligent in obedience.'

I've learned from Emyr and his literalism. You can't trick me, Gratian. 'I kept my word, that's all. I haven't given *you* my word.'

'No, you haven't.' Gratian touched the whip scar on his face.

'But you did promise me that one day you'd make this up to me.' He
stooped down, so that he could look Ansey straight in the eye. 'And
this is the price I'm asking—that you go with Lance and Rhodri.'

Ansey felt himself begin to shake.

'I want your word, Ancelin Bedwyr Cai.'

Ansey's face dropped. 'Please don't make me.' A single teardrop
fell from his cheek. 'I've got to stay with the others.' He knew his
voice sounded humiliated and desperate but he didn't care. 'There's
got to be Seven of us, Seven Days together, with the Seven Powers.'
*Oh no. There can't ever be seven anymore. I gave one to Xerxes. And we
never did find the last two, anyway.* He raised his eyes, biting his lip.

He was astonished at the stunned looks on the faces of Quystein,
Gratian and Rhodri. 'He's quite right.' Lord Ancelin surprised
him by coming to his defence. 'I haven't had a chance to tell you,
Commander—the Days have come.'

'And they're all children?' Quystein's voice was full of horror.

'Children?' Gratian's nod was slow and thoughtful.

Ansey watched the expression flitting across his face and realised
he had just lost a dream. *You hoped you were one of the Days? Is that
why you came to Auberon to search for the prophecy? Because you hoped
it would be about you?*

Gratian's recovery was swift. 'Of course. The Days would be
children. We should have foreseen that.'

At that moment, Emyr skidded to a halt next to Ansey.
Madmerry and Fern were with him. 'We've been looking for you
everywhere. Uller's here.'

'I know.'

'I've got an idea.' Emyr tried to draw him away from Gratian
as Boody, Hector and Ginevra arrived. 'It's not a good one, but…'

Gratian clapped Emyr on the shoulder. 'That's more than
anyone else has got.' He bowed, introducing himself. 'Gratian, Lord
Commander of the Knights of Renown.'

'And Chief Prince of the High Command of Ysgarde,' Emyr added.

'That's a very ancient title. Not used these days.' Gratian's brows knitted. 'Dallan! I didn't recognise you!' He shook his head as he stared at the short hair and neat glasses. 'Why, in this day of stunning surprises, am I more surprised by this than anything else?'

Emyr shrugged and turned to Ansey. 'First we need to talk to Uller and then…'

'*You* can talk to Uller,' Gratian interrupted. 'I'll escort you. But Ansey can't go.'

'Please.' Ansey swallowed hard. 'I know I've made a real mess of everything and you don't trust me, but please, I need a chance to…'

'Ansey,' Gratian broke in, 'I do trust you.'

Ansey stared at him, biting his lip, not believing a word. 'I'm sorry you feel you have to lie to me, sir.'

Gratian let out an explosive breath. 'Ansey.' He dropped down to one knee so that their eyes were level. 'This is the last way I wanted this to come out. Please believe that. This is not to do with trust. Quite the contrary. Ansey, I believe that an ancient prophecy has come to pass and that you are The King Who Guards The Gate. That's why the Jotuns are here. For *you*.'

Ansey laughed. 'That's ridiculous. I'm not a king.'

'Yes, you are.' Gratian gazed into his eyes. 'You have been since early this morning. I'm so sorry, Ansey.' He went down on both knees and bowed. 'Your Majesty.'

Lord Ancelin, Lord Quystein and Sir Rhodri all followed his example.

Father? Dead? But how? Ansey, stricken, reached for Emyr's hand to make sure he didn't drop down on his knees as well. 'Don't *you* dare!' He whirled around to glare at Madmerry and Fern, Hector, Ginevra and Boody. 'Don't *any* of you dare!'

Emyr looked uncomfortable. 'Don't dare what?'

Ansey felt a tear drop along with a sudden rush of affection for Emyr in his confusion. *I forgot to be specific.* And in that moment of diversion, he realised Emyr's gift to him: *I can put my feelings aside and deal with them later. Right now, we have to find out what it means to be the Days.*

He nodded at Emyr. 'What were you going to say? About your plan?'

'I think we need an envoy to the Jotuns. And to find out about that prophecy. There's much more to it than just The King Who Guards The Gate. Remember: *When the Days come, assuming their Power, then is the time unchancy late. Awake! It is the Daystar's hour; he brings The King Who Guards The Gate.* Now if you're the King, then who is the Daystar?'

'Where did you hear that?' Gratian asked.

'From Uller,' Emyr and Ansey said together.

'I know a different version.' Gratian took a deep breath. '*When the Days come assuming their Power, then is the time unchancy late, but lo! they come, and grace they wear to join The King Who Guards The Gate; earth is torn, the heavens rent, the sleeping dark is waking, unless the Seven become One, all worlds will know the breaking.*'

'It doesn't have the Daystar in it?' Ansey asked.

'No, but it doesn't need to. The Daystar Shield is one of the Seven Powers.' Gratian pointed to the folded cloak in Rhodri Harke's hands. 'Take it back, Ansey. There's more to the prophecy I've recited but I've given the heart of it. There was a clue in it that, if ever the Seven Days do come together, it will be in under a white canopy in Auberon, or not at all.' His eyes narrowed as he glanced from Emyr to Madmerry. 'Why do you think I stayed so long in Auberon? Because, apart from Ysgarde, it's the only location mentioned in the prophecies.' His gaze focussed on Madmerry. 'Everyday, I looked at that little white rag tent of yours, and everyday I said to myself, "No, impossible." And every day I looked for some other white canopy but never found one.'

Hector swatted his knee. 'Well, I wish you'd told me.'

'Jotuns!' Emyr put up his hand. 'I don't like to seem like I have a one–track mind, but they're going to get restless very shortly.'

'Thank you, Dallan,' Gratian said.

'Oh, he's not D…' Ansey almost let the truth out. Emyr kicked him and they eyed each other. '…dumb,' Ansey finished.

'Then let's move. Lance, find a white flag.' Gratian directed

Emyr and Ansey to the gate. Ansey let out a cry of excitement as he saw first Parment and then the man next to him.

'Tobias!'

'Well, well,' the lanky fright-haired tutor said. 'How did you get here? Delighted to see you, by the way, young scruff.'

'Are you really a mage-scholar, Tobias?'

Tobias nodded. He pointed to the soldiers grouped outside the gate in a kind of ragged queue. 'And I'm busy applying all of my knowledge ensuring that no Jotuns come through in disguise.' He raised a quizzical eyebrow. 'You're not upset, are you, over our little deception? Greywhiskers is still anguishing over the moral issues involved.'

Ansey shrugged. 'I would have liked to have helped. And there are things I'd like to have learned.'

'Such as?'

He shrugged again. 'How to make wolf's-tail cloudshadows, how to speak dwarvish, how to write on water.'

'You'll have to ask Commander Gratian about the cloudshadow, the Lord of the Nardelf about dwarvish, but...' Tobias hesitated. '...I think we owe you water-writing. So I'll ask Greywhiskers if we can bend the rules.'

'Thank you.'

'You're very unhappy, Ansey. What's wrong?'

Ansey said nothing.

'Come on...' Before Tobias could urge him further, Lord Ancelin arrived with a white flag.

Candle was with him, holding a torch and glaring at Gratian. 'This is a bad idea. But if you insist on speaking to these devils, I'm going with you.'

'Come along.' Gratian handed another torch to Emyr and pointed towards the Jotuns. 'Let's go.'

o I believe my eyes? The Lord Commander's back. Coming first out the gate, Uller noticed, was Gratian. *What a pity. Quystein would be so much easier to fool.*

Behind Gratian, Lord Ancelin was holding the white flag high.

Uller took a deep breath to steady himself. *Don't even think it. Now is not the time to avenge the kin–slaying.*

The parley group passed a line of soldiers, swords out, facing the fire–ring. *Not much more than a bowshot distance. Could try a stealth move. He's an easy target from here.*

Uller watched as Boody flew silently to Emyr's shoulder and Hector padded through the darkness, a pale almost invisible shadow, at his heels. *They're letting the King of Fyrzentsou down here? Are they mad? Unless they don't know… or unless they don't know that I know… Stupid move, either way. They should know I have a contract to kill him.*

Gratian held up his hand in a salute. 'Uller Princekiller.'

'Lord Gratian.' He felt the ravens on his shoulders raise their beaks in response to his own slight bow. 'Back home, I see. That must be an agreeable change.' When Gratian didn't respond to the pleasantry, he introduced the giant next to him. 'This is Freutim. King of the Frost Giants, Ruler of the Jotun Alliance.'

'An honour.' Freutim's voice was low, like a distant boom of thunder.

Still Gratian said nothing.

'Without wasting time,' Uller said, 'we'd like to get straight to the point.'

'You can't have him,' Candle said. 'There will be no negotiation. Read my lips: "no".'

'What did you bring *that* for?' Freutim's upper lip curled as he regarded Candle with disgust.

Gratian still said nothing.

'Here!' Uller held out the Sword towards Emyr. 'A token of good faith.'

Emyr looked at him in surprise. 'Where did you get this?'

'From your friend.' He took a step forward and bent towards Emyr. He squinted in the flickering torch–light and peered through his glasses. *Just to be sure. We wouldn't want to make a mistake at the last moment. Yes, one blue, one green.* He burst out laughing.

'What is it?' Freutim turned to him.

'Nothing.' Uller winked at Emyr. 'Just a delicious irony, which I am savouring to the full.' He turned to Gratian. *I used to think you were as sharp as a thornblade but you've disappointed me immensely. How on earth did you miss the fact this boy next to you is the King of Fyrzentsou?*

He bowed. 'As you must suspect, If not know for certain, one of the Dark Sleepers has woken. By various subterfuges, we have managed to keep it from rising.'

'This has been by no means easy,' Freutim added, 'nor is it something we can maintain indefinitely. It undoubtedly appears to you we are agents of destruction and bringers of chaos, nothing more than Servants of the Sleeper, doing its dark bidding. When the Sleeper first sent us out to search for the Seven Powers and The King Who Guards The Gate, we were—I must say—not overly diligent. We understood—wrongly, as it transpired—that the Sleeper was seeking to draw to itself Powers of Darkness. When we realised it was searching for its enemies to destroy them, we did everything we could to find what it was the Sleeper feared.'

Gratian folded his arms. 'That would be a simple deduction. The Mage who imprisoned it in this dimension.'

Uller wanted to roll his eyes and throw up his hands in disbelief. *Didn't they learn anything when they scoured Auberon from top to bottom for the prophecy?* He adopted his most confiding tone. 'I'm sure you realise there is not one, but Seven Sleepers. We have tried to locate them but have failed. They may be scattered throughout the Nine Dimensions or they may all be in this one. Either way, the purpose of this Dark Sleeper is to bide its time until it is safe to arise and walk the world. It desires to break out of this dimension but, if that is not possible, it wants as much freedom within it as it can achieve.'

He watched Gratian's eyes narrow. *Oh, you've got the picture now, have you? About time!* 'This is what the Jotuns have tried to thwart. We have attempted to put the darkness back to sleep. This has, however, been beyond our powers, vast as they are. So far, all we have managed is to prevent it from walking the world.'

'Why steal the scroll from the City of Mages?' Candle demanded. 'If all you were doing was to stop the Sleeper arising?'

'Because even though it is beyond our powers to return the Darkness to its slumber, we knew there had to be a way. If it was done before, it could be done again. The scroll told us we needed to find more than just The King Who Guards The Gate. We had also to look for the White Three, for the Masked Duo and for The Perfect Helper. These are the Seven who comprise the Seven Days. Only they have the power to combat the Seven Sleepers.'

'You think so?' Emyr asked.

'We do.' Uller made a solemn bow. 'The Ancient of Days has delegated power to the Seven Days.'

'And what makes you think that's us?' Emyr said. 'Apart from a coincidence of timing in when we were born?'

Uller pointed towards the gate of Ysgarde. 'There are prophecies about each of you, but The King Who Guards The Gate always seemed easiest to interpret. A King. At a Gate. On guard against Jotuns.' He pointed to Boody, sitting on Emyr's shoulder and Hector at his feet. 'As for the White Three, here are two. How much whiter do you want? When it comes to the Masked Duo, well, Your Majesty, I'm sorry I never thought of that fringe of hair you always kept so carefully in front of your face as a mask of concealment. But it was, wasn't it?'

'Your Majesty?' Gratian turned to gape at Emyr.

'Didn't you know?' The question was rhetorical. Uller laughed. 'Of course you didn't. You wouldn't have let the King of Fyrzentsou come down here otherwise.'

'*King* of Fyrzentsou?'

Emyr shrugged. 'Somebody called Rogin who has apparently been pretending to be my father is keeping the throne warm for me. I've given considerable thought to what I should do about this. I have even consulted my friends and I've realised it suits me just fine at present because I have a terribly busy schedule right now.' He stroked Hector with his boot. 'Something about saving the world.'

'I had this vision of how the prophecy would work.' Hector shook his head. 'I'd be the epitome of respectful service to my liege lord. But I've been a rude–mouth from the start.'

Emyr's smile was affectionate. 'You've been you.'

How many of them understood what the fox said? Uller wasn't sure but he noticed Gratian's surprised glance from Hector to Emyr. He laughed again, taking the opportunity to spread his hands out to cover the movement of his foot.

If there is any chance at all, these children are it. They are not One, but they are closer to it than any group of warriors or mages ever. They have to be very close or the Flair would not be overflowing like this. He addressed Gratian. 'Haven't you put this together yet, Commander? There are Seven Days and there are Seven Sleepers, the Children of Night. The Days have come, they have most of the Powers at their disposal. They may be children, they may be as young, fresh and innocent as the Children of Night are old, primeval and bloodthirsty, but why should that trouble you? The Ancient of Days has always had a strange sense of humour.'

'The time is late,' Freutim said. 'When the Dark Sleeper walks the world, looking for freedom, seeking to merge with its brethren, you will not believe the terror and evil it will bring. There will be no dawn, no light at all, unless you help us.'

Gratian seemed moved by this plea. 'Let us return to the castle.

We will discuss the full implications of what you've said and what assistance we can give.' He bowed to Freutim. 'You may expect an answer within an hour.'

Freutim bowed in return. Uller watched the envoys turn and make their way back up the hill. Freutim leaned towards him. 'Will they help?'

Uller considered a moment. 'No. They're playing for time.'

'The fools! Don't they understand?'

'The history of warfare between us is too long and too bitter for them to trust us.' Uller knew his eyes were gleaming and tried to shield them. It wouldn't do to give away his satisfaction so publicly. He lowered his voice. 'Still, the fox has taken the bait.'

'What bait?' Freutim sounded disconcerted. 'What double game are you playing?'

Uller said nothing for several seconds. *Don't you remember our discussion—it was only fifty years ago.* 'Endgame.' He turned to Freutim. 'If it goes wrong, you may be able to appease the Dark Sleeper by claiming ignorance.'

He could see Freutim understood.

But he would never have approved this final risk. It wasn't because he was trying to protect the Jotuns that he failed to reveal the endgame. It was because Freutim always wanted to keep some bargaining chip in reserve.

Now there's nothing. There are other works equal to the Powers. Uller could not believe Gratian had forgotten that. Watching the group heading for the gate, he strained to see Hector's pale form in the darkness. The little fox was labouring up the trail at Emyr's heels. 'But lo! they come and grace they wear…' The words felt soft and musical on his breath.

Those dwarves and scholars are just useless. They scoured Auberon from top to bottom and never even started to look into the only truly obvious line of the prophecy.

He smiled with cautious satisfaction, as he saw the bulging leather pouch in Hector's mouth reach the gate of Ysgarde.

 ven before she could speak to Emyr on his return, Fern could see he was shaking with rage. 'What do you mean you have no intention of helping the Jotuns?' The Sword jerked up and down in his hands as he faced Gratian. 'But they're telling the truth!'

He appealed to Hector and Boody. 'Tell them!' He pointed first at Gratian with his swordpoint, then at Candle. 'Tell them they're telling the truth.'

'As a matter of fact, I believe the Jotun's story.' Boody jumped onto Gratian's head and bent over to look in his eyes.

Fern was startled when Gratian replied. 'So do I.'

Does he have the Flair? Or is he like Candle—he's made an effort to learn owl language?

'Dash ish duputlee urrek,' Hector announced.

What? I can't have lost the Flair. How come fox suddenly sounds like gibberish? Fern glanced down, noticing Hector had a pouch dangling from his jaws. *Maybe he just can't talk right with that thing in his mouth.*

Candle glared at Boody. 'I believe them, too, Boudicca's Chariot.' He balled his hands. 'What I don't believe is that they want the Seven Days and the Seven Powers to foil the Dark Sleeper. I believe they have been doing its bidding so long they can't help themselves. They are its Servants.' He brushed Emyr's arm with his fist. 'Consider, lad, what and who you owe. Who are your friends? Who can you trust? I don't like to remind you, but you owe me. What do you owe the Jotuns?'

Emyr glared right back. 'Don't play games with me, Candle. You know that I owe you my sight. But I owe Uller my life. Did you save me from the manticores?'

Candle scowled. 'Only hours ago, you were swearing undying friendship with the Cavern Kin. You know that Uller saved your life for his own nefarious purposes.'

'And you're not furthering the cause of the dwarves? You've no motives but altruism? I suppose that's why we found the Powers in the travelling case.'

Steam seemed to come from Candle's nostrils. 'The reason they were in the travelling case…'

'Stop it!' Gratian stomped his boot. 'If the Jotuns wanted to divide us, they've succeeded.' He turned to Lord Ancelin. 'Call a Council, Lance. Have all the delegates there in ten minutes. And make sure the chamber is set up to honour three kings.'

'Three kings?' Lord Ancelin looked baffled.

'King of Dwarves, King of Fyrzentsou and King of Auberon.'

'Oh, of course.'

Ansey came to stand beside Fern. 'Is it to be a Council of War?' he asked Gratian as Lord Ancelin hurried off.

'Of course.' Gratian looked puzzled. 'Why do you ask?'

'Could you consider a Council of Peace?'

'Where did you hear an unusual idea like that?' He cupped his hand under Ansey's elbow and led him away from the dimly–lit gate.

Fern was left with Emyr. She could see he was fuming as he stood in the middle of the gateway. Boody was back on his shoulder. He glared at the sentry who, with Tobias, was still checking the credentials of everyone passing through the gateway. She didn't know what to say.

Hector dropped the pouch with a thud.

'What's this?' Fern picked up the bag.

'Just a little something I came across lying at Uller's feet,' Hector said.

'What's this writing?'

Boody hopped down Emyr's arm to his wrist in order to get a better look. 'It says: *Keep out. This means you! No exceptions. Confidential: Days only.*'

'Days?' Fern asked. 'Like us—the Seven Days?'

'It would appear so,' Boody said. 'This package is addressed to us.'

Emyr took it from Fern with caution. 'Has it got wardspells?'

'Nope,' Hector said. 'Maybe it did in the past but I gave it the careful onceover before I picked it up. It's just an ordinary bag at the moment.'

Fern could feel the queue of knights and soldiers watching them from the shadow of the castle wall. *Why isn't anyone rushing forward to stop us doing something rash? Can they hear us? Can they understand Boody and Hector or just Emyr and me?*

With trepidation, she watched Emyr open the pouch. He pulled out a length of red silk. Even in the feeble torchlight, the colours were vibrant. Cherry and crimson, scarlet and claret flowed from the bag. 'I think it's a cloak.' He shook it out. It was half black and half red and had a deep hem of encrusted jewels: rubies, garnets and blood carnelians.

'Not nearly big enough for a frost giant.' Fern reached out to touch the silk.

'Depends.' Ansey arrived back, his eyes red–rimmed, his voice husky. 'I don't think I've ever seen Uller the same size twice.'

'Have you killed half of Ysgarde?' Hector asked.

'No. Why?'

Hector smirked. 'I thought getting rid of most of the Knights and fighting your way out would be the only way Gratian would ever let you out of his sight.'

'Gratian thinks I'm with Rhodri and Rhodri thinks I'm with Ysanne and Ysanne thinks I'm with Ancelin.' Ansey shrugged. 'And I don't know who Ancelin thinks I'm with.'

'Here, hold this.' Emyr handed the red and black cloak to him, before pulling a swathe of orange from the pouch.

Peach, persimmon and tangerine hues tumbled out of the bag, dropping to the ground under the weight of the hem. Fern dived for the edge and held it up. It was another cloak, its hem bright with teardrops of topaz, star–shaped citrines and smooth rounds of amber. The gems were arranged in swirling fluid designs of waves and cloud.

Emyr continued to pull fabric from the pouch. Daffodil gave way to butter and gold. 'Listen!' Hector cocked his ear. 'The cloaks are singing.'

'Humming.' The yellows ended and Emyr held up a tiny cloak to his ear. 'It's more like humming. It sounds like middle C.' He held the cloak up for her inspection. It was so small only Boody might have fitted it. A gemstone forest of lemon chrysoprase, argyll diamonds and tiger–eye was embroidered with fine gold thread. 'What do you think of this?'

Before Fern could reply, Madmerry ran up. Her mask jangled, the bells chiming a paean that set the red and orange cloaks vibrating. 'Grace cloaks!'

'What are grace cloaks?' Emyr gave the yellow cape to Fern. Boody hopped over to her shoulder as a riot of greens now appeared in his hands—emerald, olive, sage and lime. Their hum was clearly audible. Emerald stars bordered the mantle, a jade moon sat high on one side and a floral sun of lustrous peridots glowed on the other. 'I think that's a D.'

'Grace cloaks!' Madmerry said. 'Haven't you ever heard of them?'

Fern was glad she wasn't the only one shaking her head.

'Did I hear grace cloaks mentioned?' Tobias left his post as Emyr handed the green cloak to Madmerry.

He's the mage–scholar. Fern felt a sense of relief. *If anyone should know what they are, it's him.*

He looked them over with a superior air. 'They look like inferior imitations to me. A real dreamcoat is a part of an octave set augmented with the colours and attributes of grace.'

'What would the colours and attributes of grace be?' Ansey asked.

Tobias didn't answer directly. 'Grace cloaks are creations of extraordinary workmanship. They are shelters and protection, they foretell the future and summon destiny—more by transforming the wearer than by any predictive power. Experts believe it's a kind of self–fulfilling prophecy. They're supposed to enable the almost effortless performance of mighty and impossible deeds.'

'How do you know these aren't real?' Madmerry was clearly disappointed.

'Because grace cloaks don't actually exist.' Tobias' smile was one of benign indulgence. 'They're just legends from the time of tribulation after the Englobing.'

A swirl of blue made its appearance in Emyr's hands. Peacock and sky rippled with cerulean and azure. 'E.' Emyr wasn't paying any attention to Tobias. He hummed along with the cloak as it slipped through his hands. 'No, E flat.'

He must have perfect pitch. Fern wondered if he'd secretly laughed at her singing.

'Can I try it?' Hector gazed at the birds and fish picked out in sapphires and lapis, aquamarine and blue topaz along the hem. 'It's exactly my size.'

'It might be booby–trapped,' Emyr said. 'It might be a Jotun trick.'

'I thought you said you trusted the Jotuns,' Hector said.

'I said nothing of the kind. I said I believed their story, I didn't say I trusted them—Uller might be telling the truth but I'm sure Candle's right and he's up to something. I don't doubt Candle's up to something as well.'

'Drop it on the ground,' Hector said.

Emyr let the blue cloak flutter down. Hector sniffed his way around it, then stuck his snout under one corner. 'It's a perfect fit.' His voice was muffled as he fumbled under it. 'Heeellp! I'm…'

Madmerry and Fern threw their arms out, just in time to catch him as he shot into the air.

'Oh, oh, oh,' he whimpered. Then, poking out his head, he smiled. 'Oooh!' His voice was a low croon. 'I've always wanted this! Hey look, guys, I'm a *flying fox*!'

'It *is* a grace cloak!' Madmerry pushed him down. 'Look! Hector, your Messenger Shoes have changed!'

Fern stared. The dark leather cuffs around Hector's ankles had transformed into gladiator sandals. With one enormous difference. They had wings.

'Oh, goodness.' Tobias was round–eyed as Hector descended to earth. 'It's the Birds and Fishes Cloak of the Fifth Day. You can fly with it and breathe underwater, too.'

'What's a Birds and Fishes cloak?' Emyr asked.

'It's very similar to the equally non–existent Sea and Sky cloak of the Second Day.' Tobias stared at the cloaks in Fern's arms and shook his head as if he couldn't believe his own eyes.

'I could fly with this?' Fern held up the orange cloak.

'If you are the Second Day, you can activate it. After that, anyone who uses it will not merely fly but go as swift as the wind. As well as be able to walk on or below water.'

Fern felt alarmed and almost dropped the cloak. If all of them had been the same, she was sure she'd feel a sense of excitement. But their differences made them somehow dangerous.

'The Second Day is Monday's child,' Emyr said. 'It *is* your cloak, Lady Fern.' He dug in the pouch once more. A length of indigo appeared, as deep and rich as midnight velvet, a sweet bell–like chime with it. 'And that's an F.'

'On the other hand, maybe F goes with Fern.' Ansey looked thoughtful.

Fern looked around the group, naming them one by one. 'A for Ansey, B for Boody, E for Emyr, F for Fern and G for Ginevra. But Hector and Madmerry don't fit the pattern of musical notes.' Fern sighed. 'For a moment, I almost thought we had a set of ordered names as well. But we're missing a C and a D.'

'Unless Dallan's a D,' Boody pointed out. 'Then we'd be missing a C and an E.'

Madmerry's mouth twisted in a rueful expression. 'Confession time,' she said with a sigh. 'You don't think I'm really Madmerry, do you? It's a nickname. My name is Cindurrah.'

Ginevra turned her pink almond eyes on Madmerry. 'That's just what the Ancient of Days called you. What does it mean?'

'Star–shepherd.'

'Really?' Ginevra seemed delighted. 'I must be one of the stars you're shepherding: 'ayelet–hashachar means *hind of daybreak*. It's a name for the morning star.'

'She's the fawn of dawn.' Hector grinned.

'But the morning star is the daystar,' Ansey said. 'Have you been the Daystar all along?'

'Don't be ridiculous.' Ginevra kicked at him with one hoof. 'In case you haven't got this yet, Prince Ancelin, this isn't about *me*. It's about *we*.'

Madmerry turned to Hector. 'Come on, foxy boy. It's time to bare your soul.'

'What?' Hector was a picture of innocence.

'Surround him, guys,' Madmerry instructed. 'He's playing hard to get.'

Fern moved behind Hector and Emyr closed the gap between Madmerry and Ansey. They all stared at him. Madmerry's lips were set in a grimace. 'Come on, you know there's something you want to tell us, Hector. You're the one spoiling the perfect line–up.'

Hector sighed. Then he moaned and mumbled under his breath. He turned on himself and bit his tail. 'Oh, all right.' He drew himself up and raised his snout in the air. 'My name's really Ector and I hate it.' He screwed up his face and let out a thin yowl. 'Hate, hate, hate, hate, hate, hate, hate it. When I was expelled from the den, I decided it was time for a break. For a new name. Something a bit more aspirational.'

Fern stared. Emyr had called him Ector long before the Ancient of Days had. *This means there's a perfect lineup of names and musical notes. What did it signify?* She turned to the cloth of indigo as she tried to understand the connection. Different animals were picked out along its border in dark jewels. There was a fox and a deer, a lion and a mouse, a giraffe and a man.

Tobias stared at the jewels. 'Jet and viollane.'

'Is that significant?' Ansey asked.

Tobias shrugged. 'Jet's neither here nor there in value—but

viollane! The rarest and most precious of all gems.' He looked around. 'This belongs to Friday's child.' Madmerry turned without a word and allowed it to be fastened around her neck. 'With it comes the power to understand and speak the language of all beasts and men.' Tobias turned to Emyr. 'There should be one more cloak, only one—and it should be violet and hum G or G sharp.'

Emyr reached into the pouch. Out came a rich mantle of purple and lilac, lavender, mauve and plum, the colours flowing together in soft, misty swirls. It appeared with a trilling peal of music. There was no jewelled border on it, no design, just a trim of amethyst along the collar. 'What can you do with this one?'

'The purpose of the purple dreamcoat, the cloak of Saturday's child, has always been a mystery. Its qualities aren't mentioned in the old lore. And in the stories, it doesn't seem to do anything.'

It's the seventh coat. From the seventh day. Fern stared at it. *It could just send things to sleep. But that would be stupid.*

Emyr was about to swing the violet cloak around his shoulders when a shout came from the courtyard.

'Your Majesties!' Lord Ancelin descended the main stairwell, a torch in his hands. He was headed towards the gate.

'Oh no.' Emyr whirled to Ansey. 'We forgot about the Council.' He stomped his foot. 'I don't want to go.'

Ansey wrapped an arm around Emyr's shoulders. 'I know there are some things hard for you to understand, Emyr. And I know you don't like dishonesty or rule–breaking. But do you get the concept of acting?'

Emyr nodded.

Ansey's face was transformed by a thoughtful grin. 'Coming!' He waved to Lord Ancelin and handed the red cloak to Fern. 'Let's go,' he said to Emyr. 'I've got a great idea.'

'Just wait.' Emyr folded his mantle and gave it to Fern. He took the Flower of Heart's Desire out of his pocket. 'Take care of this.'

Ansey dragged him off. 'We'll be back shortly.'

Boody winged from his shoulder to Madmerry's. Hector tapped the ground as he watched them depart. 'Speaking of taking care of things, anyone know where we put the White Mother's shuttle?'

'Why?' Madmerry asked.

'Because I'd like Fern to have it. Suppose things go bad, really bad. Well, I think her dimension will whip her out of here. That could happen even if things go really really good. And if she had the Wreathwatch Woman's shuttle with her, then that's a whole weight off the Kingdom of Fyrzentsou forever. Can't have the fate of its king woven if the shuttle's gone.'

Madmerry took it out of her pocket and gave it to Fern.

Hector nodded with satisfaction.

Fern felt frightened. *I don't want the Shuttle. Or the Flower of Heart's Desire. Not if they're goodbye–forever gifts.*

Hector looked at the cloaks folded across Fern's arm. 'You know, this is really quite scary. There are two Ancelins. That makes it an octave.'

'But why an octave?' Boody asked. 'It seems like a clue to something.'

'It's a frightening level of coincidence, all right,' Ginevra murmured.

'Coincidence?' Madmerry's bells jingled as she shook her head. 'This has to be orchestrated.'

'Come here, little fawn.' Tobias took up the green cloak and draped it over Ginevra, fixing the clasp carefully around her neck.

Fern held up the yellow cloak in front of Boody. 'Do you want to try this?'

Boody flapped her wings and turned to Tobias. 'What are its qualities?'

'Trees and earth. Age, wisdom, peace, solidity, bounty, shelter.'

'Right then. I'm game.' Boody swivelled on Madmerry's shoulder, positioning herself backwards for Fern to put on the cloak on. Turning, she looked set to preen herself.

Fern smirked. The golden cloak and the sunglasses looked completely silly together. Hector snortled. Ginevra broke into giggles.

'Is this how you treat an owl who's become so much instantly wiser?' Boody raised her beak in disdain.

'Are you wiser?' Fern asked.

'I don't feel the slightest difference actually.' Boody assumed an even loftier expression. 'But now that I'm a sage, I expect you all to take notice of what I say. We're getting diverted by these cloaks. We should work out how the Powers go together. The Seven becoming One is undoubtedly a reference to that.'

'I think that's an extraordinarily wise suggestion,' Tobias said.

Madmerry's gaze followed each in turn. 'Right, then. Hector's got the Messenger Shoes. No doubt that they're the real deal. Ansey's shield is surely one of the Powers too. How do a shield and shoes go together?'

Ginevra held up a hoof in protest. 'But they don't fit the same person.'

'Correct.' Boody's yellow cloak rippled as she held out her wings. 'While in theory the Helmet, the Sword, the Shield, the Belt and the Mailcoat could be carried by one individual, I actually don't think it's one of us. I think that's what the size of the Shoes tells us.'

'I agree,' Madmerry said. 'All in favour?'

They nodded together.

Madmerry raised her hand and wagged her finger. 'If anyone tries to persuade us he is the Hero of the hour and attempts to take all Seven Powers to save the Day, we're to stand firm.'

Fern could think of several dwarves and knights whom, she suspected, already had such ambitions.

'We've only got six Powers,' Ginevra pointed out.

'What's the seventh, oh wisest one?' Hector grinned up at Boody.

Angry shouting echoed across the courtyard. Emyr bawled at the top of his voice while he was shepherded down the stairs. Ansey accompanied him, bringing Candle's travelling case.

Madmerry's hand went to her mouth. 'I've never seen him like this. Dallan—Emyr, I mean—might seem scared or stupid at times but really he's a tower of strength.' She hurried to Emyr.

Fern and the others followed.

His yelling stopped.

'We're playing "good king, bad king".' Ansey patted Emyr on

the shoulder. 'It was a brilliant performance. I got to be the voice of reason and escort the bad king out to talk sense into him.'

'I acted bad, Merry.' Emyr was obviously thrilled with himself. 'I acted so so bad. I threw a tantrum. But I thought they were never going to agree to send us out.'

'And I took the opportunity to swipe this back.' Ansey held up the carrying case.

'Boody's had a great idea.' Madmerry pointed to the case. 'About the Powers.'

A wild, unearthly shriek echoed across the castle. Fern fell as the ground trembled violently. Ginevra teetered against her.

I think Ysgarde's pseudolithic cushion has failed.

Beyond the gate, the torches of the Jotuns went out, the bright rings collapsing into darkness. Night closed in. Only the lights of Ysgarde still shone and they seemed wan and unsteady in the sudden gloom.

ern staggered up only to fall down again.

'What was *that*?' Hector tottered as he lurched up. His voice was hardly above a whisper.

A whirr of wings could be heard and Gratian's voice sounded above the dying shriek. It was strained almost to a caw: 'Douse the lights, douse the lights.'

One by one Ysgarde's torches went out. Only the leafmoon and the high stars offered any light.

And then it was visible, on the horizon—a dark shape blotting out the rising stars as it strode onwards, growing in immensity as it neared the castle.

The shrieking rose in intensity then died away again.

Fern found herself being pulled up by Ansey. There was a beating of air next to her as a black shape alighted on his left shoulder.

'Hi, kiddo.'

'Munin!' Ansey was breathless.

'Look, let me put it to you bluntly. You're in big trouble, we're in big trouble. That's the Dark Sleeper.'

Fern felt a shiver of fear run up Ansey's arm. She turned to Emyr, but he was staring, transfixed, at the horizon, a look of horror on his face. Thundering footsteps sounded on the courtyard stairwell. Gratian's voice came out of the darkness. 'Who called "douse the lights"?'

'I did,' a voice croaked. A whirr of wings accompanied Huginn's sudden descent to Ansey's right shoulder.

'Thank you.' Gratian hurried up, flanked by Lord Ancelin and Candle. 'But how did you get in?'

Huginn ignored the question. 'In approximately one minute, maybe two, if we're very lucky, the Dark Sleeper will arrive. So listen good and listen fast. Uller knows you don't trust us, but understand this—we know Ansey is The King Who Guards The Gate because the Ancient of Days virtually told us so. If the Ancient of Days trusts us in this, why don't you?'

'We don't have time to work through centuries of distrust.' Gratian's gaze was locked on the looming blackness growing ever nearer. 'Even if…'

'The plan's dead simple,' Munin interrupted. 'Huginn and I are gonna try to distract the Walker. You guys probably have five minutes, if you're lucky, to work out how the Powers work together to become one.'

'So hurry.' Huginn rose from Ansey's shoulder. Then he looped back. 'And take off the grace cloaks. They'll help protect you in the last resort, but it's too late for them to be used effectively. And they'll undermine our distraction. The Walker will sense any use of their Power and be drawn to you.'

Madmerry unclasped Ginevra's cloak, and flung off her own. Boody and Hector shrugged out of theirs. The two ravens sped back down the hill, dropped to the ground, then rose into the air, carrying a burning stick between them.

Hardly visible, only the glow of the firestick glistening on a feather showed their presence. Soaring to the treeline, they turned and plummeted out of sight down the valley. The dark Walker altered its course to follow the rod of flying flame.

'How did I suddenly understand the speech of ravens?' Gratian shook his head as if to clear it. 'Quick! We're wasting precious time! The Powers—'

'We don't even know what the seventh one is, so how can we put them all together?' Madmerry asked.

Fern looked on, feeling helpless and terrified.

'It's almost caught them.' Hector's voice was full of despondency.

Fern realised he was watching the progress of the Dark Walker as it followed the firestick.

'They're expendable,' Boody said. 'They knew that.'

'The sacrifice might be in vain.' Ginevra shook her head. 'We're not going to understand this in time.'

Fern began to shiver. She knew, deep in her bones, that nothing Munin and Huginn did would change anything. *We're going to die.* And the idea that she was a Perfect Helper or even a substitute for one seemed such a mockery to her. She wasn't sure why such an incongruous thought occurred to her but all she could think of was the school's sportsday. *It's all so stupid. If this is a race, why did the ravens enter if they knew they couldn't win? For that matter, why did I do what Elsa wanted when I knew I couldn't win? When I knew that the slowest snail has an even chance of beating me?* And then the answer came to her. *It's not about winning the race, it's about finishing the course. Loyalty. Faithfulness. To the end.*

'I press on toward the goal to win the prize for which I am called heavenward…' She learned to recite it once for Mrs Ashe's memory quiz. An idea came to her. It was wild, crazy. *It won't work. But it'll buy time.* She stooped to bundle up the grace cloaks in her arms. *Anything's worth trying to gain time.* Picking out the orange one, she threw it over her shoulders.

'No!' Emyr cried. 'What are you doing, Fern? Don't wear it! Don't activate it!'

Fern pushed the clasp at her neck closed. 'Don't worry, I'll be back shortly.' She closed her eyes. 'It's a variation on "good king bad king".' A whoosh sounded in her ears. She could hardly hear Emyr's distant voice: 'What?'

A moment later, she peeked through her eyelids and realised she was in the air. Ysgarde was behind her. *The cloaks work. They really work.*

Picking up speed, she swooped over the rings of silent Jotuns, rushed down over the trees and hurtled towards the dark shape blotting out the moon. *What on earth do I think I'm doing?* A high–

pitched whistling sounded in her ears. But she had no sense of panic. Just a sense of urgent purpose. *Onward, faster, faster.* The air roared around her; she knew her cloak was an orange streak behind her. She felt the malevolence of the Dark Walker as it turned towards her.

But she tornado–spun over its massive bulk. Once clear, she pulled out of the whirlwind's spiral and dashed towards the tiny specks in front of her. 'Gimme that!' She reached out to take the firestick with one hand while still holding the grace cloaks tight with the other.

The ravens screeched and spun into an uncontrolled tumble as she grabbed their stick. Wind–swift, she turned. Without needing to look, she knew the Dark Walker was following her. It was picking up speed as it altered course. She was coming towards lights. *A city.* Plucking the blue cloak from the bundle in her arms, she dropped it behind her and risked a glimpse backwards. The Walker stopped, picked up the cloak and threw the scrap of cloth over its massive shoulders. Suddenly dark bat–like wings began to sprout and unfold, quivering for a moment as they emerged from the shape's huge bulk. *Ooops. Didn't count on that. Slight miscalculation. The Walker has become a Flyer.*

She sped on, streaking through the sky. She felt as if she were an orange blur passing in front of the moon. The Dark Flyer leapt into the sky, gaining by the second. Fern picked out the yellow grace cloak, then changed her mind. *No, not wisdom. I can't give it that. It might see through my plan.* She dropped the green instead. The sea was ahead. She went straight over a cliff, plunging into the roiling water. She was intending to ascend to the surface when she realised that she wasn't having any trouble breathing. *I'll walk along the bottom and then come up. Not too far, though, or the Flyer will remember that I'm not what it's really after. I can't risk its return to Ysgarde before me.* The orange cloak floated around her as she leapt over rocks through cool, green silence. Fish darted around her, scurrying against the current. Up she went after a minute.

The Dark Flyer was nowhere in sight as she broke the surface. *It can't have gone back to Ysgarde.* Fern rose, dripping, into the air. *Not yet.*

A swift shadow moved underneath the water. Without warning,

a dark shape lunged for her. It was a sea serpent.

She shot up as its razor jaws reached out with lightning quickness. It caught the hem of the indigo cloak, dragging it from her as she hurtled moonwards. Then it followed her, a sea serpent with dragon wings, glistening like pitch. The Flyer had become a Dragon.

The trick is to make it think I'm running out of steam. She somersaulted into a roll that brought her back towards the land. *Uh oh. Which way is Ysgarde? Without Emyr, and split-second timing, this plan is sunk.*

For the first time, she began to feel concern. She increased her lead over the Dark Dragon, looking for any landmark she could recognise. But there was nothing. *Head inland. Look for mountains.*

She sped over downs and wrinkled plains, her hair whipping against her face. She swept over hills and rivers, towns and villages, her cloak streaming behind her like the tail of a comet.

She slowed, realising the Dark Dragon was no longer following her. *It's going back to Ysgarde. It's realised I was just distracting it.*

Turning, she notched up her speed. *Cyclone level. How much faster can I go? Hurricane, slipstream. And stay away from towns.*

She wasn't even at top speed when she caught up to the Dragon. But it was already in the valley below Ysgarde. *A few seconds. It's all we need.* She threw the red grace cloak out in front of her. The Dragon hesitated, then stopped for it, catching it in its black talons.

A moment later, she alighted in front of the gate of Ysgarde. Emyr rushed to her. 'What do you think you're doing?' He hugged her and pulled her back to the gate at the same time.

'Trust me. Have you worked out the Powers yet?'

Emyr shook his head. 'Gratian thinks they form a panoply—a protective armour—but there's a piece missing.'

And then the Dragon was there. It moved lightly and easily for a creature so ponderous. Its breath was mephitic and sulphurous, its hiss cold and sibilant. 'So…' Its voice was eerie and discordant. '…you are the ones my Servants put their hopes of rescue in.' It laughed. 'How pathetic.' It laughed again. 'First, the grace cloaks. Then, the Powers.'

Without a word, Fern unclasped her cloak and threw it at the dragon's feet. The dragon grabbed it with a claw. Then Fern took the yellow cloak and threw it as well. *Oh don't touch it. Don't get suspicious.* She stuffed the violet cloak into the tightest, smallest bundle she could and hid it under her arm.

'Six,' the dragon said. 'I have six cloaks. Where is the seventh?'

'No!' Fern shouted her defiance. 'You can't have it! It's not yours! It's Emyr's! Emyr of Fyrzentsou. The purple of kingship belongs to him, not to you.'

'The purple of kingship,' the dragon said. 'Of course. Yet who but I should have it? For I will rule not just this world, but yours too, little orange flea. And you will be the first to bow to me in my robe of kingship.'

'No!' Fern flicked out the violet cloak and, with a swish, placed it on Emyr's shoulders. He stared at her as if she'd gone mad. As the dragon's raking talons descended towards him, Fern pulled the cloak from him and flung it at the Dragon.

Please, please, please... let it have been on him long enough to activate it.

The dark creature caught the cloak with a single deft swipe, hissing in satisfaction. 'You will pay for defying me.' It folded its wings and placed the cloak over its own scaly shoulders. 'The purple of kingship.' Crooning, its yellow eyes closed. Its head drooped. And then it fell sideways.

Emyr's mouth dropped open as the dragon began to snore. 'What just happened?'

Fern shuddered with delayed fright. 'The Seventh Day...' She clapped a hand to her mouth to stop it quivering.

'...is the Sabbath of rest. What else would you expect the purple cloak to do?'

Emyr stared at the Dragon. 'Send you to sleep?'

Fern trembled as she grinned. 'We must work out the Powers quickly. That's not going to keep it in slumberland forever.'

'Did you know this was going to happen?'

'No. But it worth the chance.'

On the hillside, scattered lights began to appear as the Jotuns ignited their torches. Uller sauntered up the hillside. He poked his tongue out at the dragon as he passed. 'Oh, pathetic, are we?' He blew a kiss at Fern. 'For this, I might even let you keep that whistle.'

Fern clutched at the silver chain around her neck. She had forgotten all about it. *It was Uller's? Is it the seventh Power?*

He grinned as if he read her thought. 'No, it's not. I don't know what it is but I know it's not that.'

On the ground in front of the crystal travelling case were the six Powers. Fern counted them out: the Sword for Emyr, the Helmet for Madmerry, the Shield for Ansey, the Shoes for Hector, the Belt for… *her? Or the Mailcoat? Or neither?*

Madmerry was bending over the pile, her face swathed in a veil of silk. 'Boody, let's try the Belt on you.'

Boody hopped forward in the yellow cloak and allowed the Belt to be wrapped around her several times. It flopped to the ground.

Madmerry sighed. 'Let's try the Mailcoat.'

She lifted the watersilver collar over Boody's head. It flowed into place, turning into sleek hoarfrost–coloured scales.

'It's so light.' Boody rose into the air. 'I can hardly feel it there.'

'That's definitely yours.' Hector nodded before turning to Ginevra. 'See I told you not all of them were activated.' He scrutinised her green cloak. 'Sun, Moon and Stars. Try the Belt.'

Madmerry wrapped the Belt around Ginevra's neck. At once, it became a looped collar, blinking with light. 'Stars, to match the cloak.'

Fern felt herself cringe inside.

It's me. I'm the one without any Power.

She realised they'd all turned to her. They were staring. Beyond the Days she could see Candle with the Knights of Renown, Lord Gratian in their front ranks. Behind her, she could sense the giants, watching intently.

'I've got no idea.' She wanted to burst into tears.

'It's got to be obvious.' Emyr gestured to the Days to form a circle and bring their Power with them. 'Council of peace.' He put his arms around Madmerry and Ansey, drawing them closer. 'Keep your voices down.'

They sat down and formed a tight huddle. Hector wriggled onto Emyr's lap and Boody perched on Madmerry's wrist. Ginevra curled herself into a tight ball on Ansey's knees.

There wasn't much space in the centre of their huddle but Ansey put his shield there. Its star was a jewel–beam of light, illuminating their faces. Hector put out his paw to touch it, then looked up at Fern. 'I hate to say it but it's not as temperamental as your phonelight.'

Ansey tapped his paw. 'Hush, Hector! Now listen, everyone. Let's not let anyone else take over because they think they can do better. They keep saying I am the Daystar because I have the Daystar shield. But I didn't activate it. The Ancient of Days kissed it.'

'So you think the Song is also the Daystar as well as the Ancient of Days?' Hector breathed.

'Yes.'

'Great!' Hector nodded with satisfaction. 'That means this next miracle is not up to us to perform.'

Fern wanted to drop with relief.

'I think the issue,' Boody said, raising a wing, 'is that we haven't figured out how to be One yet. How can we get the Powers to be One when we're not?'

'How do people get to be One?' Hector asked.

Ginerva was close enough to prod him with her hoof. 'It's like in Fern's song. Where it says "heart of my own heart"—when two hearts knit together and become One.'

'Beautiful sentiment.' Hector crinkled his snout. 'But we need more. We need practicality.'

'Of course it's practical!' Ginevra said. 'It's the ultimate friendship. Where you'd give your life to save another, give up your own hopes to serve another.'

'How is that practical?' Hector demanded. 'It's hopelessly idealistic.'

'You should talk!' Ginevra put her nose against his snout.

'Which little fox was it who sacrificed his dream of always waiting under a White Tree, just to help his friends?'

'There was some whining and complaining involved.'

'So what?' Ginevra started to push Hector backwards. 'You put friendship before your vows, even before your destiny. Isn't that what Oneness is about?' Before Hector could answer, Ginevra turned to Fern. 'Then there's this girl from another dimension who risked her life against the Dark Sleeper on what seemed a hopeless chance. Isn't that what Oneness is about?'

Uller's face appeared above their huddle. 'Actually,' he whispered, 'you must all be very close. Everyone can hear and understand you. And that's one of the great signs of Oneness. When all creatures understand each other without the need for the Flair.'

Ginevra kicked the Shield with her hoof. 'Close is not good enough. Without the single heartbeat within this armour, without the single song in all its harmonic splendour shaping its form, this is a pile of useless junk.'

Even before Ginevra had finished, the answer came to Fern. 'The Song! That's my Power!' *It can't be!* 'But I sing like a cricket.'

'Ansey's not the Daystar and you are not the Song,' Boody whispered. 'But the Ancient of Days has given part of himself to both of you. Besides, these grace cloaks hum musical notes for some reason. And that's why there's two Ancelins. To give us a clue about an octave.' She took off her cloak and shrugged herself out of the Mailcoat.

Without a word, they followed her actions, layering the grace cloaks with the panoply pieces in the centre of their huddle. It all seemed instinctive. Hector's Shoes were at the bottom, Madmerry's Helmet at the top.

'I still can't sing.' Fern looked around the circle.

'Of course you can.' Madmerry wrapped her scarf around her head so only her eyes were visible. 'We'll help.'

'How does that song you sang on the Airbridge start?' Boody asked.

Fern took a deep breath: '*Be thou my vision…*'

By the second word, Madmerry, Boody and Ginevra had joined in.

By the end of the first line, the armour was floating, the cloaks swaying like limbs within it. *O Lord of my heart; Naught be all else to me, save that Thou art, Thou my best thought, by day or by night...'*

They leaned back, opening out the huddle, but they didn't stop singing.

'Waking or sleeping, Thy presence my light.'

When Ansey, Emyr and Hector learned enough to join in, the panoply suffused with light. They had to shield their eyes.

'...heart of my own heart, whatever befall, still be my vision, o ruler of all.'

Fern could feel the words lingering in her heart. The Days truly were the heart of her own heart.

And then, there were many voices singing.

The Jotuns had joined in.

And the dwarves.

The voices of the Knights swelled above them.

And then she felt it. Cool and light against her forehead.

She looked up in surprise, almost faltering in the song. But there were so many singing now, it didn't matter. The Song went on.

She saw Ansey looking around and realised he had felt it too. So had the other Days. It had been a kiss.

The panoply was solid light. The grace cloaks swirled into a unity and as the armour lifted itself tall and straight, they became like limbs of living light. And they were humming.

With a bound, the winged panoply picked up the dragon and flew off. The echoes of its song drifted down from an impossible height.

Uller ambled over to them. 'Now it makes perfect sense why it had to be you lot.'

'It does?' Ansey smiled up at him.

'No one could have persuaded us to work together and, at the end, it was obvious the Song needed all of us—giants, dwarves and humans. We all knew the task was beyond a bunch of emotionally crippled kids so, out of pity, we decided to help.'

Excuse you! Fern wanted to thump him. *I am not an emotionally crippled kid.* She folded her arms. *Am I?*

Uller was beaming. 'We lost our pride and our mutual distrust in a moment of pity. And for that moment, we were all one.' His smile turned to a sudden frown. 'Imagine that. That it needed all of us to build a panoply that hums a lullaby of eternal sleep.'

'Are we still the Days?' Hector held up his bare paws. 'I feel a bit naked without the Shoes. Like part of me is missing.'

Uller's great throaty laugh rang out like a bell. 'You will always be the Days. You have made peace possible.' He grinned at Ansey. 'I admit to being surprised you were the one to create the Daystar Shield.'

'I didn't,' Ansey insisted. 'It wasn't me.'

'You must have had something to do with it. It had to be made in a crucible of obedience.' Uller raised his hands. 'Not always easy to know when to obey and when to refuse. Not always easy to be sure when disobedience is rebellion and when it is a legitimate search for independence.'

'Nah, it's dead simple, boss.' Munin flapped down in a tired pile of feathers onto his shoulder. 'Rebellion is a unilateral declaration.'

'And independence…' Huginn descended onto Uller's other shoulder. '…is a bilateral agreement.' He tilted his head, listening to the music drifting down from the high heavens. 'Oh, that's beautiful!'

Munin blinked his red eyes at Fern. 'Thanks, kiddo. We were goners without ya.'

Ansey grinned at her. 'I'm so glad you're still here. Hector always thought that, as soon as the crisis was over, you'd be zapped back to your own…'

A light as sharp as a needlepoint speared towards her. She reacted too late as it snaked around her waist and yanked her upwards. Hector threw himself at it, snapping in a wild frenzy as a frost–white bubble popped into place around her.

'No!' she screamed. 'Not now! I don't want to go home now!' She beat her hands against the bubble. 'Let me out.'

Voices rippled, tinkled, chimed, whirred. It was the snowflakes, still arguing over copyright.

Beyond them she could hear a song. *Heart of my own heart…*

'No! I'm leaving my heart behind.'

The bubble bounced…

and bounced…

and bounced…

roup work was a classroom activity Fern came to love over the next few months. Where she'd once hated it, now she looked forward to building the oneness she'd experienced as the Days joined with the Jotuns, dwarves and Knights of Ysgarde in the Song.

She knew she'd changed. She'd even stopped trying to be invisible and had gone to speak with her step–dad.

For the first time, she recognised the pain and perplexity in him. 'I don't understand why your mum left.' Nick only just stopped himself from crying. 'There were no signs anything was wrong. And I've never understood why she left you behind.' He hugged her then. 'Fern, you're always welcome here.' Tears finally dripped down his face. 'Always.'

As Hector said, it was probably about as good as you could get in the happy ending stakes. Given the circumstances, that is.

When the bubble had finally opened, there he'd been. Hanging on by a thread of light. The moment he'd seen her emerge from the bubble, he let go of the thread and howled. He turned pathetic, beseeching eyes on her. 'Is this your world?'

She'd looked around. Smelled the air. Sensed the quality of the sunlight. It wasn't a firerose up there in the sky: it was a hydrogen smelter. 'Yes.' *I think it's even the same day I left. Maybe no one will have missed me. I'll be able to fit back into my normal life, no questions asked.*

Hector had howled again. After several seconds he stopped, mid–yowl, and sighed. 'It could be worse, all things considered. Dwarves have obviously been here. They've been keeping it secret, but that's not the point. If there's a way here, there must be a way back.'

The moment he'd said it, the pall of despair Fern had felt smothering her just dissipated. Hope swelled inside her.

'Looking on the bright side,' Hector said, 'what's the chance of getting a mobile phone of my own?' A twinkle appeared in his eye and he grinned. 'I realised I don't need an opposable thumb to operate one.'

Fern grinned back at him. 'Oh, Hector, you're just going to love social media. On Facebook, no one will be able to tell you're a fox from another dimension.'

Her prediction proved correct. Hector adored computers. He treated them with the utmost respect and became delicate and precise in his use of a keyboard. 'In my dreams I own an iPad,' he told Fern. 'But I am prepared to suffer with an outdated PC because I'm such a noble self–sacrificing fox.'

'At least you didn't say "humble".' Fern rolled her eyes at him.

He lived in secret under her bed and spent the day while she was at school on Nick's computer, searching for any evidence of the dwarves' presence in the world.

'It's hopeless,' he said one Saturday morning after Fern had sneaked some bacon back to her room for his breakfast. 'This world of yours is drowning in information. It's absolutely impossible to sift genuine knowledge from raw data. At least when it comes to all things dwarvish.' He put on his most pleading look.

'What do you want?' Fern had become used to his expression when he'd come up with a new scheme.

'Flower of Heart's Desire.' His mouth formed a smooch. 'Come on, sweetie. You've still got it, haven't you? If your heart's desire was for me to find the dwarf portal to this world, I think we could break through the data mountain and find their hidden access point.'

Hmmm. 'What about the White Mother's shuttle? Wouldn't that do?'

'You wouldn't try to fate–weave, would you?' Hector looked horrified.

'No!' Fern shook her head. 'All I meant was… oh, never mind.' She took the Flower of Heart's Desire out of her pocket, along with the Shuttle. She always kept them together. She threw the Shuttle at Hector as she felt for the whistle around her neck. *I don't like using these together. I don't know why.*

'Hey, Fern darhhling!' It was Elsa's voice and she was coming down the hallway.

Elsa had changed as soon as it became clear Nick was on Fern's side. She made an effort to be publicly polite. Still, Fern hated the overly–sweet 'darhhling' Elsa insisted on using. She suspected Elsa knew it irritated her but it was impossible to complain about it to Nick.

Hector dived under the bed a moment before Elsa poked her head in. 'You've got visitors.'

Puzzled, Fern went to the front door. She was even more puzzled to find Goliath Jones there with Mrs Ashe standing behind him. 'Hi.'

'Hi.' Goliath didn't smile. 'Can we come in?'

'We need to speak privately,' Mrs Ashe said. 'Can we go to your room?'

Fern nodded. 'Sure.' She raised her voice. 'Sure you can come to my room.' She knew Hector would get the message and make sure he was well–hidden.

But when she got to her room and ushered her visitors in, he was in plain sight, right in the middle of the carpet. Splayed out, he was gripping the wool pile with his claws. 'Over my dead body,' he yelled.

'Hector!' She looked where he was staring.

Uller was in the corner. 'Hand it over, fox!'

Fern didn't know whether to be relieved the Jotun had found them or alarmed at Hector's attitude.

'Uncle Uller!' Goliath exclaimed. 'What on earth are you doing here?'

Fern slewed to him, unable to believe her ears. 'You're related to Uller?' *But you're a midget, not a giant.*

'Fern McDey.' Uller Princekiller stood up, his head touching the ceiling. 'Ector, son of Danika. Hear me out.'

Mrs Ashe, frowning, stepped into the room. 'I'm here as Goliath's case worker. I wanted to speak to Fern about a race.' Her frown became a smile. 'You're Goliath's uncle? Our case history doesn't show any record of any relatives. So it's wonderful I'm here just at the same time as you happen to be here.'

'Actually I'm his uncle's uncle.' Uller reached over her head and closed the door. 'You have a fast car? You'll need it.' He turned to Hector and then to Fern. 'I am here to beg for help from both of you. It's taken a while to find you, even though I had a head–start.' He smiled at Fern. 'I knew you had to know Goliath to have possession of the whistle.'

Fern touched it. She glanced from Uller to Goliath and back again.

Uller took a deep breath. 'Fern McDey, it was a mistake to bring a fate–weaver's shuttle to this world. You have drawn the attention of the Mage who englobed the cosmos of Auberon–Zamberg.'

'Uh oh.' Hector jumped up, kicking the Shuttle he had been lying on to one side. '*That* Mage?'

'Did that fox speak?' Mrs Ashe was goggle–eyed.

Goliath took a step back.

'Grab your things,' Uller commanded, nodding at Fern. 'You must go now… before you endanger everyone and everything you hold dear.' He inclined his head towards Mrs Ashe. 'Take her away from here. Quickly.' And then, in a collapsing wink of light, he was gone.

Mrs Ashe squeaked in fright but then she seemed to collect herself. 'Right. Let's move first and ask questions later.'

Fern threw a few clothes in a bag with her mobile phone and the Flower of Heart's Desire. Hector jumped into the bag and she zipped it up, leaving just enough room for his snout to push out. A minute later, she thundered down the stairs after Goliath and Mrs Ashe. 'Hey Elsa,' she yelled. 'Tell dad I've got to go for a while. Tell him I love him and I'll be back when it's safe.'

'What?' Elsa stared. 'Where are you going? Shall I tell him you're with Goliath?'

Fern slammed the front door and dashed after Goliath and Mrs Ashe. She followed them out the gate, straight to Mrs Ashe's car. She flung herself onto the back seat, pulling in her bag after her.

Mrs Ashe sped off.

'Down!' Goliath shouted from the front seat.

Fern threw herself onto the back seat.

A black stretch limousine went past. Fern peeked out the back window, watching it slow and then stop as it reached Nick's house.

Her bag started jiggling on the seat. She unzipped it and Hector pushed his way out. He glared at the limousine as it dwindled in size the further Mrs Ashe drove up the street. 'I'm not the predicting type,' Hector said, 'but I have this bad feeling we're about to take on a Mage who makes the Dark Sleeper look like a fluffy teddy.'

He looked up to the rear vision mirror where he could see the reflections of Goliath and Mrs Ashe. 'How about you introduce our new assistants?'

Fern took a deep breath and hugged him tight. 'Hector, I'm so glad you're here.'

The little fox sighed. 'Strangely enough, kid, so am I.' He winked at her. 'So am I.'

Boy Wonder: A slightly sarcastic nickname used by Hector for Dallan

Bramble: A dwarf who watched the flight of the tutors from Fastness Height

Callum: A march–lord with responsibility for keeping watch on the border forts of Auberon

Candle: A dwarf; the anointed High King of the Cavern Kin, also titled Lord of The Nardelf, Enthroned Serenity on the Rock of Time, Master of The Deeping Ways, Keeper of the Secret of the Wreathwatch, Warden of the Scimitar Mountains, Well–Builder of the Stars, Son of Earth and Child of Ancient Dream

Cato: An injured runner

Cavern Kin: Dwarves

Cindurrah: See Madmerry; means *star–shepherd*

City of Mages: A place visited by Uller in search of the scroll about *The King Who Guards the Gate*

Companion to the Heir of Auberon: See Candle

Dallan: A blind and autistic sheep–herder; a friend of Madmerry

Danika: Mother of Ector

Dark Dragon: See Dark Sleeper

Dark Flyer: See Dark Sleeper

Dark Sleeper: A malevolent entity which is waking but, while in sleep, constantly tugs at a 'blanket' formed by the surface of the land

Dark Walker: See Dark Sleeper

Daystar: A title of the Ancient of Days

Daystar Shield: One of the Seven Powers; cannot be awakened except by a kiss from the Ancient of Days

Doctor Much: One of Ansey's tutors

Eagle Legion: A troop of dwarves watching the Bowl of the Field of Stars

Ector: See Hector

Efreets: Ally of the Jotuns

Elsa: Fern's step–sister

Emyr: Prince of Fyrzentsou; he can be identified by his one green eye and one blue eye

Fateweaver: A weaver with the ability to twine the fates of individuals using a special shuttle

Fern McDey: A girl who finds security in being 'invisible'; one of the Seven Days (although originally a substitute); Monday's Child

Fifth Dwarf Legion: Dwarf troop that appears on the rim of the Bowl of the Field of Stars

Flair: An instinctive ability to understand the language of a different species; the two main varieties are Beast Flair and Bird Flair; a sign of the bloodline covenant over the rulers of Auberon

Fletch: A strategy board game, combining skill and strange chance

Flower of Heart's Desire: A gift given to Emyr by Candle; a crafted living daisy

Freutim: King of the frost giants, ruler of the Jotun alliance

Fyrzentsou: A kingdom ruled by the usurper Rogin; one of the seven kingdoms carved out of the ancient principality of Auberon–Zamberg

Ginevra: A white baby fawn; one of the Seven Days; Wednesday's Child

Goliath Jones: A fast midget who fights anyone who calls him 'Golly'; he has an eye for Elsa

Grace Cloaks: Rainbow–coloured mantles with different gifts to bestow; each hums a different musical note

Gratian: The new captain of the King's Shield; the commander of Ysgarde

Harper: One of Ansey's tutors

Harrowfell: A steep cliff–face with a dangerous switchback road running up it

Hector: A white baby fox; one of the Seven Days; Tuesday's Child

Helmet of Providence: One of the Seven Powers; in the care of the Kingdom of Fyrzentsou; disguised by an over–mask; also called 'The Helmet of Time'

His Q–ness: See Quystein

Hobbit: A nickname of Goliath Jones

Huginn: One of Uller Princekiller's ravens

Humble: A dwarf sent to Fyrzentsou to help Gratian and the tutors

Imri: The murdered king of Fyrzentsou; nicknamed 'The Whirlwind'; father of Emyr

Isles of the Colossus: A place visited by Uller in search of *The King Who Guards the Gate*

Jens: A boy who once lent Ansey his practice sword

Jénève: The first wife of Maurtz, king of Fyrzentsou

Jotuns: Giants; Jotuns could be frost giants, storm giants or fire giants

Khufu: Pharoah of ancient Egypt; builder of a pyramid

Kindle: A dwarf sent to Fyrzentsou to help Gratian and the tutors

Kingdoms Beneath the Sea: A place visited by Uller in search of *The King Who Guards the Gate*

King Who Guards the Gate: A scroll of prophecy about the end of the age referring to king set to guard a gate against giants and also referring to the coming of the Daystar

King's Shield: A troop of soldiers specifically assigned to protect King Maurtz and Castle Auberon

Knights of Renown: An independent band of knights from Ysgarde, famed for their integrity which is shown by the brightness of their shields

Lal: One of the servants at Ysgarde; also called Lally

Lance: See Ancelin, Lord of Tariquhaven

Land–bond: A spiritual bond between the rulers of Fyrzentsou and their land for the health of the land; a sign of the bloodline covenant over the rulers of Fyrzentsou

Lyndark: A distant kingdom; one of the seven kingdoms carved out of the ancient principality of Auberon–Zamberg

Madder's Crossing: A river crossing with an old decaying bridge

Madmerry: A girl whose face is so scarred she wears a fantastic mask to hide it; a herbalist; one of the Seven Days; Friday's Child

Mailcoat of Justice: One of the Seven Powers; in the care of the Sovereign Isles; stolen by the Jotuns; looks like a silver collar

Malveraine: A distant kingdom; one of the seven kingdoms carved out of the ancient principality of Auberon–Zamberg

Manticores: A rust–coloured human–faced lion with the tail of a scorpion and green blood

Mara–mares: Embodied spirits of nightmares

Merry: See Madmerry

Messenger Shoes: One of the Seven Powers; in the care of the Kingdom of Malveraine; lost and found by a den of foxes

Mintaka: Captain Gratian's horse; it is the name of a star in the constellation Orion.

Mistmurk: A vast swamp

Mistmurk Height: A high ridge jutting into and overlooking the Mistmurk swamp

Mistress of Illusion: A title used for female Jotuns who can skinchange or shapechange (that is, disguise their appearance by a 'second skin')

Mistress Wildling: A title Candle used to address Madmerry

Mouse: A nickname of Goliath Jones

Munin: One of Uller Princekiller's ravens

Nardelf: An underground kingdom ruled by Candle; the realm of the dwarves; the hidden one of the seven kingdoms carved out of the ancient principality of Auberon–Zamberg

Nero: Emperor of Rome; owner of a vomitorium; a mad ruler who set fire to the city

Nick: Fern's step–dad

Nine Netherhells: A reference in a curse by Gratlan

Nobble: A dwarf who escorted the Days to Ysgarde

Old Greywhiskers: One of Ansey's tutors

Olethea: Emyr's mother; former queen of Fyrzentsou

Olien: Emyr's aunt; queen of Fyrzentsou

Osiirians: An ancient race, long disappeared; green–hued

Parment: Patricus Percival Parment; usual gatekeeper at Ysgarde

Professor: See Old Greywhiskers

Puddle: A dwarf, a Subtle Gentle, an artist whose greatest work of art was her own life

Quade: A boy Fern knew at school

Quystein: Acting commander of the Knights of Renown

Rhodri Harke: A cowardly knight

Rigel: A horse ridden by Ansey and calmed using the Flair; it is the name of a star in the constellation Orion.

Rogin: King of Fyrzentsou; a usurper

Rubble: A dwarf who watched the flight of the tutors from Fastness Height

Ruēl: Name of the Creator, see Ancient of Days

Seven Days: The seven chosen ones of prophecy; unexpectedly discovered to be children; not all of them are human

Seven Powers: Six are known, one is hidden; the Seven Days need to use the Seven Powers to defeat the Dark Sleeper

Snow Citadel of the Wreathwatch Wraiths: Solveigra's castle in the Wreathwatch Mountains; abode of snow demons

Solveigra: An ancient queen who wished for immortality; her legend is told more fully in *Many–Coloured Realm*

Sovereign Isles: A distant kingdom; one of the seven kingdoms carved out of the ancient principality of Auberon–Zamberg

Speaking Sword: One of the Seven Powers; in the care of the Kingdom of Vircontium; stolen by the frost giants

Squeak: A nickname of Goliath Jones

Subtle Gentles: Dwarf artists whose works of art are their own lives

Summerheight: Middle of the season of summer

The Q: See Quystein

The Song: See Ancient of Days

Tobias: One of Ansey's tutors

Toddle: A dwarf sent to Fyrzentsou to help Gratian and the tutors

Trolls: Allies of the Jotuns

Tybold: Ansey's step–brother; son of Barbizca

Uller Princekiller: A frost giant who has sought for the identity of The King Who Guards the Gate for many centuries

Van: One of the servants at Ysgarde

Vircontium: A distant kingdom famous for its swordmasters; one of the seven kingdoms carved out of the ancient principality of Auberon–Zamberg

White Mother: See Solveigra

Winterdeep: Middle of the season of winter

Wobble: A dwarf who escorted the Days to Ysgarde

Wreathwatch Mountains: A range of mountain peaks forming part of the border between Auberon and Fyrzentsou

Wreathwatch Pass: A high mountain pass between Auberon and Fyrzentsou; part of it glaciated; guarded by the White Mother

Wreathwatch Woman: See Solveigra

Xerxes Xenophon: Human resource manager and slave trader; disguise of Uller Princekiller

Ysanne: A knight at Ysgarde

Zippy: A pony